Bello:

hidden talent rediscovered.

CW00571038

Bello is a digital only imprint of Pan Macmillan,
established to breathe new life into previously published,
classic books.

At Bello we believe in the timeless power of the imagination,
of good story, narrative and entertainment and we want to use
digital technology to ensure that many more readers
can enjoy these books into the future.

We publish in ebook and Print on Demand formats
to bring these wonderful books to new audiences.

About Bello:

www.panmacmillan.com/imprints/bello

About the author:

www.panmacmillan.com/author/pamelahansfordjohnson

Pamela Hansford Johnson

Pamela Hansford Johnson was born in 1912 and gained recognition with her first novel, *This Bed Thy Centre*, published in 1935. She wrote 27 novels. Her themes centred on the moral responsibility of the individual in their personal and social relations. The fictional genres she used ranged from romantic comedy (*Night and Silence, Who Is Here*) and high comedy (*The Unspeakable Skipton*) to tragedy (*The Holiday Friend*) and the psychological study of cruelty (*An Error of Judgement*). Her last novel, *A Bonfire*, was published in the year of her death, 1981.

She was a critic as well as a novelist and wrote books on Thomas Wolfe and Ivy Compton-Burnett; *Six Proust Reconstructions* (1958) confirmed her reputation as a leading Proustian scholar. She also wrote a play, *Corinth House* (1954), a work of social criticism arising out of the Moors Trial, *On Iniquity* (1967), and a book of essays, *Important to Me* (1974). She received honorary degrees from six universities and was a Fellow of the Royal Society of Literature. She was awarded the C.B.E. in 1975.

Pamela Hansford Johnson, who had two children by her first marriage with journalist Gordan Neil Stewart, later married C. P. Snow. Their son Philip was born in 1952.

Pamela Hansford Johnson

NIGHT AND SILENCE WHO IS HERE?

BELLO

First published in 1963 by Macmillan

This edition published 2012 by Bello
an imprint of Pan Macmillan, a division of Macmillan Publishers Limited
Pan Macmillan, 20 New Wharf Road, London N1 9RR
Basingstoke and Oxford
Associated companies throughout the world

www.panmacmillan.com/imprints/bello
www.curtisbrown.co.uk

ISBN 978-1-4472-1555-4 EPUB
ISBN 978-1-4472-1554-7 POD

Copyright © Pamela Hansford Johnson, 1963

The right of Pamela Hansford Johnson to be identified as the
author of this work has been asserted in accordance
with the Copyright, Designs and Patents Act 1988.

Every effort has been made to contact the copyright holders of the material
reproduced in this book. If any have been inadvertently overlooked, the publisher
will be pleased to make restitution at the earliest opportunity.

You may not copy, store, distribute, transmit, reproduce or otherwise
make available this publication (or any part of it) in any form, or by any means
(electronic, digital, optical, mechanical, photocopying, recording or otherwise),
without the prior written permission of the publisher. Any person who does
any unauthorized act in relation to this publication may be liable to
criminal prosecution and civil claims for damages.

The Macmillan Group has no responsibility for the information provided by
any author websites whose address you obtain from this book ('author websites').
The inclusion of author website addresses in this book does not constitute
an endorsement by or association with us of such sites or the content,
products, advertising or other materials presented on such sites.

This book remains true to the original in every way. Some aspects may appear
out-of-date to modern-day readers. Bello makes no apology for this, as to retrospectively
change any content would be anachronistic and undermine the authenticity of the original.
Bello has no responsibility for the content of the material in this book. The opinions
expressed are those of the author and do not constitute an endorsement by,
or association with, us of the characterization and content.

A CIP catalogue record for this book is available from the British Library.

Visit **www.panmacmillan.com** to read more about all our books
and to buy them. You will also find features, author interviews and
news of any author events, and you can sign up for e-newsletters
so that you're always first to hear about our new releases.

To my Son
ANDREW MORVEN STEWART

Contents

'Night and silence! who is here?
Weeds of Athens he doth wear.'

Puck, *M.N.D.*, Act II, Scene 2

1. Dear Old Dr. Parke

Under the maples, burning like bonfires, pure yellow and pure red, walked Dr. Dominick Maudlin Parke, his hands clasped behind his back.

The day was mild. The sky, behind the flagrant leaves, was almost white, almost as white as the hair of Dr. Parke, dear *old* Dr. Parke, though no more than fifty-seven years of age, who walked in generally admired perplexity, though he was not perplexed at all.

He knew precisely, as he had always known, what he had to do.

He had to welcome, at 4 p.m. on the dot, the latest and last of the Visiting Fellows.

His soft shoes trod soft leaves, amazingly coloured, though his eyes had long ceased to heed them. The scarlet maple leaf, when turned on to its backside, becomes the most fragile of mauves, rose-mauve, tender as the word Mauve or as the flesh of an odalisque in shadow on a couch of crimson plush: such flesh Dr. Parke trod all unseeing, but all-knowing.

Any old how, such was his reputation.

In this pause of the day, when the boys were in their classes and the sky was quiet, he inclined his head towards the chapel in playful but reverent salutation. The ivy rippled politely at him in reply. Below the campus, New Hampshire plunged down to the Gropius airport, twenty miles away; above, it soared to the ski-slopes. To the left of Dr. Parke, the Faculty houses, their lawns strewn with bicycles, toys, hosepipes, broken garden chairs: before him, chapel, Old Hall, library. To his right the Boosie House (1912), the new dormitories (1958), the classrooms. Behind him, the gymnasium and the Centre for Visiting Fellows, flashing its glass, its lambent mahogany, back at the sun. Behind the Centre, more Faculty houses, including the President's, and houses of a random character put at the disposal of the Visitors.

One of the Visitors was coming across the grass now from the library, little Miss Groby, laden with books and muttering to herself. For an elderly woman she moved fast, with a mouselike scuttle. She nodded briefly to Dr. Parke, glancing at him from beneath her beetling brows, but did not speak.

'Good day, good day, good day!' he called after her, sweeping the air with his goodwill, 'and what a day!'

Miss Groby scuttled on towards the Centre.

'And *what* a day!' Dr. Parke repeated, this time for the day's own benefit. The whole of his teeth moved slightly, like the keyboard of a piano. He had forgotten his dental powder. As he passed on he forgave Miss Groby for her lack of response. After all, he supposed, she had just had a splendid late lunch in the Boosie House, and replete after such delights, perhaps even a little drowsy, was eager to get back to her work.

He turned for a moment to see her disappearing through the glass doors. He felt sorry, as he often did, that Carlo Tiepolo and Miss Corall made the building so untidy by propping their balcony windows open with chairs. From where he stood, the seats of Swedish leather, peacock and scarlet, stuck up from the face of the building in gross disharmony. It occurred to him that had they an alternative device by which to open the windows they would certainly use it: but he did not know what this device might be or how to go about discovering it. He was not, although he believed himself to be one, altogether a practical man. And he was Head of the Centre.

A man of small stature, with stooped and skinny frame but cheeks still round and rosy, he contemplated the impossibility of making changes. Changes ought to be made, perhaps, but he simply didn't see how they could be. Meanwhile, Miss Corall's chair was withdrawn and Dr. Tiepolo's fell over.

Old Dr. Parke looked at his watch and began to hurry. It was already twenty-five past three. Oh dear, he was going to be late at the airport!

2. An Englishman's Home

Matthew Pryar, fifty-one last week but looking like a well-preserved thirty-eight, fastened his seat-belt. He was humming dulcetly to himself, without knowing it, 'Sheep May Safely Graze'. He was rather tired, but also happy in the foreknowledge of comforts to come. After a rough night in New York he had not felt like his breakfast, nor had he felt very much like lunch, either. By the time he was on his way to Hamelin he had recovered his appetite, but on this flight no meals were served. The President had promised, however, when inviting him to pursue his Merlin studies at the Centre, to look after him in every way, and within an hour, perhaps, would be implementing that promise.

The bright sky drenched the windows to port: to starboard, rich earth swamped them: great hills and sunny fields, the fuzz of trees, chalkline of roads, and now, visible as the plane banked steeply, houses, backyards, motor-cars, men, even, and at last the Gropius wonder itself only a couple of bumps and a trundle away.

Matthew unbelted himself, brushed himself down, passed a comb quickly through the sleekness of his hair, still brown, with a discreet ripple in it. He felt the pleasurable anticipation not only of one who is about to eat, but who is about to enter a new avatar. He was delighted by the idea of being accepted as a scholar among scholars.

Having done almost no work of any description since he came down from Oxford (he was well-heeled), and devoting his attention solely to the sweetening of social life both for himself and others, he had been nagged by Dorothy Merlin into making a study of her work. Since he mildly liked her work, he saw no reason why not to: and as her total *œuvre* consisted of twenty shortish poems and four slim verse-dramas, the labour was not demanding. He had all the luck of those who find themselves, by accident, first in the field. He was immediately accepted as the world authority on Dorothy Merlin, because he was literally the only one. And so, a rich American liberal arts college had desired him.

He had prepared his attitude of arrival. He was not going to make scholarly noises: others might see through them, and at Cobb, anyway, scholars would be two a penny. He was going to play safe and be himself, bringing the elegant world to them, the elegance of London and the shires: and when they got used to that, they would wonder all the more that so urbane a head should carry so rare a speciality.

The plane swung round before the airport building, stopped, and stopped purring. Everyone stood up to grab at coats, hats, brief-cases. Blithe as a boy, Matthew stepped out on to the tarmac, his mothy smile at the ready, and walked towards reception and checking.

There were several people awaiting the new arrivals. Seeing a tall, ascetic-looking man with literary eyes, Matthew advanced upon him confidently, hand outstretched.

'Good-morning, Dr. Parke. I'm Pryar.'

'Fingleton,' said the man.

'From Cobb?'

'General Motors.'

Matthew turned away. He eyed the others: pretty obviously, none were for him. More perplexed than irritated, he went to collect his bags, eight matching cases in Hunting Stewart tartan, with M.J.P. in gold letters on their sides, which came skidding off a moving belt. Matthew stood among them and waited.

The building was remarkably handsome, a pride to the world in which it existed, clean, glaucous, infinitely spatial and far too hot. There was a news and cigarette stand, a gift shop, a device for drinking water. No sign of food. His stomach gave a terrible rumble, which made him start and blush. All bodily noises are controllable by will except this one. He would almost as soon have died than greet Dr. Parke, when he came, with another noise such as this. He looked about him again, hoping, at least, to see a bar of chocolate somewhere. There was none.

'Take your bags?' said a Negro porter.

Matthew replied, well, perhaps not now: he was waiting for somebody.

It was now twenty-five minutes past four, and all the passengers on his flight had gone their several ways. A new crowd came in: a new flight, Hamelin to Chicago, was called. He wanted to go to the lavatory, but dared not move lest Dr. Parke should miss him.

After a while he began to have a curious feeling that he was part of the airport, that Gropius had built him and his cases into it for decorative effect. Though he was cramped, some instinct deterred him even from moving from one foot to the other.

Five to five. One of the automatic doors swung magically open, and through it came a little elderly gentleman, beaming, bright-eyed, a *craquelure* of rose upon his cheeks.

'Ah, Mr. Pryar, Mr. Pryar! Welcome to Hamelin. Welcome to Cobb. A little late, I fear, but better late than never.'

For one hungry, unmagnanimous moment, Matthew doubted this.

'Well, well, let's get along, shall we? No need to hang around. A little trouble with the car, that's what I had. She was a naughty girl, she broke down on the parkway. Nothing serious, but it took time, it all took time. Well, Mr. Pryar, welcome once more to Cobb! These are your bags? I think we can manage them ourselves, eh?'

He seemed able to manage two: Matthew had to carry all the others.

Outside, an old Ford awaited them. Dr. Parke looked at it as if he had never seen it before. 'Well, well, we'll have to make do somehow. No room in the trunk, sir, there's the eggs and my wife's phonograph. We'll have to put your cases in back.' He pulled the front seat forward and helped Matthew to heave the bags over it. 'You sit by me, there's plenty of leg-room.'

All this while Matthew had said nothing. Even now, as the Ford burped into life and, with a faint stench of hot rubber, began to move away from the airport, he said nothing.

'Pleased to have you with us, Mr. Pryar, very pleased. You'll find we're a friendly community at Cobb. We're honoured by the presence of our Visiting Fellows, we treat them well. We know you'll be very happy. Are you acquainted with Miss Corall? I'm sure you are.'

Matthew was. She was one of the sights of Cambridge (England).

'Mediaevalist, most distinguished, honoured to have her. I'm afraid I haven't read your papers on Dorothy Merlin. I've never read anything by Miss Merlin, either. But as I always say, what are omissions for, if they're not meant to be repaired?'

Dr. Parke sniffed delicately. 'I don't think it's the brake linings. No, I'm quite sure it isn't.'

Matthew found that the road wound uphill all the way, yea, to the very end. It wound past frame-houses with shrubs before them that looked like huge, swollen swags of pinkish-white lilac, past gas-stations, cabins labelled 'Antiques', endless advertisements for maple syrup. And all around was the officious beauty of the mountains, of the incandescent trees, of distances blue as Patenier's. (He made a note to mention Patenier in his first lecture, if a lecture should ever be forced upon him.) Dr. Parke's car seemed ill-adapted for climbing. It stopped more than once, while the smell grew worse. On one occasion it gave out a strange hostile growl, which, fortunately, coincided with, and obliterated, a protest from Matthew's empty stomach.

Now they seemed far from human habitation. There were no more small towns, small villages. Nature was supreme in her imperial colours. Of course there was no sign of human life, but Matthew, having been in the United States before, had long since ceased to be surprised by the total lack of pedestrians outside built-up areas. (Not that there were many inside them, either.)

'We're remote at Cobb, perhaps,' said Dr. Parke, 'but we like it. A little place all to ourselves. Yes. And the college shop is excellent, quite compendious, ah yes! Twenty miles each way to the nearest township, what do you think of that? Aaaah, here we are!'

And there they were on the campus, the Ford running smoothly now, as if it had dismissed some intense moral anxiety from its mind and was simply relieved to be home again. The chapel clock announced the hour: a quarter past six. Bells rang. Young men in sweaters and dirty-white trousers, very tight across the buttocks, were hurrying in all directions. Matthew salivated. Now, he thought, for a drink!

'First of all we must show you the Centre,' said old Dr. Parke. He swung the car dangerously and pitched it downhill again towards a brick building having a lot of glass in it which had not been there at the time of erection. The Centre had been built in 1902 and converted in 1959, with facings of glass and mahogany and a great amount of steel. The first things Matthew observed were gay projections of some incomeprehensible nature from two of the first-floor windows.

'Chairs,' Dr. Parke explained, 'they will prop open the windows with their chairs. I must see about it. Something must be done.'

He led Matthew into a polished foyer, where there were two empty desks, obviously vacated by the secretaries at the day's end. Rapidly he exhibited an old-fashioned general lounge which conversion had not touched — 'That's where you Fellows will have your little get-togethers, I suppose' — and indicated the position of the lavatories. 'You're upstairs.'

They went up. On the first floor it was even hotter. With the air of one bestowing a marvel, Dr. Parke flung open a door. 'This is for our Dorothy Merlin expert! May I take leave to hope that you will be truly snug here?'

It was a light, handsome room equipped with all a scholar could desire, big desk, typewriter, two telephones, sofa, peacock and red armchairs, infinite shelves, clothes closet, college directory, stationery cupboard. The mercury must have stood at eighty degrees.

'Do smoke, my dear fellow,' said Dr. Parke. 'I never do myself, but I quite like to see it in others. Do smoke.'

Matthew had been smoking all the way from the airport.

He now expressed appreciation of his working quarters.

'Shall we take a brief tour of the campus before we install you in your new home, or would you prefer to go there right away?'

'Right away, please,' said Matthew, trying to clutch his drink and his dinner a little closer to him.

Back in the car, they shot off into a maze of side lanes embowered in woodland, where the Faculty houses stood. Dr. Parke gave a comprehensive *curriculum vitae* of who lived in each. He indicated a splendid piece of neo-Georgian, orange and cream. 'That's President Pickersgill's. We shall meet him soon.'

('Tomorrow,' Matthew thought.)

'And here' — the car dashed off at right-angles into another lane — 'is your own castle. An Englishman's home is his castle, and so shall yours be. Eh? No one shall come and worry you. You shall be undisturbed to work all you wish. We'll expect great things from you while you are at Cobb. Your castle!' Dr. Parke added, with a wave of the hand and a splintering beam of satisfaction.

3. A Tour of the Campus

It looked by no means unlike one. Built at the turn of the century, out of a local, liver-coloured brick, it even had a suggestion of castellations. The door was ogival, and at the apex hung a fancy lantern with panes of mauve glass in it. The front lawn, the short path, were wild with leaves.

'Enter,' said Dr. Parke, 'and take possession of your heritage!'

Matthew stepped into something which seemed to him pitch-blackness.

'The switches, the switches,' a voice said, 'we shall soon find them — aha!'

The lights sprang up over a vast gloomy room, papered with orange flowers. Dr. Parke was revealed, proud and joyful.

'There! What do you think of that? This was old Mrs. MacLaughlin's home for ninety years. She died just where you are standing, in an attempt to touch her toes. She kept up her exercises to the last — a wonderful, wonderful old lady!' He dreamed about her for a moment or so, then said briskly, 'But we must press on. The hour grows late.'

He proceeded to lead Matthew on a nightmare tour.

'Kitchen — washing-machine, dryer, dishwasher, steam-iron, coffee percolator — all here, you see . . . refrigerator . . . What's in it? Ah, an egg. Milk. Bread. A little piece of butter. You will find the garbage cans just outside the screen door. Five rooms on this floor, two living-rooms, dining-room, study, breakfast corner. . . . Upstairs, now: careful, we have to find another switch——'

Matthew found it.

'Ah! And up here, as you will see, four bedrooms, living-room with television set (only one channel, I'm afraid, but you will find the Hamelin station very enterprising, you will enjoy College of the Air at 6 a.m.), three bathrooms, two small rooms … make yourself at home, Mr. Pryar, consider yourself one of our community. And now we must just pay our brief respects to the President.'

The house appeared to be full of flying brown dust, though it was, as Matthew later discovered, perfectly clean. It was the first time in his life that he had ever caught himself expecting to see a ghost. The spirit of Mrs. MacLaughlin, doubled like a jack-knife, was almost visible.

'Sir, I think I had better perhaps have a wash, and perhaps a drink——'

'Ah, drink!' Dr. Parke stopped dead. 'Now that, I think, we didn't allow for. But if you drive down to the liquor store in Hamelin tomorrow, or, alternatively, drive up to Piltdown, I am sure you will be able to stock yourself handsomely.'

'I don't drive,' said Matthew. 'If someone could be so kind——'

The clock chimed seven in a voice of sickly charm.

'Quick, quick, we must be on our toes,' said Dr. Parke, 'if we want to catch the President before his dinner.'

Even the thought that the President would have to offer him a drink did not silence Matthew now.

'I think I might pay my respects to the President tomorrow. To be absolutely honest with you, I am rather hungry——'

'Ah, but he goes to Dartmouth tomorrow, he and Mrs. Pickersgill will be away for a week. So it's now or never, my dear fellow, now or never!'

He helped to stow Matthew's bags in the hall, then bundled Matthew back into the car and they were off again.

The chapel clock sang the quarters as they passed beneath the President's neo-Georgian portico.

The door was opened by a small, smudgy man with eyes like a lemur's, darkly ringed, and a fuzz of black hair standing up like an ill-placed tiara well to the back of his otherwise bald head. His clothes hung on him; they might have been bought to allow for growth. Matthew gave the faint sweet greeting he reserved for butlers, and wondered that the President couldn't get a better one.

'Ah, Tim!' cried Dr. Parke, 'we are just paying you a brief visit. This is Mr. Pryar, Mr. Matthew Pryar, not the poet but doubtless as distinguished, I'm sure——'

'How do you do?' said the President gloomily. He looked at his watch. 'A bit late, but better late than never.'

(That was what they all seemed to believe.)

'I can manage twenty minutes, then we're due elsewhere. Come in and sit down. Sit down, Dom, you must be exhausted. Now, Mr. Ryan,' he said to Matthew, 'let's get right down to brass tacks.'

'Delighted,' Matthew said, feeling giddy.

'Your proposition seems to the Trustees perfectly sensible taxwise. But if we look at it from the angle of the ten-year plan, that's a different matter. Say we raise twenty thousand on the first project, and then, for the sake of argument——'

'Tim,' said Dr. Parke, 'I did tell you. This is Mr. *Pryar*. Not Mr. Ryan.'

'Not?' The President jumped. 'Then who——'

'Mr. Pryar, the latest and last of our Visiting Fellows for this semester, the greatest English authority on the works of Dorothy Merlin. I told you,' he added plaintively, 'not the poet.'

'I thought she was a poet!' The President looked distraught.

'No, no, no, she is, but Mr. Pryar is not. A small academic joke.'

The President looked for the joke, failed to see it, offered Matthew a belated, a hunted welcome. At that moment something beautiful happened: a sound: the tinkle of ice in crystal, the rattle of glass on metal. Matthew had a vision of liquid gold and silver, gold of maples, silver of stars, all bound within a lovely singing, circumambulatory in galactic mist like the music of the spheres.

Not even a lifetime of good manners could prevent him from turning his head. Coming through the handsome corridor into the handsome room was a six-foot handsome woman, dark and grave, bearing a salver on which were four glasses.

She spoke with a foreign accent, and in her voice was a strong and beautiful boom.

'Good-evening, our dear Dominick, good-evening, Mr. Pryar.'

'Mrs. Pickersgill,' said the President hastily, 'my wife. Trilby, this is Mr. Pryar.'

'I know it to be Mr. Pryar, Timon, you heard me speak his name. And you should not have thought that he was Mr. Ryan, who is not coming until Tuesday week. Refreshment, Mr. Pryar!'

She held out the salver. His hand clutched the icy glass, which tinkled at him sweetly and also (he realized) with a kind of horrible innocence, like the giggle of an idiot. What he had got was a glass of ice-water.

'I pledge you,' said Trilby, 'I welcome you. I pledge you one and all.'

'Drink deep of the Pierian spring!' cried Dr. Parke, exhilarated.

Matthew felt a heat rising up behind his eyes. Dumbfounded, he believed it was tears.

'We are sorry,' said Trilby, when the refreshment had been consumed in silence, 'that we must now leave you. But we shall see you often, Mr. Pryar, and you must count upon us. Truly so. I am sincere.'

Then they were out again in the car, in a night which had turned so icy that it stung the nose and ears; Matthew and Dr. Parke.

'Well, Mr. Pryar,' said Parke, stopping before a fine building in Regency style, 'Mrs. Parke will be keeping my dinner hot for me, so I mustn't delay. You know what women can be, when it's a question of tardy menfolk, I'm sure! This is the Boosie House — B-O-O-S-I-E — the Faculty take luncheon in the Pump Room, which you will find on the first floor, and there is an excellent cafeteria below where the boys wait upon us and themselves. I shall leave you on your own to get a nice little snack, and then "dig in" comfortably into your quarters. You remember your house? First right, second left. It is good to have you with us, Mr. Pryar. You will find that at Cobb we are all members one of another. And now, let me wish you a very good night!'

He was off and away. Matthew, without his overcoat, was shivering in a deserted road. He approached the Boosie House cautiously: it seemed very ill-lit. A stranger and afraid, he tiptoed up the steps and pushed his way through. the heavy portals. Night and silence. A light burned below. He stumbled downstairs, found himself at the cafeteria door. On it was a notice which read:

'BREAKFAST 6 a.m.–9 a.m. SNACKS 5 p.m.–7 p.m.'

The chapel clock had just struck seven forty-five.

He found his way home somehow and into the kitchen, where he stood looking helplessly into the refrigerator.

Now Matthew had never done a single domestic chore, for himself or anyone else, in his whole life. He did, however, believe that an egg could be made edible by boiling it in water. It took him fifteen minutes to find a saucepan, another ten to discover how one turned on the hot plate. With tears still gathering, to his surprise and shame, in a thick clot stretching from the back of his nose to the middle of his forehead, he cooked that egg. For safety, he gave it thirty minutes. Then he ate the result (there was no egg-cup but of course he did not need one) with a piece of bread and butter (he could not find any salt), went upstairs and slept like a log till the sun awoke him, flashing from a transformation scene of peerless snow.

4. Friend and Fellow

The habits of Matthew's life had always been regular and sweet.

He drank and smoked moderately: low-sexed, he made love very moderately indeed, and only to women who were very nice. He woke at eight o'clock, ten minutes before his man came in with a pot of tea. During these ten minutes he lay on his back, quietly reviewing the events of the day before and the probabilities of the day to come. After his tea he arose, did a few moderate exercises, bathed, shaved, evacuated: returned to his room and ate a moderate breakfast set for him on a table in the window, where he could look out upon the manly elegance of St. James's Street.

These excellent habits helped him now. Even after the ordeals of his first day at Cobb, he was able to lie sweetly and calmly, staring up at the snow-light on the ceiling and trying to decide how he should overcome his difficulties. No one, of course, came in with a pot of tea: but Matthew bathed, shaved and dressed as meticulously as usual, thanked the Lord for giving him the foresight to bring a pair of rubbers, and looked forward optimistically to making a new beginning.

He had only one frightening thought, which was, that perhaps nobody would come to make his bed for him, and wash up the plate and saucer he had used the night before.

Oh, but surely, he said to himself, surely someone will. Of course someone will.

Closing his eyes as he passed through the drawing-room, just in case the ghost of Mrs. MacLaughlin might still be hanging about, he went out into the dazzling, freezing day and back to the Boosie House.

It looked cheerful this morning, with carefree young men in extraordinary caps of wool or fur streaming in and out of it. Clouts of snow flopped from rooftops, squirrels disappeared up trees like puffs of grey smoke, a bird red as a cocktail cherry caused Matthew to pause for a moment, stricken with delight.

He was humming 'Sheep May Safely Graze' again, though he did not realise it.

Heat hit him as he went down to the basement, so inhospitable the night before, so welcoming today. Faculty and students were lining up with trays: Matthew joined them, anxious to begin immediately the pleasant friendships lying ahead. Since he had been in America several times he was not unfamiliar with cafeteria practice; his heart singing, he took his tray, chose eating implements, and asked the serving student for orange juice, fried eggs, bacon, toast and coffee.

'Thank you most enormously,' he said, when all this arrived, and he meant it. At last he was going to eat.

The student gazed earnestly at Matthew's open, lineless face, at his blue eyes, his sharp profile, his hair cut by Mr. Crisp of Trumper's. He seemed puzzled. Perhaps he was puzzled by Matthew's speech, which, a sharply-recognisable brand of upper-class English, featured an introductory hooting noise followed by a slow drawl neatly an octave and a half lower down the scale.

'You're welcome,' he said.

With tray piled high, eggs like marguerites, bacon like medlar flowers encrusted in gold and pearl, Matthew chose to sit sociably at a table where two elderly gentlemen, with that wonderful snowdrift hair seen only on Americans, were finishing their coffee.

'Good-morning,' he said, 'I'm Matthew Pryar.'

Courteously and gravely they rose to greet him.

'You're from England?' said one. 'How do you like Hamelin?'

The other said, 'It's most unusual for the snow to be this early. What did you think of the fall colours this year, Mr. Pryar?'

Matthew replied that he was sure he should like Hamelin when he had seen a little more of it, and that the fall colours could not have been more excellent.

They enquired politely what was his mission at Cobb.

'I'm a Visiting Fellow,' Matthew said, and was surprised to see both faces very faintly cloud over.

'Well,' said one of the men, 'there certainly seem to be some excellent people among them this year. Dr. Tiepolo. Miss Corall. Professor Hefflinger. I'm sure you'll all be getting together.'

Matthew said he looked forward to this, and he plunged into his breakfast in a delirium of hungry bliss. The two gentlemen forgot him.

'If we assume there is a high-concentration of π-mesons——' said one.

'That's not paying enough attention to what we know of this range of particles,' the other rebuked him.

'Well, I'll grant you we might have to allow for K-mesons too,' conceded the first.

The conversation proceeded along these lines for some time. At last they rose, bade Matthew a courteous but rather startled farewell, as if surprised to find him still there, and went away.

Nobody else approached him, nor did he care. He too, at last, rose, went out into the stinging brightness and made his way in the direction of the Centre. Here would be friend and Fellow. Here, at least, would be Edith Corall, who would certainly know where you got food and drink. He had never been very fond of Edith, who was far too strident for his tastes, far too bonny an extrovert, streaking round Cambridge on her bicycle, wearing an artist's smock, tapered slacks, and a bright green cap of the fez variety on her canary hair. But at least he knew her: and at least she was fond, almost immoderately fond, of physical comforts.

As he passed into the heat a bright little secretary rose to greet him, explaining that she was Miss Ehrlinger, but everyone called her Pat. She had a stack of mail for him, it was on his desk in his room.

Nobody else seemed to be about; only, as he was told on enquiry, Doug Ruddock, the Emily Dickinson Fellow, who got as mad as all get out if disturbed. He wouldn't even answer the telephone. 'But there's something good about Dr. Ruddock,' Pat said, tautening her little, low-slung buttocks 'something real good!'

Matthew certainly hoped there was. He enquired about Miss Corall.

'Oh, she never shows up till eleven, if then. Neither does Dr. Tiepolo. And Miss Groby only works here in the evenings.'

When he enquired who the other Fellows were, Pat said he would find a list on his desk. 'And when you want one of the secretaries, you just give me a ring.'

Safe in his own room, he felt splendid, he felt important. The stack of mail, which he had not yet opened, ensured that importance: So did the telephone, the splendid desk, the lamps blooming like onions on stems of steel, the Swedish chairs. Alone, he opened the window and propped it open with one of those chairs, in the manner deplored by Dr. Parke but necessary to an Englishman if life were to be lived. Then he looked at his mail. There were eleven envelopes. Ten contained printed invitations to unenticing lectures. The eleventh contained a letter from Dorothy Merlin.

'I hope you are really going to put your back into the book and *not* slack about it, because it is all very well writing essays about my work, I have to have something between hard covers. And incidentally, why do you say you don't slack when you *know* you do? You should have every opportunity to *finish* it at Cobb. By the by, I have found an early draft of *Should Seven* which ought to be of supreme interest to scholars. I am sending you a copy, and trying to find out whether Texas would like to buy the original. I am NOT going to let Yale have it for nothing, even if they ask for it. (Which they haven't — doesn't that go to *show*?)

'No news here. Duncan is making a fool of himself with some horrible girl who says she is a deb but I think she is a housemaid. Do you know there is a so-called "revival" here of that unspeakable man, Skipton? Uttersons are bringing out what there is of some frightful book he was writing when he died. I told Billy Utterson I thought he was off his head — Billy was, I mean. Cosmo has bronchitis.'

This left Matthew with no mail to answer (though he had longed to use the secretaries), since he did not, of course, propose to answer Dorothy.

Having forgotten the distresses of his arrival, he began to feel very happy. Matthew, who had been bone-idle all his life (except during the war, when he had fought with considerable verve), had, during the past two years and under Dorothy's bludgeonings, perceived the romantic charm of the scholarly life. Its glow sank deep into his vitals. For the first time he regretted leaving Oxford without a degree. How delectable it would be if Cobb, after a decent interval, decided to give him an honorary one! He would have a hood of emerald corded silk and white velvet. He would not, naturally, let people call him Dr. Pryar: but Dr. Pryar he would be thenceforward to himself.

Unfolding the list of Visiting Fellows, he realised how meagre were his qualifications to exist in this world at all, and he was swept by the disagreeable, utterly unfamiliar, emotion of humility.

'PRYAR, Matthew. Educ. Eton and Oxford, England. Author of monograph, and essays in various periodicals (*Encounter, London Magazine, Observer, Times Lit. Supp., Botteghe Oscure, Paris Review, Queen*, etc.), on the works of Dorothy Merlin.'

Not good. Not in comparison with his new colleagues.

'CORALL, Edith Laventie, Fellow of Madingley College, Cambridge, since 1944, mediaevalist. M.A., D.Litt., 5 hon. degrees. *Pubs: "The First Crusade"* (3 vols.), *"The Counts of Flanders", "Household Records of the Gravensteen, Ghent".*'

'GROBY, Maud Foster, Chair of Slavonic Languages, Latimer College, Stamford, England. M.A., Ph.D., Hon. D.Litt. (London), Litt.D. (Columbia), L.H.D. (Amherst), *Pub:* (in progress) *"New Recensions of the Patristic Hagiographies among the Slavs in the Light of the Hesychast Doctrines and the Cyrillo-Methodian Tradition"* (4 vols.).'

'HEFFLINGER, Rudolf. Zoologist. Ph.D. (Tübingen), Hon.Sc.D. (Princeton), D.Sc. (Pennsylvania), D.Sc. (Chicago), D.Sc. (Oberlin). *Pub: "Araneae of the Andes"* (3 vols.), 116 papers in scientific journals.'

'RUDDOCK, Douglas Parmelee. Ph.D. (Wisconsin). Professor of American Literature, Osborne College, Utah. *Pubs: "Emily Dickinson, Steps towards a Synthesis", "Emily Dickinson, a*

Preliminary Enquiry into Sources", (in preparation) *"Emily Dickinson: a Tentative Appraisal of Imagery"*. EMILY DICKINSON FELLOW, Cobb College, 1959.'

'TIEPOLO, Carlo. Sociologist. Ph.D. (Harvard). Assoc. Prof. University of Illinois. *Pubs: "A Crowd of Hermits", "The City — The Vacuum", "Stylites on Main Street"* (Pulitzer Prize, 1956).'

'WOHLGEMUTT, Herman. Ph.D. (Princeton). Professor of Mathematics, Atlanta Polytechnic. *Pubs:* 77 papers in mathematical journals.'

Matthew, with only one meal inside him during the past forty-eight hours, was tempted once more to cry. But this he resisted. He was here to work. He was here to begin the book on Dorothy, the one he had deceived her into thinking he had begun already. In one of the drawers of his desk he found a stack of ruled paper. He took it all out and set it before him. He straightened his Hardy Amies tie, he shot his pale grey cuffs. Taking a tip from Douglas Parmelee Ruddock, he set down a title:

'DOROTHY MERLIN: TENTATIVE STEPS TOWARDS A SYNTHESIS OF IMAGERY.'

That, he thought, would do the trick, would make his name, would set his feet on the path towards the emerald hood.

He took Dorothy's entire *œuvre* from his briefcase and weighed it thoughtfully: just under eighteen ounces he supposed. He hoped she wouldn't write anything more till he was through.

Outside, above the garden, the sky was butcher-blue, with dazzling clouds whipping about it. Tiny little birds hopped hopefully about the snow. An aeroplane scrawled its slow silver eastwards. Though the garden lay at Matthew's back, he saw all this, because he had swivelled his chair round in order to look at it. For he found he could not write a word. All in good time, he comforted himself. You are a bit disoriented at the moment. Be peaceful, and it will come.

He wished he had brought an interesting book with him, not one of Dorothy's. He hoped somebody would drop in soon, one of his colleagues. He wanted the radiant scholarly get-together to start.

Half an hour passed, and he could bear his loneliness no longer. Jumping up with an air of resolution, he left his office and walked along the superheated corridor, studying the names on the doors. Edith Corall: her door was ajar, the room empty. Miss Groby wasn't there during the day. Hefflinger, the zoologist, he didn't fancy, and though he heard a cough from the office of Wohlgemutt, Matthew did not know how to open a light conversation with a mathematician. Tiepolo's room was empty. But Douglas Ruddock was in, banging away on a typewriter.

Matthew hesitated for a moment. Ruddock might be 'mad as all get out' (he admired the American gift for the perfect phrase), but he would soon rise above that. Matthew, in his loneliness, risked it. He knocked loudly and blithely, and was rewarded with a sort of snarl which he interpreted as permission to enter.

5. Miss Dickinson's Secret

What he saw before him was something like an owl convulsed and swollen with rage. A round white face with a beak in it, round pale eyes behind round glasses, a crest of pale hair. The owl sat silent and glaring.

'Do forgive me, Dr. Ruddock,' Matthew said airily, though his step towards the desk was uncertain, 'I hate disturbing you, but I thought it would be nice for us to meet. I'm Pryar.'

The owl swallowed once or twice, then, deliberately, swept all its books from table to floor.

'Oh, Lord,' said Matthew, 'what a nuisance! No, don't you move. I'm in a perfect position to retrieve.' He dropped gracefully to one knee and scooped up books and papers. 'There!' he cried at last, offering them as if they were glass slippers on an heraldic cushion.

'What gives with you?' said the owl at last.

This was incomprehensible. 'Gives? With me?'

Dr. Ruddock rose slowly, and in doing so became less owl-like, since he was far taller than he had seemed while seated. 'You say you're Mr. Pryar?'

'Indeed, yes!' Matthew said with a gay smile and an air of revelation, as if he had not truly realised it himself until that moment. 'I'm working on Dorothy Merlin. You're the Emily Dickinson Fellow, I know. I've always thought she must be fascinating, so simply deadly in white dimity, always lurking, and thinking thoughts far too large for her. I do wonder why she had to lurk.'

Dr. Ruddock sat down again, and with a hopeless wave of the hand motioned Matthew to a chair. He said nothing. His round eyes studied Matthew's face.

'I know it's quite shocking to disturb you, my dear fellow, but how else does one get to know one's colleagues?'

'One doesn't,' said Dr. Ruddock.

'Not ever?'

'Not much. Not often.'

'But don't you want to?'

Dr. Ruddock began to pant and swell again. 'Now see here, Mr. Pryar, some of us want to work. Some don't. Groby drinks. If you get to know people you get no work done. Still, since you're here —' he pushed a packet of Marlboroughs at Matthew. 'Pleased to meet you,' he muttered.

'I won't stay a moment. But I'm delighted to meet you, I really am. Emily Dickinson has always been a passion of mine, and I know you're the world authority.' He saw a gleam that might have been of gratification moving across the white, pasty face. 'Pretty well everyone knows that, don't you think?' Matthew continued engagingly. 'In fact, I was at a party — *not* literary, in the least — just before I came away, and Mildred Shropshire (that's the dowager duchess, not the new one) said, "If you want to know why she lurked you must read one of those marvellous books by Douglas Ruddock." I assure you, she did. Now if Mildred were an intellectual that wouldn't be significant: but when you realise that people like *Mildred* know, then you realise it's got around.'

Gratification was palpable now. Something like a smile appeared. Matthew was delighted with the words he had put, somewhat implausibly, into Mildred's mouth. He leaned forward, earnest, a fellow scholar. '*Do* you know why she lurked?'

Dr. Ruddock sprang up suddenly, wrenched the chair out of the window, which swung to, and made sure the door was shut. 'Are you close-mouthed, Mr. Pryar?'

'Oh, do call me Matthew.'

'Doug.'

'I'd love to call you Doug. Yes, I can keep a close mouth. I'm terribly discreet, in fact.'

'Well — she drank.'

Matthew was so startled that he dropped his cigarette. When he arose from picking it up, it was to see Ruddock irradiated by a smile of infinite cunning.

'She drank?'

'Listen, this mustn't get out. Not till I've collected all the evidence. I'm working on the imagery in the poems and the letters.' The man was obviously wild with excitement, with *furor academicus*. 'She had to lurk, as you put it, because half the time, I suspect, she could hardly stand.'

'The little tippler reeling against the sun, or whatever?' Matthew suggested knowledgeably.

'That!' Ruddock gave a ferocious sneer. 'That's only one of a thousand pieces of suggestiveness! And do you know what her tipple was?'

'No,' said Matthew, locked in with a madman and thinking now of escape.

'Rum. I think so. Rum. That's what *she* meant by "Manzanilla". Or it could have been sherry — she talked about sherry.'

'Has anyone been through the household books?' This seemed to Matthew a very scholarly suggestion, and he was proud of himself.

'Just try and get at them,' said Doug Ruddock, darkening, 'if you ask me, there's a conspiracy.'

' "Thunder in the room," ' said Matthew, just for the sake of something to say.

Ruddock gave a roar. 'By God, that's great! Just you think! "That stop sensation in the soul, And thunder in the room!" Ever been drunk, Matt?' Friendliness was complete.

'Oh, often. Often.'

'Then isn't that the perfect description of the sensations felt by the inexperienced drinker?'

'I thought you said she was frightfully experienced.'

'Ah, but she was remembering the days when she wasn't. That's 1860, that poem. Now think, man, think! Could there be anything more revealing?'

'But the context——'

' "I got so I could speak his name," ' said Ruddock

24

contemptuously. 'Pure window-dressing! Shoved in to put us off the scent. No, the whole poem is written for the sake of those last two lines. *She couldn't hold them back.* She had to reveal the truth in her own — admittedly magnificent — way. So she tried to kid us she was talking about love, when she was really talking about what happens when you suddenly find you've hit the bottle a bit too hard. "That stop sensation" — do you ever go deaf when you're drunk, Matt? That's what she's getting at. "And thunder in the room." Your ears unstopper themselves and there's a sort of subterranean roaring — after which you sometimes pass out like a light. Now then: have I got something here or have I not?'

Ruddock's gaze bored into Matthew's. The silence in the hot room developed an inward ticking; there might be thunder in it, too. A great slab of snow fell from the roof on to the balcony.

Matthew was saved from the necessity of reply by the bursting open of the door, the bursting in of a large ginger cat, man-propelled, and the bursting out of a loud, harsh voice.

'Pussy wants in!'

Standing in the opening was a huge, hot-eyed, blue-chinned man, wearing a bright check shirt, a brown parka and a multicoloured woollen cap pulled down over his ears. He was about thirty-five or -six and, though he was not fat, must have weighed at least two hundred and ten pounds. Eyebrows bushy as moustaches started out below the hat brim, from them depending a fleshy nose and a mobile, fleshy mouth.

'And keep him out of my room, because I damned well don't want him there!'

Leaping on to Ruddock's papers the cat began to purr loudly, to make dough.

Matthew rose hastily, sensing trouble, but there was none. Ruddock merely gave the cat a passionate, reciprocated embrace and said, 'Thanks. Chuck, this is Mr. Pryar. Matt, this is Carlo Tiepolo. Social Studies.'

Tiepolo shook hands crushingly. 'You English? I was there in the war. Broadway, Worcestershire. Know Broadway?'

'What,' said Matthew enviously, 'all the war?' It had been his misfortune to spend most of it in the Western Desert.

'Till the Normandy landings. What are you doing here, Matt?'

Matthew explained about Dorothy Merlin.

'Well,' said Tiepolo, 'that's a gap in my knowledge.'

Ruddock continued to drool over the cat. 'He just walked in one day,' he explained to Matthew, who had not enquired about its provenance, 'he just walked in here, through the open window and started to purr. Just like that. Listen to him.'

'Well, you keep him away from me, he's just piddled in my paper-basket.'

'He never does that to me. I guess you frightened him.'

'I'll frighten the tail off him if he comes back.'

'Well,' said Matthew, intervening, 'I'd better be getting back to work. So delightful to meet you both. I hope I shall see a great deal of you.'

He left hastily, but was followed by Tiepolo. 'That guy's a nut. Sits there with his cat, hour after hour, riffling through books, never seems to put a word on paper.' (Matthew was learn later that Chuck Tiepolo believed nobody worked but himself.) 'You settled in all right?'

'Well, yes,' Matthew said, seizing an opportunity. 'But I was wondering whether there was any means of transportation either to Hamelin or Piltdown. I want some Scotch.'

'Don't you have a car?'

'No.'

'If you like to take mine——'

'I don't drive.'

'Don't *drive*? Then how the hell do you think you're going to get around?'

'It does seem rather remote here.'

'I'd take you myself, but I have a class this afternoon. I do a little teaching here. Are you going to teach?'

'I'm not sure,' said Matthew nervously.

'Well. About the Scotch. I don't think you'll get a lift today because it's the Cobb-Dartmouth game.' Tiepolo looked at Matthew with sudden, villainous intensity. He said, 'You a moral man?'

'Well, I hope — reasonably. I mean, in what way?'

'If you're a moral man I don't know how you'll get your Scotch. But if you can go easy on the scruples——'

'I think,' Matthew said delicately, 'that if it didn't involve some actual criminal offence, I might.'

'Come on, then. And this is some actual criminal offence.'

Tiepolo led the way to Miss Groby's room and knocked. Satisfied that no one was there, he led Matthew in to an appalling pig-muddle. Papers and books were everywhere, on the chairs, the sofa, the floor. Everywhere there were full ashtrays. Over the typing-chair hung a brown wool cardigan and a pair of thick blue woollen stockings. On the desk was a large blotting-pad, scribbled over with the words, 'It is hell, hell, hell, hell, hell, hell, hell.'

'She gets low,' said Tiepolo.

He opened a filing cabinet. In it were six bottles of Scotch, half-full.

'Nutty, isn't it? She has to pick and choose. Likes to keep them at the same level. Here, you take this one, and you can put it back Monday.'

Matthew said he couldn't possibly. She would be sure to find out.

'Never, she's too fuzzy. She can't count any more. Now do you want it, or don't you?'

Matthew did feel like a criminal, and didn't care for the sensation: but his moral sense was overcome by desire. 'Yes,' he said.

'So that ought to keep you going. I've got to run over to Piltdown myself Monday morning; I'll bring you back some liquor.'

Tiepolo closed the cabinet door. Matthew, a bulge under his jacket, crept out into the passage. He was asked abruptly whether he thought he would like it at Cobb.

'Oh, I'm sure I will.'

'Hah!'

'I beg your pardon?'

'I said Hah.'

'I am, I confess, a little bothered by my domestic arrangements, but I thought if I had a word with Dr. Parke——'

'Hah! Parke! You wait and see. You just wait.'

'And of course I look forward to meeting some of the Faculty——'

'Faculty? We don't see them. We're lepers here.' Tiepolo said this with an air of dark, seething satisfaction. 'You wait. Well, I hope you've got something to eat in the house. So long.'

He was off and away, plunging down the passage and into his own room. Matthew was alone once more, in silence, with his Scotch.

6. A Smell of Roast Beef

He went to his house first, to have a drink from the bottle and then conceal it. (No servant had been in yet, but he supposed the bed would be made later.) Afterwards, he went across creaking snow, hyacinth-coloured from the reflected sky, towards the Boosie House. He realised for the first time what an exceptionally beautiful building it was, labelled 1912, but created in Regency style, half-serious, half-playful, stiltedly delightful. Charming ironwork, now sparkling black and white, sustained the verandahs; delicate stairs swept up to the porch like the gesture of an inviting female hand. Over the door was a plaque:

THE GIFT OF
ELEANOR GREENFIELD BOOSIE
IN MEMORY OF
THOMAS BURNS BOOSIE
PRESIDENT OF COBB COLLEGE (1879–1910)
'HOSPITABLE BE THY HOUSE'

This was soothing, rooted in a pleasant past, and made him hungry for his lunch. He realised, however, that it was only eleven-thirty, and that he would have to wait for half an hour at least: so he walked happily about the campus, watching young men erect astonishing animals out of old iron, of emerald and orange crêpe paper, outside fraternity houses, and putting up fighting slogans in preparation for the big game. They all seemed very cordial, and many said 'Hullo' to him, turning upon him their cheerful, snow-flushed faces. He thought how happy a day it would be when English undergraduates offered so spontaneous a welcome to the stranger within the gates, instead of looking glacial and stuffed, like so many *bombes surprises*. He realised, with regret, that he had been just such a *bombe surprise* himself: one of the reasons the English were not universally popular became plain to him.

Whisky-warmed, filled with American euphoria, he waved to the young men as he went by. Twelve o'clock came. There was a great bustle around the Boosie House, colourful youths streaming noisily in and out. Bursts of random cheering sounded beyond the trees, snatches of song about Always on the job for Dear Old Cobb.

Matthew pushed his way confidently through joyous crowds to the Pump Room which, seen through a stately archway, glimmered with wax polish, glass and silver. A fine smell of roasting meat filled the air. An elderly woman came blithely forth to greet him.

'You must be Mr. Pryar. Welcome to Cobb! I'm Mrs. Untermeyer, I'm in charge of the Boosie House. I'm afraid there's no lunch here today, only for the teams. But on Monday I'll keep a place for you. Have a good time while you're here!'

Undaunted, despite this considerable jolt, Matthew ran downstairs to the cafeteria. But here his way was barred by a bland young man with a beard, who also seemed to know who he was.

'Mr. Pryar? Glad to see you, sir. I'm Hubsner, Mathematics. I'm afraid we've had to pre-empt this room today for the geometers — the teams have taken over upstairs, you know otherwise . . . Of course,' — a shade of doubt appeared on Mr. Hubsner's face — 'you could sit with us if you liked.'

This invitation did not seem to Matthew sufficiently cordial for acceptance. Politely declining, he raced upstairs again and out into the air. He stood beneath a scarlet maple charmingly tufted with snow and puffing off powder with the slightest breeze. He realised the full extent of his dilemma. There was no food. Tomorrow would be Sunday: and there would be no food. He had already eaten his egg. Taken by an access of hebephrenia, he stood without moving, unable to move, incapable of coherent thought.

But coming over the campus towards him, a cashmere scarf of orange and green checks wound twice about his throat, a plastic rain-hat on his head, was little Dr. Parke.

'Ah, Mr. Pryar! Getting your bearings, eh? Settling down among us?'

Matthew was released from the horrible trance.

'I'm most terribly sorry to be a nuisance,' he said with his own brand of airy firmness, 'but do you know where I can get something to eat? Apparently this delightful house has been pre-empted by the teams and by geometers. If you'd be so very kind as to direct me somewhere——'

'Ah,' cried Dr. Parke, 'that reminds me! Mrs. Parke is going to ask you to tea next week.'

'I couldn't be more pleased. Do thank her so much from me. But it is actually a question of food *now*.'

'Of course it is, my dear boy! That's easy. If all the questions asked me were as easy as that one, now, my job would be a sinecure. At Piltdown, on Main Street, just two blocks beyond the Citizens Savings Bank, there is a splendid delicatessen, kept by Mr. Balyai — quite a character — you must draw Mr. Balyai out, make him talk to you. I suggest you run along there and stock up! Eh? He has everything you need, everything the heart could desire. Yes, yes, certainly you must make Mr. Balyai's acquaintance. It is a real experience. He's been there . . . let me see . . . as long as I've been here! Twenty-five years, yes, all of a quarter of a century.'

'A quarter of a century', delivered by a man of Dr. Parke's spiritual weight, takes on the thud of a hundred years. The past came down between the trees, ghosts debated together the tactics of Bull Run.

'I have no car,' said Matthew, 'and I cannot drive.'

'Oh dear! And it is, of course, quite a long way. Quite a long way to walk.'

'I understand that it is a matter of twenty miles.'

Dr. Parke agreed to this. He paused for a moment in thought, then flung his hands up in the air. 'Ah, now, I think I have it. Yes. If you go to Anderson's gas-station — not twenty miles, my dear fellow, not more than two — you will be able to hire a cab. How's that, eh? Go straight on past your house, turn right at the intersection and keep steadily on. You can't miss it.'

Matthew thanked him with restrained enthusiasm and set off on the bitter walk. The road ran steeply and he fell down twice. He did not sing to himself. He very much doubted whether any cab would be available.

In this, however, he was wrong, since one of Anderson's *aides* skidded him up to Piltdown, where he visited Mr. Balyia (whose voluble and gesticulatory eccentricities might have charmed him in circumstances quite different) and bought some tins of food. He also remembered, at the last moment, buy a can-opener, just in case the kitchen of his house was not fully equipped. He was almost elated by his own good sense in doing this. Think of it, himself sitting hungry before pile of tins, unable to get at the contents! 'Old Ugolino's grief.' he thought. He also bought six bottles of whisky. On the drive down again, where the skidding was far worse, he began to contemplate his administrative capacities. He would know how to run the Centre, given half a chance. And it would be a pleasing job. Dr. Parke couldn't be far from retirement; if Matthew went about it the right way, might he not induce the Trustees to appoint a successor from outside? It might be as well to make contact with a Trustee or two, when an opportunity arose. He lost himself deeply in this fantasy, and did not awaken from it till he found himself carrying the bottles and tins into his still unservanted house. He had forgotten to buy bread, but he remained philosophical. He ate some liver pâté, some ham, some cheese and a bag of pretzels.

He thought — Fantasy? Why fantasy?

Invigorated, he went out for a long walk. When he returned, it was to find general mourning. Cobb had lost the game to Dartmouth, 27–0.

7. Poor Edith

Sunday was not an easy day and Matthew had no variation of diet. It occurred to him to try to contact his colleagues, but all seemed to be away for the week-end. They knew a thing or two.

After the promise of thaw, the weather had hardened up and the little waterfall on the edge of the campus was a chandelier of radiant ice. The trees held their fluff stiffly; the paths were perilous.

In the evening, having successfully performed the feat of bed-making for the second time, he decided to go down to the Centre and replace Miss Groby's Scotch before she returned from wherever she was. He made his way by flashlight, slipping and sliding, clutching at the trees, to the deserted building, let himself in to darkness and crept upstairs. He switched on the corridor lights, which could not be seen from the outside. Fourth door, Dr. Maud Groby. He opened it and went in.

Matthew, unused to vulgarisms of speech or thought, nevertheless registered unconsciously the fact that she had given him a Turn. For there she was at her desk, slumped over her messy papers, but raising at him, nevertheless, in the glare from the doorway, her fine wild animal's eyes. He was so taken aback that he shot out at her, at arm's length, the bottle half-full of whisky, prepared to the precise level of the one he had borrowed. He heard himself saying, 'I brought you this,' and he switched on a lamp.

'My dear boy,' she said without surprise, thickly, plummily, 'how very, very kind! To bring me a gift, a gift!'

She was pretty drunk, but able to stand. Rocking up on to her feet she grasped the bottle firmly, opened the filing cabinet and placed it within. Matthew noticed that only two bottles now contained any liquor. 'A gift,' Miss Groby muttered, 'a gift. Sit down, dear man. Who are you?'

He told her: she seemed none the wiser.

'It shows,' she said, 'that there are still good people in this world of ours. Gift-bringers. Good, good men. It restorsh onesh faith in human nature.' Her tongue slurred here: up to now she had spoken quite plainly, though on the soft side. 'It restores one's faith in human nature,' she repeated with clarity. 'Yes, Mr. Pryar, sit down. It is sad here. Often lonely. You will discover.'

He told her he had already discovered it, and enquired with interest where she had found anything to eat over the week-end.

'Scosh and peanut butter,' said Miss Groby, 'is a truly balanced diet. Scotch,' she added firmly. 'Take my advice, Mr. Pryar, lay in a store. You will find all the calories you need. There is peanut butter at the college shop. Behind the Boosie House.'

'The shop? What does it sell?'

'Behind the Boosie House. It sells razhor-blays, shaving-shoap, shtamps, peanut butter, jam.'

Matthew enquired politely whether it also sold scented rushes and was kept by a sheep.

Miss Groby appreciated the point of this, and she smiled, pushing back the nested hair from her face. 'You might think so.'

'How long have you been at Cobb?'

This was fatal, since it made her relapse into gloom. 'Months and months and munsh. And more munsh to come. The academic year.'

'I am so truly sorry,' said Matthew, meaning it. 'I am only here for two.'

'Doing what?'

He explained about Dorothy Merlin. This went home. 'A rude woman,' she said, 'I remember her lecturing at Stamford. A silly, rude woman. She knew nothing. Nothing whatsoever.'

'Oh, come! We can't expect too much of poets.'

'Nothing what-so-ever,' said Miss Groby, and forgot about Matthew, totally. Reaching for his gift, she poured herself at least four fingers into a paper cup. 'Rude, rude, rude. Silly and rude.

She was a mother, she said. Of seven. Poor brats, poor brats. Seven poor brats.' She began to weep, not unhappily.

Matthew slipped out.

At breakfast time on Monday, in the cafeteria, he was hungry and resolute.

He joined a table at which sat Dr. Parke and two members of the Faculty, to whom he was introduced. They were drinking coffee.

'I say,' said Matthew, 'is that all you have for breakfast? What Spartans you all are!'

The strangers looked away.

'Breakfast, my dear boy?' Dr. Parke silvered over with mirth 'This is our mid-morning break! Now, what is it o'clock? Twenty-five minutes past nine. Why, we were all breakfasting betimes, at home, with our good ladies, no later than a quarter of seven!'

'You are very stalwart,' Matthew replied. 'I fear I am merely English.'

He noticed that the strangers seemed determined to ignore him, but since he had other things to worry about, they did not bother him.

'Ah, England! Mrs. Parke and I went to Scotland last year and to Stratford-upon-Avon. Well, I expect you are truly settled in by now. If there is anything I can do for you, let me know. Don't hesitate to let me know.'

Matthew raised his voice so that, by no means noisy, it was crystalline enough to cut across the din of the room. It sounded beautiful to him: he would have been audible, without the slightest strain, to the little deaf boy at the back of the gallery.

'I was only thinking,' he said, 'what a pity it is that the delightful house you have so very kindly lent to me is going to be in such poor trim in eight weeks' time. I shall do my best, of course, but I am simply inept — I can't help it. I suppose I could use a duster. I must certainly learn to use a duster. I wonder how one does?'

That same afternoon, an angry-looking woman arrived at Matthew's house, telling him she was prepared to help out for two hours a week, though she was only doing it to oblige Dr. Parke, who had enough on his hands already.

'How absolutely splendid of you!' he exclaimed, with such relief that her expression softened. 'Isn't it going to be terribly hard work for you, cleaning up after someone totally and irreparably helpless? Because I am,' he added, to leave her in no doubt.

All the same, he decided to confine himself to two rooms only.

It seemed to him, when he had made certain telephone calls to old friends who lived in Connecticut and up the Hudson Valley, that life was straightening itself out for him at last. He had fixed up every week-end in the future except for the last two; and all those friends were rich, with butlers. The two he had not yet contacted were even richer.

In the evening, Edith Corall telephoned him. 'Hullo, Matt. How are you? I'm in the apartment block behind the gym. 207. Come round and have a drink.' These were not at all like Edith's normal tones, which were unsubdued. He ate the last of the ham and went to visit her.

When she opened the door he got a shock. She was wearing an ordinary tweed skirt and a miserable-looking grey sweater. The cigarette, in familiar jade holder, stuck out of a grayish face: the canary hair had greyed and flattened.

'My darling Edith,' Matthew cried, kissing her hand, 'as marvellous as ever! It is really most splendid to see you.'

She gave him an unblinking stare. 'You know what Captain Scott said at the South Pole?'

' "God, this is an Awful Place",' Matthew supplied her, with feeling.

'And you see what it has done to me.'

'Believe me, dear Edith, I cannot see the slightest difference——'

'The time for flattery has passed, Matt. I am telling you, it has got me down.' She led him into a pleasant, bright, untidy room, fortunately stocked up with bottles and cocktail bits. She gave Matthew and herself a stiff drink. 'I have only another five weeks to go. If it were six weeks, I think I should die.'

He was alarmed. This was not the brilliant parrakeet of Cambridge (or perhaps the kingfisher, flashing through the grey undergrowth), not the bird he knew, not the bird on the bicycle, beak cocked at the sky, golden crest flashing up Petty Cury, down King's Parade. Ah, bird on a bicycle! he thought, *Bonjour tristesse!* He begged her to explain.

'There is a hairdresser in Hamelin,' she said, 'and a barber in Piltdown. It takes me days of organisation to get either to one or the other — and I have been reduced to the barber before now, simply because someone happened to be driving that direction. There are three mediaevalists at Cobb, one is of the highest world standing — pretty well as good as I am. None has called on me. The food at the Boosie House is unspeakable; I do not like pears with cream cheese, pineapple with ham, or marshmallow in my lettuce. The Pickersgills asked me to dine once, and took me to the Pump Room. We sat down to eat at six forty-five. At eight sharp they left to go to a play-reading. *Krapp's Last Tape*, if I remember. Can there be a play-reading of *Krapp's Last Tape*? Or is it a monologue? Anyway.'

'The Faculty can't bear us, they think we are blacklegs. Some of us can't bear each other. Tiepolo is a silly big thug, Ruddock is mad, Maud Groby is even more broken than I am. Hefflinger is a merry old bastard, but I am afraid of his pets.'

'Pets?'

'You will see. Wohlgemutt adores it here,' she went on, 'and sees nothing wrong in it, which makes *him* a blackleg, so *we* don't like *him.*'

Edith Corall sank down and burst into tears.

Matthew more alarmed than ever, tried to embrace her, remembered that she did not much care for embraces and tried to withdraw: but she clutched him around the neck and would not let him go.

'And I have to get up and go out to breakfast. I have a kitchenette but I can't cook. I never cook. Oh, Matthew, I haven't had to *dress before breakfast* since I was twenty-five!'

He reminded her that Americans were a sturdy people, accustomed to roughing it, and to working longer hours.

'They may work longer hours but they don't get any more done than we do. Anyway, this is supposed to be the land of luxury.'

'Luxury,' said Matthew, 'but not comfort. Bless them, they are the most generous, the most magnanimous people on earth, but their real standards are those of the Frontier. The only two things that persuade them of their comfort are overheated rooms and admirable water-closets. Compare America with Switzerland, with Holland, with Belgium! I, too, am living in a covered wagon, Edith,' he added with gentle firmness, 'and it is worse for me than for you because there are twelve rooms in it.'

At that moment there was a knock at the door. She dried her eyes and rushed to open it. On the threshold was a gay-looking, squat man of about fifty, with twinkling glasses and red hair *en brosse.*

'Ach, my dear Miss Edith Corall!' (He had an accent.) 'I was just passing, and I thought I would look in for a little chat. We are all lepers, no? So lepers should be happy together.'

She backed away. 'Dr. Hefflinger! What have you got in your pockets?'

He burst into merriment and wagged a finger. 'There you go, so foolish, for such a wise woman! Perhaps I have nothing.'

'You don't bloody well come in here till I'm sure you have nothing.'

'Look, I turn my pockets out——'

'No, you don't! You just *tell* me!'

'I turn just one pocket out, then, and you will not be silly——'

She screamed and jumped on a chair.

'Now, now, I tease you! My pockets are empty. I have not even Susie. Be good, come down, and introduce me to this gentleman, who must be Mr. Pryar.'

'You swear?' she cried.

'I swear. See!' With the rapid movement of a conjurer he turned out all his pockets. Nothing emerged but money, matches and keys. He helped Edith down, and knelt to retrieve his property.

'All right,' she said grudgingly, 'sit down and have a drink.'

Matthew introduced himself formally and was pump-handled.

'You are the great Merlin scholar, you need not tell me,' said Hefflinger. 'I had the great pleasure once of meeting Miss Dorothy

Merlin.' He twinkled largely. 'I thought that in appearance she was a little bit like my Susie.'

Matthew, who had guessed what Susie was, nodded appreciatively. 'But she is tremendously impressive when you really know her,' he said, on the defensive.

They settled down together, Edith still trembling slightly but looking less tearful. Dr. Hefflinger explained, modestly, the true reason for his visit. Tomorrow night he was to lecture in the Pump Room, because the lecture room in the biology building had been pre-empted by the Structural Linguists. He was sure everyone would be muddled about the new *venue*, and that, apart from students, few people would come. 'So please do support me, it means much to me to see a friendly face, and besides, you will not have anything else to do.'

'*No*,' said Edith.

'There will be lantern-slides. Only slides.'

'You promise?'

'On my soul,' said Hefflinger.

Matthew, who had been regarding him with interest, now concentrated his attention upon something like a tiny black thread which had appeared against the whiteness of the handkerchief in Hefflinger's breast-pocket, and was waving gently to and fro.

'Edith,' he said swiftly, 'be a dear girl and give me another drink. I do so apologise for my greed, but life is just too much. Please.' He held out his glass. As she turned her back on them to refill it, he mouthed passionately at Hefflinger who, by happy chance, latched on at once, glanced down at his chest and rammed both handkerchief and mobile thread out of sight. He mouthed back ruefully, smiling, 'So silly. I had forgot. But it is only Titine, after all.'

'All right,' said Edith, 'I will come to your lecture. But I shall sit near the door.'

He bounced up. 'You are a great and wonderful woman! Mr. Pryar is a wonderful man. It will honour me to have your support. And now, sustained by this so wonderful drink——'

He had, Matthew thought, adopted the speech of the professor in *Dracula*.

'— I shall run along, back to my work.'

He kissed Edith's hand, making a better job of it than Matthew had done, since he was born to the gesture, and trotted off.

Edith did not refer again to his visit. She and Matthew got rather drunk together, and she wept a little more. She had always known, she told him, that he was a gentleman, but now she knew he was also a scholar. 'You are a *scholar and a gentleman*, Matt,' she said. 'I always wondered what it meant and now I know. And I don't care if I do sound vulgar, I always do when I am a little tiddley. I was born in Brixton and you know it, Matt. So why should I pretend?'

He murmured something highly complimentary concerning her birthplace.

'Yes, you are a scholar and a gentleman. Matt, they have broken me. Forgive me.' She added, in Provençal,

> 'Merce quiér a mon compaignon
> S'anc li fi tort qu'il m'o perdon.'

'What *does* that mean, Edith? You really mustn't show off, you know.'

'It means, "Do forgive me, my friend, if I've hurt your feelings." '

'But you haven't! How could you? I adore to be a scholar and a gentleman! Dear Edith, you really must put on your wonderful green fez again and let us see the old You.'

'If that brute had brought Susie,' she mused, 'I'd have killed him.'

8. Meeting with a Trustee

It was a splendid afternoon. The young men sparkled down the ski-slopes like lovely little aeroplanes caught in the sun. By nightfall the infirmary would be filled with broken collar-bones and the six psychiatrists would be hard at work on students who resented their athletic failure and thought their mothers might have something to do with it.

Matthew, leaving the Boosie House after a horrible lunch (hashed corned beef, rigid, surmounted by a rigid poached egg), ran slap into a friend.

This was Tom Helliwell, once a Rhodes Scholar, whom he had known at Oxford, and who now came crunching over the snow to meet him, his young-old face lit with pleasure, his blue eyes glittering, his silver-gilt hair prettied by the dust of snow.

He and Matthew exclaimed with surprise at finding each other so high up the slopes of New Hampshire.

'I'm a Trustee of this place, didn't you know?' Tom said. 'I'd no idea they'd had the brains to appoint you this semester, Matt, or I'd have been on the spot to meet you. Have. You had your lunch?'

Matthew said, 'In a sense.'

'I've got the car here. Let's run over to the inn at Monkshill — it won't take forty minutes.'

Monkshill, he explained, was a few miles above Piltdown, and the only decent food for miles around was to be found there. He did not suppose Matthew had eaten very much: he could surely manage something light and a drink.

So they drove until they came to a Pickwickian hostelry full of heat and darkness and pleasant odours. (On the drive Matthew had discovered that his friend, through an unexpected inheritance, had become rather rich: which explained the trusteeship.)

'Now are you settled down and comfortable?' Tom asked anxiously, after they had ordered. 'And is your work coming along? What work are you doing, if I may enquire?'

Matthew, no fool, launched immediately upon the latter subject, outlining for his host, with a skill he had not even suspected in himself, a plan for his book on Dorothy Merlin which he had not even conceived until that moment. 'Yet,' he added diffidently, 'I often wonder whether I shall really bring it off. My only real gift, such as it is, is for administration: that comes easy.'

And when Tom had demurred at his doubts, it was easy to slide into an objective discussion of certain matters that needed administering pretty badly.

Tom was shocked. 'My dear Matt! If only I'd known! Unfortunately I have to go back to New York tonight, or I'd certainly see to things myself: but I do suggest you have a word with dear old Dr. Parke.'

'I am sure Dr. Parke would always do his best,' Matthew susurrated, 'but he has a lot on his plate anyway, and I'm by no means certain he's up to coping with all these domestic things, which must seem to him very minor. I imagine he can't be far from retirement.'

'About eight years,' said Tom, giving Matthew a shock. 'He may look like Methuselah, but he's not much older than you or me. I doubt whether he'll want to stay on after sixty. Or even as long as that. I think he'd like to get back to his Björnsen. It's going to be the standard work.'

'I think he *ought* to get back to his Björnsen,' Matthew said eagerly. 'My impression of him, for what it's worth, is that he's a really great scholar — for all his modesty, one feels the impact of a tremendous mind, don't you agree?'

'Does one?' Tom was doubtful. 'He's such a nice old guy.'

'Oh, *I* do! And it does seem to me hard that he should have to waste his time running the Centre when he could be working on that perfectly splendid book.'

That should be enough: further hinting might defeat its own end. This was, Matthew hoped, the first whiff of marijuana which could turn into a craving for heroin — a craving for Matthew Pryar, and he alone, to come and put the whole place to rights. He changed the subject to one which had always been a favourite of Tom's — women; for though Tom might wear a white satin tie with a silver stripe in it and look like an interior decorator, he was, in fact he had always been, a ram. The years had not changed him, though he was now married and had four children, so an hour passed pleasantly, for Tom, anyway.

As they swerved back down the hills he said to Matthew, 'If you should ever have any thoughts about the Centre, just let me know. You might hit on exactly the right man. I'd be more than eager to hear your recommendations.'

And he, Matthew thought, is the power behind that particular throne. Good old Tom.

They found, to their mutual pleasure, that they were to meet at Mrs. Cowper Nash's, in Connecticut, in a week's time.

9. Dr. Hefflinger Closes the Pump Room

Dr. Hefflinger shone out as over a crowded auditorium.

In fact, the Pump Room was by no means crowded. In the front rows were twenty-five or so students. In the centre back was Matthew, and near the door, waiting to run, was Edith Corall, a woman of her word and of honour. It was as hot as a tropical forest, the heat damp round the feet, damper in the region of the neck.

Behind Dr. Hefflinger was stretched a white sheet. Before him on the table, was a heap of books, and something which resembled a covered box some two and a half feet in length. The lantern operator, a youth in blue jeans, stood against the wall, just behind Matthew. Dr. Hefflinger's title, designed to trap the young painlessly into his own subject, for there was a journalistic component in his nature, was: *Our Amiable Araneae*. He was well away.

'The little *Lycosa tarantula* — ah, so little, by the standards of us big men! — is poisonous hardly at all. She is very lazy homemaker. She spins no web, the idle one, but ah! — she catches her prey by speed of foot. Harm you? Not at all. She may try to bite, if she feel naughty, but her poison is so small, so small——'

Matthew saw Edith take a grip on herself, swallow a pill: doubtless, some tranquilliser.

'The spiders of two families only, *Uloboridae* and *Heptathelidae*' — he spelled them, and waited, while these happy names were scribbled into notebooks — 'have no poison glands. The others — ah, yes! But harmless to man. They are *no* enemies to man. They are his friends, his very good, his very dear friends.'

Matthew recognised the tendency of arachnologists (he had met a couple before) to drool sickeningly over their pets.

44

'And he,' said Dr. Hefflinger, irradiated, 'is theirs! To my own specimens — though I think not of them as specimens but as my friends — I feed the food they love best. Little pieces of raw, raw meat, each attached to a tiny thread, so that I can run it up and down in front of them. And how they gobble! Ach, but now I show you!'

He gave a sign to the dark operator at the back of the room. The screen was brightly illuminated. 'My Susie,' he began, 'who alas is not with us tonight, though later, possibly, I might show you——'

Edith, quick on the uptake, slipped through the door and was gone. A wave of cold flooded the room, subsided.

'— I might show you her clever, funny relations — is a real gourmet. If the meat is cooked, she will not take it. I have tried her with corned beef hash, but no, she is coy. Things must always go her way, no other.'

On the screen appeared a picture of Dr. Hefflinger and the Leaning Tower of Pisa, upside down.

'No, no, no, my dear young friend! You have the wrong slide.'

'Oke, sir,' came a confident voice. The slide turned the right way up. 'That better?'

'No, Jim, no, you have the wrong slide altogether.'

A fumble. This time, a picture of Dr. Hefllinger, in whites, on the quayside at Cannes. This was removed quickly.

'I think you have the wrong *box* of slides, Jim. Those are my holiday records.'

More fumbling. The students began to snicker. They did not do so because Dr. Heffiinger had failed to hold them with his discourse — he had: but because the young tend to welcome interruption merely for its own sake.

'It is the wrong box, Doc. Sorry. But it's the one you gave me. No spiders in this bunch.'

It seemed impossible for Hefflinger to lose his temper. He breathed quietly in and out for a few seconds, then said, 'It must still in my room be, then. No, Jim — you must not fetch it. It would take too long and you would never find it. I have another idea. Lights, please!'

The screen blacked out, the room lit up.

'So we will do altogether without our lantern, eh? And have something perhaps better.' He peered towards the back of the room. 'If my colleague, Dr. Corall, is here, perhaps she had better leave ——Ah! I see she has left. Now, if you will all come and stand round me——'

They came, Matthew with them, but still keeping to the rear.

With the air of a conjurer about to produce some delightful surprise, Dr. Hefflinger lifted the cover from what had seemed to be a long box. It was, in fact, two glass cages set end to end, with tops of perforated steel, and each was tenanted.

Even Matthew, who prided himself on having no phobias, felt the hairs prickle on his neck.

In the first box was something that looked like a furry glove for a baby, thick, stubby, silky: but it was disquietingly mobile, running up and down as if it were practising five-finger excercises.

'This is Hannah, of the genus *avicularia*, "*avis*", a bird, which means she eats little birds who are not too smart for her. Do not jump, you foolish young man there at the front, she is prisoner of Zenda, she cannot get out. And if she could she would do you no harm. You could hold her in your hand, cosset her, stroke her — as if she were a dear little kitten. Now this fellow' — he pointed to something worse — 'is Romeo. I captured him myself, in the forests of the Amazon, and though he eats too much, he is my great chum.'

Romeo was not moving around, though he pulsated somewhat. He was at least eight inches across and covered with thick floss-silk, ranging between shades of apricot and flamingo. Everyone backed a little at the sight of him, and Matthew found himself swallowing.

'There is no larger than he in the world, and he is good and tender to woman and man. If you permit, I show you.'

Shooting back a glass panel (before anyone could stop him), he picked Romeo up and displayed him at arm's length. This cleared the room of four or five weaker persons. The rest stuck it out, and one fat, grinning student even gave Romeo a loving stroke.

'You see?' said Hefflinger in high delight. 'You see how there is no need to fear him? He is, in any case, comatose, he is sleepy after an enormous feed. He is lovely to touch as the downy breast of the swan, and his colours are as pretty as the sunset——'

At that moment Romeo came to life, gave a convulsive wriggle, and heaved himself out of Hefflinger's hand on to the floor. Matthew and three other men got on chairs. They saw Romeo disappearing into the gloom behind the grand piano. Matthew saw something else. He saw the fat student, heaving with mirth, slip the panel of the second cage. Hannah, more volatile than Romeo in any case, tumbled out in a flash and went scrambling around the platform, with Hefflinger in hot pursuit. One boy, a football player, most regrettably screamed. Most of the others had now backed against the wall and two lads had joined Matthew (not without dignity and an air of leisureliness) on chairs. Three Spartan boys went chasing after Hannah, who was trapped by one of them at last beneath a flower-vase, released by the doctor and put back in her cage.

But in the confusion Romeo had completely vanished and was not to be found.

'Yet he must be somewhere!' Hefflinger protested. 'He is a great enormous guy. Anyone should be able to see him. My eyes are not good, not so good as young ones. If you boys will be so kind as to hunt this very funny thimble — what a comic thimble he is, to be sure! — then we will pop him back into his boudoir. If you find him, lift him very gently — his tummy is full, he is perhaps a little irate, a trifle testy.'

But he was not to be found.

'Has anyone opened the door since he got away from me?' Hefflinger demanded.

They all looked at one another. Apparently nobody had. But Matthew opened it a little now and slid cautiously out through the crack, making quite sure that Romeo did not follow him.

He had had enough for one evening.

Next morning when he went to the Boosie House for breakfast, he enquired at the cafeteria whether recapture had been made.

'No, sir!' said the waiter smartly. 'No, sir! Not a hide nor hair of him. He's a smart spider. Doc Hefflinger's fit to be tied.'

47

'I trust,' Matthew said, 'that Romeo has not joined us down here. I should find him distracting.'

'Don't worry. Doc's had the Pump Room shut up all night, so he knows it's still there. He's got another search going on right this minute.'

All the same, Matthew did not enjoy his bacon and eggs quite so much as usual. Since all *araneae* have a tendency to manifest themselves suddenly out of nothing at all, he could not but feel that Romeo, despite his enormous size, was capable of doing the same. And indeed, the morning crowd appeared to have thinned a little; Edith Corall, for instance, did not put in an appearance.

At lunch-time, after a struggle to put down a few chapter-headings relating to Dorothy, he had worked up a good appetite.

The thaw had come, rushing in with the joyful violence of Widor's Toccata in F Major: snow plopped, snow melted, waterfalls ran once more, and though the full glory of the fall colours had been nipped away, there were still patches of gold and red among the woodlands and a golden shine upon the nearer slopes. Great white stars with crumbling silver at the edges sparkled still beneath the sweeping fir trees, but the open grass was green as peridot and the sky was a light and perfect blue. Matthew raced across the campus and streamed with the crowds to the Boosie House: only to find a notice on the Pump Room door:

'NO LUNCHES SERVED HERE TODAY.'

So Romeo had still not been found. Furious, Matthew sought the cafeteria: little was left but warm roast beef sandwiches (having had experience of these, he wondered why Rimbaud had ever tolerated ham *à moitié tiède*) and salads with cottage cheese. As he gloomily ate his way through a slab of banana cream pie, his gaze fell on the fat student who had let Hannah out of her cage.

He was on him in a flash. The student had been guzzling at a table for two in a corner of the room. Matthew took the vacant chair, effectively penning him in.

'Where did you put that damned arachnid?'

'That what, sir?'

'That pink chap. Romeo. You hid him, didn't you? And so the rest of us have damned well had to starve!'

'No, honest, sir, I swear——'

'I saw you pick him up,' Matthew said, lying. 'Where you stuck him I don't know, but I'm a good enough witness to make it hot for you with the Dean.'

The student succumbed at once. Matthew must not give him away, it would be the finish of him. He'd been getting bad grades, he was in the dog-house as it was, the Dean had already warned him. He wanted to do Zoology himself; picking up Romeo had just been a sort of a test. 'Sir, I'd go down on my knees if you'd give me half a chance to move, I'd do anything——'

'Oh, be quiet, you stupid chap,' said Matthew, 'I've no interest in getting you into trouble. All I want is the Pump Room opened up again. If you just tell me where——'

The boy whispered. Matthew inclined his head, uttered some stern words of rebuke, and crept upstairs. On the notice-board he found a bill advertising *Waiting for Godot* and some drawing-pins. On the back of the bill he wrote, in large capital letters,

'ROMEO IN GRAND PIANO'

and pinned this notice to the Pump Room door.

Then he went away. He might be gnawed by hunger, but he was no poor sportsman. He walked to the gas-station and had himself driven to Monkshill, where he ate an indifferent, but by no means repulsive, dish called 'English kidney stew'. Of course, all this left him with no time to do any more work on Dorothy Merlin that day.

10. Rich-Rich

'When citizens something the south and west,
And maids go out sprig-muslin dressed,
        And so do I———'

Matthew hummed quietly to himself, as he stepped from the bathroom which was heady with Floris scents, into his bedroom, a haze of sun and muslin —

'And so do I,'

he repeated, without thought for the appropriateness, or otherwise, of the words. All Matthew's songs welled from his unconscious mind, to surprise him whenever he paused to consider what he was, in fact, singing; also from his unconscious mind came a sting of repugnance, as his feet sank into the thick eggshell-blue carpet, which made him reach for his slippers. (Just for a shock of a second, it had felt like treading on Romeo.) But otherwise all was joyful, all lovely. He had been served with breakfast in bed — scrambled eggs with chicken livers, raspberries flown in from somewhere improbable — he had read the best part of the *New York Times* Sunday edition, he had adored the Renoir (only one, since this was only the second-best bedroom), coveted the Harpignies and Diaz, he had stretched himself on the day-bed, which, like the cradle of a very rich infant, was frilled with sprig-muslin, he was going to read, before lunch, a little out of three books among many left at his bedside: ghosted reminiscences of a Vanderbilt and a Pierpont Morgan; a real book, unghosted, by a Saltonstall.

A fine morning. Muslin shimmered. So did the pots of pink azaleas on chryselephantine tables scattered here and there with a kind of daisylike inconsequence. As he had never visited Mrs. Nash in the country before, he was permitted to ignore the hunting-horn with which she summoned her regular guests to riding or to church. She proposed, she said, to see that he had a really fine rest.

He was happy. He decided to forget that Mondays ever came. One of the things middle age had taught him was that if you want to make time last, you must live it moment by moment, never looking ahead. Of course, if you wanted to get something over and done with, the reverse was true: if it was Sunday and you were to be hanged on Tuesday, it would be best to keep your mind firmly fixed on Wednesday. By that means, you would soon polish off the difficult period in between.

The valet knocked and entered with Matthew's clothes, beautifully spruced, his ties steam-pressed, his shoes shining like chestnut fire-coals.

' "Glory be to God for dappled things",' Matthew murmured, his unconscious mind busily dictating again, ' "slow; sweet, sour; adazzle, dim——" '

He dressed slowly, luxuriantly, read a little in Mrs. Nash's interesting books, and at last strolled out into the library, where there were three Renoirs, a Sisley, a multitude of flowers, a dazzling tray of drinks and, thank God, nobody about. The butler came in and hovered. 'Don't bother, Briskin,' Matthew said, 'I'll look after myself.' He did. Briskin brought in *canapés*: caviare, *pâté de foie gras*, asparagus, smoked salmon.

Matthew knew several duchesses, all well-heeled, but no one within touching distance of Mrs. Nash for sheer blinding wealth. He was very fond of Mrs. Nash, he would have liked her even if she had been poor and would doubtless have made her a small allowance. There was no question, however, that living with the rich-rich suited him right now. He went easy on the *canapés*, deciding that his stomach must have shrivelled after the privations of Cobb, and that it might be quite a long time before he could eat entirely normally again.

At that moment, the horn sounded. He heard them come into the hall, Mrs. Nash, Tom Helliwell, and somebody else, whose voice he did not recognise. He hoped the voice was only coming to lunch. He wanted food, not a social life; and he had still found no time to discuss the Centre further with Tom. In Matthew, ambition was beginning to seethe, and he liked the feel of it. He had never had any ambition before: he had never had the faintest idea how very nice it could be.

He saw himself directing the Centre like a god, making the lives of the Visiting Fellows utterly delightful. The Boosie House should never shut: he would turn one of the smaller dining-rooms into a club. The college shop should sell comforting and nutritious goods, both for male and female. (Let not poor Edith starve.) As well he knew, Cobb was extremely rich: possibly the third richest college *per capita* in the United States. Edith Corall should be gay once more in parrot colours, she should whistle as she rode her bicycle. There should be a regular car-hire service *on the doorstep* for unmechanical persons like himself. Buds should break. Streams should flow. In the Centre itself there should be a small, relatively elegant canteen. And out of all this, great works should come, works to make the Cobb Press famous throughout the world. It was not for himself that Matthew wanted power: it was for Cobb, it was for Learning, it was for the new Enlightenment!

The first thing he meant to do was to retire old Dr. Parke right off the campus, far, far away.

Mrs. Nash burst in, fat and tall and jolly, her silver-mauve hair flashing off sunlight, her eyes blue as her own star-sapphires.

'Poor Matt, all, all alone and deserted! Well, it's your own fault. You should have come to church. We had a sermon on the Unjust Steward — can you understand it? I never can. But no one can say the victor didn't try, which is why we're so late.'

She swept him into her arms and let him drop out of them. 'Have you got a drink? That's right. Briskin!' Her voice rang out. 'Look after Mr. Pryar and give me a daiquiri.'

Into the room came Tom, who had changed out of his

church-going clothes into whipcord trousers, a fawn cashmere sweater and tangerine cravat. He was followed by a small smudgy man whom Mrs. Nash introduced as J. L. Walters. 'Now everyone knows everyone else,' she said with satisfaction.

J. L. Walters did not drink. He shivered over tomato juice and said he thought he had caught cold. He smoked Mrs. Nash's cigarettes and looked depressed. Matthew concluded that he was probably a solicitor, a minor member of the firm she employed, who had to be asked now and then as a charity.

For lunch, sixteen people arrived, so there were twenty at table. Matthew knew some of them personally and knew the names of most of the others. Those who knew him understood immediately what he was saying, those who didn't were disconcerted by his preliminary hooting and took a little longer. At three o'clock all sixteen swept off again, and Mrs. Nash retired for a nap, Tom went riding, and Matthew was left alone with J. L. Walters.

'Have you known Mrs. Nash long?' Matthew enquired politely. 'She is quite adorable, isn't she?'

'Years and years,' said J.L., with a snuffle. He remarked on his cold, added repulsively that Diogenes had believed in letting the nose run rather than blow it, to effect a quick cure. 'Which reminds me, Mr. Pryar. Coming on me like this, it's made me short on handkerchiefs. I don't know if you——'

Matthew gave him a spotless one.

'Thank you. Oh, yes, years and years.' J.L. peered into the cigarette box and found it empty. Matthew offered him his case.

'May I take one or two, just to tide me over?'

J.L. took five.

This might not have seemed such a deprivation, since it could not be long before Briskin discovered the shortage and made it good; but it happened that Matthew's own cigarettes were the only ones he really cared to smoke.

'This house is glorious at all times of the year, isn't it?' Matthew said.

'Sure. But the cost of upkeep . . . I always say, take care of the pence.'

'But she has already,' Matthew suggested delicately, 'a good many pounds.'

'I dare say. But if you want to keep the pounds, you have to watch the books.'

'Do you suppose she does watch the books?'

'I'm hoping,' said J.L.

Matthew was dead sure he was a solicitor, but this seemed such a humble thing to be, in the ambience of Mrs. Nash, that he did not make further enquiries. He only hoped J.L. had not some sort of hold over her.

'I think I'll take a nap too,' said J.L., 'that is, if you won't mind.'

At the door he paused. 'Look, Mr. Pryar, like a fool I've let myself come away without money. Pearl' (Mrs. Nash) 'will get me to New York tomorrow, but I'll have to tip the chauffeur. If you could let me have five dollars——'

Matthew did.

'And I'd better get your address. At Cobb, eh? Like it? I imagine they keep you busy.'

J.L. retired to rest and later to change into a rusty-looking dinner-jacket.

Before the meal (only fourteen people arrived this time) Matthew had a brief chat with Tom.

'Who on earth is Walters?'

Tom was vague. He was, he replied, an old chum of Mrs. Nash's, had known her late husband, something of that sort. A corporation lawyer, he thought. A bit dim. He was a Trustee of Cobb, incidentally — had been on the board for ages, but didn't turn up often to meetings. In fact, Tom had met him only twice before in committee, and, so far as he could remember, he hadn't uttered much. He was a Cobb alumnus.

'Does he always borrow one's handkerchief and five dollars?'

'I wouldn't know,' said Tom, 'he didn't borrow anything from me.'

The beautiful week-end came to a close. On Monday morning Matthew flew back from New Haven to Hamelin, feeling that the golden coach had turned back into a pumpkin and the horses into rats. He was, however, fairly content. In the few minutes with Tom before they went their several ways (J.L. left very early) he had dropped a couple more discreet hints as to the way the Centre might be improved under a really inspired administrator, and he fancied Tom had not failed to latch on. The next thing to do was meet some of the other Trustees. J.L. was obviously not much use, since Matthew wanted men of real influence behind him: but there must be at least two others of Tom's weight.

He saw himself as Alexander, mapping out a whole world: no, as a Machiavelli without respect for the Prince, prepared, in fact, to sling that prince out on his ear and take over.

11. A Protest Party

He found another letter from Dorothy.

'*Will* you write to me, Matthew? You have had plenty of time to answer my letter. Say it takes 2 days (or 3 at most) to get to you, and you reply by return, I should have had your answer *yesterday morning*!!!!

'I insist on knowing how you are getting on with the book, please send an outline for me to approve. Also, please devote a *whole* chapter to *Joyful Matrix*, and do try to rid yourself of a certain superficiality which I have warned you about before. You can if you want to, perfectly well. It only needs a bit of guts.

'Would you believe both Mortimer and Nicholson devoted their entire space in the Sunday papers to Skipton, of all people? Why do they say he's interesting when they know he's not? I am writing to them both, telling them certain things about S. they may not *be aware of*. When I think the reading edition of *Joyful M.* only got a quarter of a column and on the wrong page at that, it makes me SPIT.

'Cosmo still coughing. He could stop it if he wanted to. No sign of Duncan. I suppose he is on the drink again — revolting! When I think of what I do for people and how they repay me, I could——'

He turned over.

'Spit.'

He sighed. Dorothy was a boring and repetitive letter-writer.

'Please reply AT ONCE. I am at a crucial stage in my career and I must feel I am getting *some* support. It is little to ask of you, Matthew, when you remember how I took you up, and how Cosmo and I took you abroad, when you were only a hanger-on of the smart set and knew no literary people at all.

'Not that we don't love you, you know we do.'

This last statement was an afterthought, scribbled in tiny letters above a caret mark.

'Now do get going, *immediately*, love from all, D.M.'

He called up one of the secretaries. The girls were for use, and he would use them. He asked her to write to Miss Dorothy Merlin as follows.

'As instructed, I am opening Mr. Pryar's mail in his absence, as he is at present making a tour of eastern universities and does not wish his letters to be forwarded. Be assured that I will bring your letter to his attention immediately he returns.'

He blushed slightly, seeing the pretty girl smiling over her notebook.

'I'm terribly sorry to ask you to tell fibs,' he said, 'but Miss Merlin, as you will see for yourself, tends to press one. And as I am working like a dog on her *œuvre*, it seems unreasonable for me to interrupt it just to answer her letters, don't you think?'

'Sure, sure,' said the girl, running an expert eye down Dorothy's text. 'Sure. We'll keep her quiet.' She looked at Matthew dreamily, as if she were not up to mischief. 'If you've got some manuscript for me to type, I'll gladly——'

'You know perfectly well,' he said, 'or I am sure you must guess, being as clever as you are charming, that I haven't written one blind word of it.'

She smiled, and said she Only Thought.

'No, you didn't,' said Matthew. He added, after the manner of Dorothy, 'And why do you say you Only Thought when you know you didn't?'

She giggled delightedly and went back to her duties.

Meanwhile, Matthew wrote out five invitations to the other Visiting Fellows, asking them to join him for drinks at his house at 9 p.m. that night. He asked the secretary to distribute them, telephoned the garage and had himself driven into Piltdown, where he bought enough drink to keep even his old friend Duncan Moss busy for three weeks.

The Help had paid her solitary visit, so the place did not look so bad. Matthew rummaged in cupboards for glasses, jugs, ashtrays, and was proud of himself when he found them. He went to the college shop and bought cigarettes — those, at least, were available to the unhopeful shopper.

All was set.

Joy filled him as a tap fills a crystal glass with chlorinated springs, right to the top, and fizzing. He waited for the gay greyness to settle, for the water to clear. Now he was poised, secure, ready to act.

His first visitor was half an hour early. Doug Ruddock came tapping smally at the door and entered like a conspirator, whispering, 'Am I the first?'

'Indeed you are.' said Matthew, who was only just out of the bath and who had not yet brushed his hair.

'Good. I wanted a word with you. I've really got something, Matt! Wait till you hear it!'

Ruddock went up and down the room with a prancing gait, his face brimful with a kind of surly glee.

'Better come on upstairs,' Matthew said, 'I don't use this floor.'

His guest took no notice. 'I haven't finished the letters yet, but I've got all the image-clusters out of the poems. Drink! Booze! Smashed from morn to night!'

'I really think, my dear Doug, from what I know of Emily Dickinson (which I confess is not much, and I shouldn't dream of disputing with a scholar like yourself)' — all this while Matthew was nudging Ruddock towards and up the stairs, addressing himself to the reluctantly retreating back — 'that you are barking up the wrong tree.'

They had reached the upper living-room, now fully in trim for the party.

'Wrong tree! Now just you listen!

"I would distil a cup
And bear to all my friends——"

or better,

58

"The Ditch is dear to the Drunken man
For it is not his Bed——" '

'Come,' said Matthew, 'metaphor surely? I wonder if I'd better
leave the front door open? I don't want to tear up and down——'

' "A Lady red — and the Hill
Her annual secret keeps——"

Don't you see what that means? She went on a yearly bender.'
Ruddock's excitement soared. He took to the prowl again, knocking
over a pile of paperbacks and trampling them in his happy certitude.

' "Glowing is her Bonnet,
Glowing is her Cheek,
Glowing is her Kirtle,
Yet she cannot speak."

Why couldn't she speak? Tell me that. Isn't it as plain as the nose
on your face?'
  'Doug, I should very much like a word or two with you before
the others come — you know, about our conditions as Visiting
Fellows. You may, of course, consider me effete, and if so, you
have only to say so, but the constant fear of finding there is literally
no food——'
  'Listen, listen, listen. She can't keep off it, even when she's doing
her math.

"Logarithm — had I — for Drink —
'Twas a dry wine——"

And half the time she couldn't walk straight. That's why she didn't
go out.

"A Doubt if it be Us
Assists the staggering Mind

59

In an extreme Anguish
Until it footing find."

Metaphor, oh, sure. But what metaphor! Drunk again. You can't
miss it.'

At that moment, fortunately, Matthew heard the grinding of his
bell. He raced to the stairhead, shouting, 'Come up!' while behind
him Ruddock persistently droned on.

' "I fitted to the Latch
My Hand, with trembling care,
Lest back that awful Door should spring —
And leave me — on the floor——"

On the *floor!* That was the usual place for her, wasn't it? Huh!'

Miss Groby came weaving softly up to them. She was wearing
a purple sweater with a tight round neck, but had not used a comb
since pulling this garment over her head, so that her hair looped
and slopped downwards over her small sad face like thatch upon
an African kraal.

'Good-evening, Mr. Pryar! How kind, how very kind. Hospitality
— so very welcome. We get little enough hoshp——' She stopped
and gave him a smile.

Matthew, dispensing hospitality for his guests and himself, assured
her eagerly that her complaint was, he hoped, to be discussed
confidentially between the Fellows that very night.

She nodded with more than common firmness, adding in a voice
not free from belligerence — 'You just try working on the Hesychast
Doctrines on an empty stomach. But Scotch feeds — thank God,
good Scosh feeds.'

He agreed, and offered her a bowl of pretzels. 'Thank you, no,'
said Miss Groby. 'I have long since ceased to eat.'

Edith Corall came next, looking, he thought, more chipper. The
first thing she said was, 'Hefflinger come yet?'

'No.'

'Mind you frisk him.'

She cast a cold eye on Ruddock, gave Miss Groby a sympathetic pat. 'Getting any work done, Maud? We never seem to meet.'

Chuck Tiepolo was next, a bully-boy making more noise than the rest of them put together. 'God Almighty, it's a Convention! Well, good for you, Matt. Doug, that damned cat of yours was in my room again. If you don't keep it to yourself, I'll poison it.'

'If you touch my cat, I'll poison you!'

'Now, now, boys,' said Edith, 'break it up. This is our first social occasion for God knows how long, not since——'

'We all had that glad and giddy reception with pink stuff in a bowl and pieces of apple in it a couple of months ago,' said Chuck. 'I threw up when I got home.'

The merry voice of Hefflinger rose from beneath. 'Hullo, there, my good friends!'

'Frisk him!' Edith pleaded. 'Don't let him come up before you have.' She had turned pale.

Matthew ran down and checked Hefflinger's ascent.

'My dear Doctor, how good of you to come!'

'Good? It is good of you to ask us. What could be more pleasant than a reunion of kind, of very dear friends, leagued in a common enterprise? For I am sure,' Hefflinger added with startling irony, 'that if we ever happened to set eyes upon one another we should indeed be the best of friends.'

'Miss Corall has already arrived,' said Matthew, 'so if you would forgive me for enquiring whether you are quite free from pets——'

'Mr. Pryar!' This was reproachful. 'You think I would alarm my dear Dr. Corall, foolish as she may be where innocent creatures are concerned? Ah, no! I have come alone.'

'Nothing in your pockets? Not even Susie? Not even Titine?'

Dr. Hefflinger crossed his heart and hoped to die.

Matthew, however, who had more character than many people, Dorothy Merlin included, gave him credit for, asked him if he would kindly shake out his handkerchief. Dr. Hefflinger obligingly did so, and turned all his pockets out as well.

'*Is* he all right, Matthew?' came a faint voice from the stairhead.

'Perfectly all right, Edith dear. Not to worry. We're coming up.'

The last arrival was the one Visiting Fellow whom Matthew had not yet met, the mathematician, Wohlgemutt. This was a heavy, squat, pale, dead-eyed man dressed with excessive trimness in a Brooks Brothers suit, shining linen and a pinspotted tie. He offered a minimal greeting, refused alcohol, and finding Matthew had omitted to provide soft drinks, stiffly accepted a glass of water. 'Without ice,' he said tensely, as if this were a well-known foible of his asceticism. It was certainly a nuisance, since Matthew had put ice in the water-jug and had to go and fill Wohlgemutt's glass from the bathroom tap.

It occurred to him that it was going to be a pretty sticky party, and that it would be unwise to introduce any business until it had thawed a little. Luckily they were all, the mathematician excepted, drinking fairly heavily. In a while Edith began to look almost cocky, as in the splendid days of Cambridge: Maud Groby wore a faint, wondering smile. Ruddock and Tiepolo were growing weary of fighting over the cat, and Dr. Hefflinger had regretfully stopped trying to explain to Edith that all creatures were the friends of mankind, especially the soft, the cosy, the furry ones who loved best to know man, to be his little lieutenants. Wohlgemutt said nothing except once, in answer to Matthew, who had rather foolishly begged him to talk about his work. 'You aren't a mathematician? No. Then it wouldn't be any use. You do Merlin. I know. She's no good.'

Giving him up for lost, Matthew thought it was time to address the others. He did not intend that they should be too fuddled to understand him.

Taking his position before the empty fireplace, he smiled down upon them.

'You must know,' he began, 'how awfully glad I am to see you all. It is most frightfully nice of you to interrupt your work to come and see me. Believe me, I am terrifically grateful.'

' "Those thirsty lips to flagons pressed——" '

Ruddock, addressing Edith, was back to his subject. His voice fell clear in the suddenly silent room. 'Oh, sorry,' he said.

62

'We're grateful to you, Matt,' said Edith, 'it makes a change.'

'But I didn't get you here without *arrière-pensée*. I know some of you may think it's frightful impertinence of me, as a newcomer, to take the initiative, but I do feel that we at the Centre have certain problems in common.'

'We do, we do,' Miss Groby breathed, less to encourage him than to draw his attention to herself and to the fact that her glass was empty.

'Do please give Miss Groby——' Matthew murmured to Edith, who obeyed. He went on, 'We are all madly lucky, if I may so put it, in our working conditions. I can't thank Cobb enough, and I'm sure you can't. Cobb has, we know, all the money in the world, and it was a perfectly wonderful idea to spend it in this manner. But I do feel that what I might term the — ah — domestic side of our lives here has been handled with less imagination.'

'Ho!' Miss Groby interpolated, rancorously.

'I need not remind you——'

Matthew was surprised at his own eloquence. He could have described himself, with justice, as unaccustomed to public speaking: yet he had just discovered that he was extremely good at it. Good at it, perhaps, in a rather too formal way; his periods flowed too smoothly, he was not going to be able to think of any good jokes to lighten the whole thing. But good at it, in his fashion, he was.

'— that we are many miles from the nearest shopping centre or public restaurant. Twenty miles each way, in fact, as near as makes no matter. I need not also remind you that at least three of us — Miss Groby, Miss Corall and myself — do not drive motor-cars. The food at the Boosie House, however delightful the surroundings, is not entirely satisfactory (though I know our national tastes differ — indeed, I have often congratulated my American friends on the delicacy of their palates: they really can taste food that seems tasteless to me, which is *not* to praise my own country, for I am sure that we, let alone France and Italy, have fallen into the habit of *seasoning* our food, which really must be quite unnecessary when you come to think of it——)'

He had lost himself, bang in the middle of a parenthesis. He was not so sure, for the moment, of his own gifts as a speaker. He began again.

'However, the food at the Boosie House is perhaps not up to your national standard. And furthermore, there is apt to be no food at all upon occasion, say, if the dining-room is pre-empted for geometers. I have often thought they might meet elsewhere——'

'Even geometers have to eat,' said Wohlgemutt without expression. From the others, however, had come a faint murmur of applause.

'Also, we have no central meeting place: and as, so far as I can see, Cobb comes to a dead stop somewhere around seven forty-five p.m., some of us may lead an existence which might without injustice be described as solitary.'

'Bloody solitary!' Edith cried. 'Damned, bloody solitary!'

'I should be surprised,' Matthew continued, with this encouragement, 'if we were especially popular with the Faculty.'

Tiepolo snorted, and grinned.

'They may consider that we are paid too much for too little. In my case, I am sure,' he put in gracefully, 'they are dead right. In yours — no, no, of course not. But I do detect a *feeling*.'

'They hate our guts,' said Ruddock simply. 'I've been here for over eight months. Do you know how often any one of them has asked me out? Twice. Old Parke for tea. Mrs. Pickersgill for lunch — at the Boosie.'

'Now I can suggest,' said Matthew, 'a way in which all these things could be rectified. If we had an inn, like Dartmouth, or Williams——'

'And I have to do my own charring,' said Edith. 'I don't know how to. I have never learned how to. My place gets filthier and filthier. If I try to char, I don't get my own work done. If I do my own work I can't char——'

'I think,' said Matthew delicately, having more or less solved his own problem in that direction, 'that perhaps we in England are a little spoiled. Americans still live near to the Frontier. They are far more used to looking after themselves, which is wholly admirable. And besides, with all those splendid machines——'

'I broke my washing-machine the first day,' said Miss Groby, who had begun to cry a little in a manner by no means unenjoyable, 'and it cost me thirty-two dollars to put it right.'

'But leaving this aside,' Matthew persisted, 'an inn would ensure food, and serve as a social centre for us all.'

'They won't build any inn,' said Chuck, 'they say it won't pay off. They've been arguing that out for the past ten years.'

'It doesn't need to pay,' Edith put in, 'not with all the money they've got. Though it would pay. Any fool can see it would.'

'But,' Matthew said in a higher, clearer voice, 'this is only dealing with the fringes of the trouble. In my view, the whole direction of the Centre might with profit be a trifle re-vitalised. It does seem to me to lack real leadership. Forgive me, all of you. As I say, I am a newcomer. But I should so enormously like to hear your views on this subject.'

Their views broke out at once, and were concerned with the subject of dear old Dr. Parke.

'He just doesn't understand——' (Edith)

'He doesn't give a goddamn, is what you mean.' (Tiepolo)

'He is perhaps, though a good man — really a fine fellow, I think — not fully seized of our little problem.' (Hefflinger)

'I used to eat once. I used to love my food. It is his fault.' (Miss Groby)

Wohlgemutt had not spoken. He seemed to swell above his glass of untouched water. Matthew watched him with growing apprehension, which was soon justified.

'If you don't like it here, Mr. Pryar,' said the mathematician slowly, and with weight, 'I wonder you stay. Some of us don't want a social life, we get plenty of that back at base. Some of us manage O.K. on the food we get. (And I got that crack about our palates.)'

'But I assure you, I was perfectly sincere,' Matthew broke in, alarmed. 'I honestly do think they must be far more fine than ours in Europe——'

'I got that crack, Mr. Pryar. And the point is, some of us are here to work, and, as you have the goodness to admit, we have optimum working conditions. Also, some of us don't mind a good healthy walk. So you can count me out of the protest, whatever it is. As for Dr. Parke, a man for whom I, with everyone at Cobb, have the highest respect, if more people were like him this world would be a better place. Thanks for your hospitality, but I must be getting back. To work.'

He rose, in a stunned silence which was not altogether a surprised one. Apart from Matthew, all of them knew him. But they were stunned, if not by his opinions, by his vehemence. In silence, Matthew escorted him, to the stairs.

And then the bell rang, the door opened, and the merriest of voices cried, 'I heard of your little gathering! May an outsider hope to join in the festivities?'

'Do come in, Dr. Parke,' said Matthew.

12. An Invitation to Tea

Dear old Dr. Parke rose up with alacrity, almost colliding with the departing Wohlgemutt. 'Who's that? It's dark, I can't see. Ah, Herman! And how is Herman?'

'Fine, thank you, Dom. How are you? How's Bea?'

They exchanged courtesies.

'But you're not going, just as I arrive?' Dr. Parke protested. 'Really, I shall think I'm the cause of your departure!'

Wohlgemutt said he was sorry, he had some work to get through.

'Ah, that's the way! Work, nothing like it. A glutton for work, aren't you, Herman? That's what we like to see. That's what our President likes to see.'

Wohlgemutt went away. Dr. Parke advanced into the party, beamed on everyone, accepted a little drop of Scotch in a great deal of water. 'No, I don't smoke, Mr. Pryar, but I like to see others smoking, indeed I do. And it no longer troubles my chest.'

The room was so dark with smoke that it resembled the set of a Nineteen-Twenties Expressionist play.

'Now this is pleasant, very pleasant indeed! Harmony among our Fellows is what we like to see, fun after school, as it were! An exchange of minds, a meeting of the Two Cultures — or perhaps the three or four or five cultures! And how,' he asked Miss Groby, 'is the *New Recensions of the Patristic Hagiographies* going? Let me see, that will be volume five.' Like Royalty, he forgot nothing when he chose to remember it, and, like Royalty and ships' pursers, was deeply admired for the feat. He made a little, informed remark about the work of each of them, not seeming to notice their somewhat grudging response.

We do look rather like conspirators, Matthew thought, we look caught out. And moreover, we are all feeling pretty damned cowardly. He hoped Chuck Tiepolo might raise directly the reason for the gathering: but Chuck only slumped forwards on to his feet, straightened up and took his leave.

'And how goes your labour on Dorothy Merlin?' Dr. Parke demanded, with a beam. 'You are to introduce her to this continent, I recall. A work of pioneering. I have been reading her poems lately.' He quoted a few lines:

' "Mother and Mother seven times again,
Grief-given, ruth-riven, O joy O pain!
   In the antithesis
   My joy it is,
Seed-breeding, need-feeding, O sun O rain!"

Fine stuff, Mr. Pryar, I envy you your exercise.'

They had listened sullenly to this recitation, or rather, declamation: for Dr. Parke had a sense of drama.

'What the hell's it mean?' Edith murmured, but not very loudly.

'But I am not here,' said Dr. Parke, 'to spoil the revel, or even to stay more than a minute. I came with a specific purpose.' This was to ask Matthew to tea on the following Friday, which was in two days' time. 'Mrs. Parke is agog to meet you. She keeps saying to me, "When is Mr. Pryar to visit our home?" So I said to her this morning, "Bea, I shall corner Mr. Pryar this very night and bring him in triumph" — not right now, though,' he added hastily, 'on Friday. Well, now you must forgive me.'

At that point they all got up to go.

They did not, perhaps, wish to outstay him and have Matthew comment on their collective pusillanimity.

Miss Groby went first, lost her footing and hurtled down the entire flight of stairs. This caused a great commotion, for nobody found it possible to believe that she had arrived at the bottom quite unharmed. Hefflinger and Edith volunteered to take her home, Dr. Parke prodded her wrists, ribs and ankles with diagnostic panache to see if she had broken anything (he would have had her screaming in agony had she done so), and Matthew ran lightly down with some reviving whisky, which was by far the most sensible action of all. It was quite fifteen minutes before they were all gone: he heard their voices upraised on the night air, for the moment exhilarated by the excitement of Miss Groby's mishap.

On Friday he went to tea with the Parkes. They lived about a mile (uphill) out of Hamelin, in a rather imposing framehouse with dark green shutters, a ragged but extensive garden all about it. Standing in the long grass by the door were two wooden flamingoes, and above the portico was a diagonally-swaddled infant, Delia Robbia type. Matthew's heart sank somewhat. Yet as Dr. Parke admitted him he was conscious of very considerable comfort, of shining wood and silver, a log fire, an infinite number of books, and broad windows clotted with cross-draped muslin, with rubber plants and with sunshine.

'Welcome, welcome, welcome!' his host cried. 'Come you in. Let me take your overshoes. Ah, I see the rain has gone and the voice of the turtle is heard in the land. Well, well, how good it is to have you with us! Mrs. Parke won't be two minutes. Sit down. And please smoke. I don't myself, but I don't mind it in others. An ashtray — have we any ashtrays? Surely, surely—— Ah, yes!' He found a piece of pottery shaped like a chipmunk with a hole in its back, just large enough to take a couple of butt ends. Matthew knew he would have to control his craving for cigarettes that afternoon.

Steps sounded along the flagged hall. He looked up, and was chilled by a sense of *déjà vu*. Advancing upon him was a dark, grave woman all of six feet high, who addressed him in a strong and beautiful boom. 'Ah, Mr. Pryar! We are rejoiced to see you in our home. I am truly sincere.'

He jumped up. 'Mrs. Pickersgill——'

Dr. Parke gave out a jet of silvery laughter. 'There, Beata, he's been fooled like the rest! No, Mr. Pryar, this is Mrs. Parke, my wife, not Tim's! The President is my brother-in-law.'

'There is the most terrific resemblance——' Matthew began.

'Trilby and I are identical twins, so thus it should be,' said Mrs. Parke with composure. 'Only I part my hair on the other side, for it is psychologically bad to lose the sense of identity. Also I wear brown shoes, Trilby always black. Therefore it is quite easy to tell us apart.' At that moment she hurled herself upon the window, flung it up, and began to shout in accents of hoarse rage and in a tongue Matthew did not recognise. Dr. Parke smiled upon her and waited.

After a moment or so of noisy denunciation she closed the window again, and sat mildly down at Matthew's side, smiling sideways like a Byzantine madonna. She tapped the ashtray with her forefinger.

'Our guests from England, they think the little chipmunk is so cute. Now this little one is cute indeed, because he is petrified. But the real ones are to us not cute, but a most distressful nuisance. So when I see a naughty in the garden, I shoo him off.'

Her English was, in a quiet way, the most extraordinary Matthew had ever heard. (He wanted to know her nationality, but as the information was not volunteered and he felt it impertinent to enquire, was in fact never to know it.)

She soon rose to bring in the tea: and a splendid tea it was, with sandwiches, hot biscuits, and three kinds of cake. Whoever starved in Hamelin, Matthew thought, the Parkes certainly didn't. He ate as heartily as he could as an insurance against future hunger, though it occurred to him, dismally, that like Miss Groby he was losing the habit of eating and would soon be incapable of swallowing solids.

Dr. Parke munched away. 'Well, well, we have a most interesting collection of Fellows this semester. Most gratifying to Cobb. Dr. Tiepolo is, I am sure, writing another book for the bestseller list — which is not to disparage it, for though he has a light, discursive style, his mind is profound. Indeed, I know of no one in the field of the behavioural sciences——'

'But he is rude,' said Mrs. Parke, 'truly he is a rude man. I do not myself care for him.'

'Come, come, my dear! A rough diamond, but sound at heart.

Yes, I may say sound. And Miss Groby, what a scholar! She makes me feel like a child.'

'She is given to drink,' Mrs. Parke stated.

'No, no, I am sure you are wrong.'

'You say she fell downstairs.

'Anyone might fall downstairs——'

'Especially in my house, if I may so call it,' said Matthew, getting in a small and quite unheeded blow. 'Despite its great wealth and ingenuity of light switches, it is really extraordinarily dark on the staircase.'

'And your own work — ah! That's pioneering, if you like. As I think I said. As for Dr. Ruddock, there, I confess, I am partial. Emily Dickinson is dear to me, as she was dear to the late Professor Gombricht, who founded our Memorial Fellowship. Indeed, I may say I make something of a cult of her. So it pleases me to think of the lustre dear Doug Ruddock is adding to her name, under Cobb's aegis and under Cobb's very roof.'

'You should not let Dr. Ruddock have cats in the Centre,' said Mrs. Parke, 'they bring diseases. I would take his cat away, if it were within my province, I would truly. Cats are phthisical.' She added to Matthew, 'My husband is very good, very kind, but he is also weak.'

Matthew seized his chance. 'Oh, I'm sure he's not. But he is the soul of kindness, everyone here spots that at once. And I was wondering, Mrs. Parke, whether I could interest him, or perhaps interest you, in the idea of an inn, or some sort of meeting place where we poor strangers——'

She gave him a dark, uncomprehending stare.

'It is a bit quiet in the evenings,' Matthew said with an air of boyish simplicity, 'honestly.'

There was a moment of impending thunder, not emanating from Dr. Parke, who was smilingly emptying the two butts from Matthew's chipmunk into an envelope, but from his wife.

'*Nobody,*' she said at last, 'has felt that. I am sure nobody. Or it would have been said.'

'I'm sure it would have been said,' the doctor put in. 'The Visiting

Fellows are encouraged to be entirely open with us, to speak as among equals. When they are with us, they are of us. I do hope you feel that, my dear Matthew, if I may so call you.'

Matthew had a few moments in which to think, since Mrs. Parke at that point raged up and went for the chipmunks again.

When she had returned to her chair he said cautiously, 'My dear Mrs. Parke, nobody is conceivably complaining. You are all so splendid to us. But the Boosie House is shut by eight o'clock, and to a stranger in your midst' — he was proud of this phrase, which he felt contained the correct proportion of dignity and soap — 'the evenings can be rather long.'

'Ah, there now,' said Dr. Parke, 'I believe you are thinking along the wrong lines. What do we need of you here, what do we hope to enable you to do, when the day's task is ended? To loaf and invite your souls. That's it. To loaf and invite your souls.'

'Besides,' said his wife, much less pleasantly, 'a scholar needs sleep. If he has laboured in a way that is proper during the day, then he needs quiet, he truly needs rest. Dominick and I are always in bed by nine-thirty. We have our supper, we play our chess or perhaps our Scrabble, and then we are to lullabies. We do not want an inn here. We should become like Dartmouth, have no repose.'

Matthew, who had adored what he had seen of Dartmouth, began to lose hope.

'You are not afraid of cancer?' she enquired then, seeing him light a third cigarette.

He smiled noncommittally. He was not to be bullied.

'Well, well, well,' said Dr. Parke, stretching his little length in a manner cordial and luxurious, 'these problems will not be for me, much longer. No, no, I don't mean smoking. I mean the Centre. For a long time past I have been getting in arrears with my own work, and that won't do, that won't do at all. My Björnsen hangs fire. So I am proposing to retire before long and leave the job to a younger man.'

Matthew held his breath.

'There is,' the doctor continued, with a twinkle, 'quite a little competition! That surprises you, eh? But it's so. My job's no sinecure, that's what I tell them all. But at least three people from outside would like to take over from me, and more than one of the Visiting Fellows. For instance — let me breathe a little secret — our good friend Ruddock.'

Matthew was stupefied: this had never occurred to him.

'Of course, the final choice must lie with the Trustees.'

'Of course.'

'Dr. Ruddock is a rude man, too,' said Mrs. Parke.

'Ah, my dear, you are too rooted in a more graceful past! *Küss die Hand*, eh, eh? No, no, I admire Ruddock. He is a sound fellow. And I think his work will bring great lustre upon Cobb.'

It would be unjust to Matthew to say that the opportunity for ruining the hopes of at least one candidate occurred to him immediately. He was by nature a kind man, who loved to feel that everyone was happy around him, and who would even go out of his way to bring this about, if he did not have to go excessively far out of it. There was nothing of the villainous in his composition and not really very much, though he would have been surprised to learn this, of the oblique. But he did feel the stirring of an emotion whose source he failed to recognise, something between excitement and mischief.

'We have, you see, only one Memorial Fellow,' Dr. Parke went on, 'and so it is inevitable that Cobb should be associated with one great name above all. Yes, I think Ruddock will do us proud, I do indeed.'

'Are there any other claimants?' Matthew asked, perhaps a trifle too airily; for Dr. Parke wagged his finger and said that perhaps discretion was the better part of valour. 'I may have been too indiscreet already, my dear Matthew, but I know I can trust you. A still tongue in a wise head, eh?'

'Dorothy Merlin is no good,' boomed Mrs. Parke.

At this point the door-bell rang and her counterpart entered: to Matthew, with terrifying effect. As the two women embraced, he failed to see the slightest difference between them, except for hair parting and shoes; and even the hair partings gave the effect of mirror-image. Furthermore, the women were far too big. The room was full of them.

Trilby Pickersgill advanced on him warmly and apologised for having neglected him so long. 'But Mr. Pickersgill and I mean you to dine with us, we mean it most sincerely. I will call you up, that is my promise, I will call you up tomorrow. You are happy with us? Good, good, of that I am certain.'

'I was saying,' Mrs. Parke continued conversationally, 'that Dorothy Merlin was no good.'

'Ah, Beata! You are so wicked. You tease our friend. Mr. Pryar, she is a most terrible tease! Now I have read some poems of your subject, and I find she is all mother. I adore her that she is all mother. So you must not let Beata pull your leg.'

'But she is not all poet,' said Mrs. Parke.

Mrs. Pickersgill had dropped in for a reason, to advise her brother-in-law that the Trustees would be meeting the following week. 'Mr. Egan cannot come, but Tom Helliwell and J. L. Walters will be here on the Tuesday night and will stay with us, and perhaps you and Beata can have Dr. Perse and Mr. Van Eyck. It is a great nuisance that Mr. Walters and Tom will both arrive together, for there is only one guest room decent.'

Matthew suggested very diffidently that he would gladly put Tom up, that is, if they thought Tom would care for the idea. 'After all, I've loads of room.'

'So you have, so you have!' Dr. Parke looked enraptured. 'And I believe he is an old friend of yours. I am told so.' (Was there anything he did not know?) 'Would that help you, Trilby?'

She looked very pleased. It would indeed help her: her house was full of painters, and she really had not known how she and her husband were going to manage. Taking Matthew's hands in her own, she wrung them painfully.

When he left the house, Matthew made arrangements with the gas-station to be taken into Piltdown for supplies: he also, and this was a triumph, induced a promise from Anderson that he would persuade his sister-in-law, resident in Hamelin, to come in and cook breakfast during the three days Helliwell was there. 'I don't know if she will,' Anderson added doubtfully, 'she helps out sometimes, but it's not her job.' However, Matthew felt that for three dollars a morning she probably would; and he went on his way humming, though he was not aware of it, a sturdy hymn of his schooldays, which began, 'God is Working His Purpose Out'.

13. Matthew and the National Press

But before the arrival of Helliwell, Matthew had something to look forward to, which was another lush weekend with Mrs. Nash. It should, he thought, be delightful, for the weather was mild again, and though the trees were leafless, the turquoise sky, between bare and velvety branches soft as the antlers of young deer, was far more evocative of early spring than of the coming winter. Mrs. Nash was to send a car for him on Saturday afternoon, to meet him at Hartford airport. On Saturday morning, early, he went for a walk in the woods above Hamelin.

Now there is something very few visitors to a campus ever notice at all: which is, that there are students. Most of these visitors, set to formulate a mental picture of the place, would see topography, buildings, Faculty members themselves: despite the fact that it would necessarily be swarming with young men in the peculiar uniforms of contemporary fashion, the grey-white trousers, bulky sweaters, Parkas, woolly caps, these young men would somehow never entirely enter the consciousness. Students contrive to make a rather pleasant background noise, not unlike a hum of bees, but their physical presence, even when they are almost knocking the visitor down as they stream from dining-halls or Faculty houses, is singularly unobtrusive. Nor do their hopes and fears, their dissatisfactions, their demands, impinge very often on the visitor's ear. Thus Matthew, who had by no means failed to observe Cobb's dreadful isolation, had never even begun to consider what the very first dissatisfaction of the young might be.

He was walking uphill, over soft coniferous earth, through spare and delicate trees, loving the delightful sun. Far away to the right, the skiers sped down the bouncing slopes; to his left the bright chain of ponds (he would himself have called them lakes) where the young men rowed were sparkling and pale as a rope of Mrs. Nash's aquamarines. Through a clearing in the woods, as he looked up, he could just see the gilded pinnacle of the Sabine Leake College for Women, twenty miles away, but projected by the clarity of the air. He thought he would walk on for another half-mile till he struck the highway, and then stroll back again. His thoughts were so pleasant and so absorbing that the swelling of faint yells, squeals and tramplings into a positive din made no impact upon him. In fact, the woods were filling up: with young men, and with others. Cars were double-parked along the road, could Matthew have only seen them, and from these cars couples were tumbling in their scores.

He was suddenly aware of a figure hurtling in his direction, a female figure, which gasped, shrieked, tripped over a root and fell smack at his feet.

'I say, steady!' Matthew exclaimed, and automatically bent down to haul it up. He had the girl in his embrace at the very moment when a rush of students burst through the trees, embroiling him in what seemed to be an extraordinary game of tag. He felt rather like St. Peter Martyr set about by murderous woodsmen in a painting by Giovanni Bellini which is in the London National Gallery.

'Save me, save me!' the girl screeched, but did not cling to him for refuge. As she squirmed through his arms and darted off, he had a confused impression of flying fair hair, glasses, and red sweater. He looked about him in bewilderment, and might have stopped someone to ask what was going on, except that by this time the hunt had swept past him, undulating on its way to Hamelin.

Well, well! he thought: and that was all. He resumed his walk, grateful for the restoration of quiet, and in another hour was back at his house, packing his week-end case and singing 'My Heart Ever Faithful', as he thought of Mrs. Nash. There was still a good deal of noise going on about the campus, but as he drove in Anderson's cab to the airport, he failed to notice it.

It is not an easy journey from Hamelin to New Canaan, but by timing planes carefully it can be done in about three hours.

He arrived just before six o'clock. He was as joyful to see her as she him. 'We're going to be all by ourselves this weekend, Matt, and if the servants think it's sin, what do we care? Though they know I'm too old for sin, more's the pity. Jane Merle might just look in for lunch tomorrow,' she said with a touch of wistfulness, 'she's back from Arizona. Anyway, I've asked her. But she's always madly busy, what with her Foundations.'

Matthew knew about Mrs. Merle, though he had never met her. She was one of the three richest and best-known women in America, a forthright, beautiful, dominant widow who was a law unto herself. Mrs. Nash had once referred to her, in a moment of pique at yet another rejected invitation, as 'the fairy princess'; then, being a just woman, had added reluctantly, 'Only you don't think of her as a princess. She's a prince. In the Tudor sense. Elizabeth I called herself a prince. You know, just as some duchesses used not to be duchesses but dukes.'

Mrs. Merle had an enormous estate bordering upon the not-inconsiderable estate of Mrs. Nash: which made Mrs. Nash's look like a cottage-garden. They did, of course, know each other pretty well: they kissed when they met; but on the rare occasions when Mrs. Merle had paid her friend a visit, it was usually for fifteen minutes only, *en route* to a school, a hospital, a college, a clinic, of her own founding. This made Mrs. Nash sad, and as she was without self-consciousness or false pride, she not infrequently said so.

It was not, of course, quite true that he and she were to be alone. He was, indeed, the only house-guest: but fourteen came to dinner that evening, and another twelve were expected to dine on Sunday.

Saturday's party was for relations and neighbours, wind-blown farmers, male and female, with enormous herds in other parts of the country: *grandes dames* in black velvet with beautiful sunken eyes who came from monstrous mansions on the Hudson River, a young playwright rich as Croesus in his own right, and the nice, penniless cousin who lived in a fanciful cottage at Mrs. Nash's gate and had never felt like Lazarus about it in her life. All stayed late

— neighbours because they lived only a stone's throw away — relations because they were staying with other relations — so Matthew and his hostess had little time to talk alone. He was tired after his journey, and she had been out riding most of the day.

They had a nightcap together.

'Well, darling,' said Mrs. Nash, 'and is it still as dreadful?' She glanced sideways at the looking-glass. 'Oh, dear, I'm getting so fat!'

'I am a little more organised,' Matthew replied, 'and dear, you simply are not.'

'A fat old, sad old woman.' She screwed up her nose at him.

'Not a bit of it. Pearl, I am beginning to plot.'

'Plot what? Are you going to ask me to marry you, so that I can rescue you from your dire straits?'

'No, because you would refuse me.'

'Certainly I would. Once bitten, twice shy. What plots?'

'I wouldn't mind running that place,' Matthew said. He watched her warily. The ramifications of her influence were wide, but no one ever knew in which directions they spread.

'Oh, no, no.' She was firm. 'You'd be crazy as a coot in six weeks. I wouldn't hear of it.'

'Would you be in the way of hearing of it?'

I don't get you, Matt,'

'Pearl, dear, is Cobb anywhere within your empire? You see, I am brutally frank.'

'No, it's not. And if it were I wouldn't lift a finger. I know what's good for you, darling. I always know what's good for people.' She patted his knee.

'But Pearl——'

'Beddy-byes, Matt dear. You know you can hardly keep from yawning in my face. I won't make you come to church tomorrow, you heathen, so you can sleep late. I'll rouse you when I get back.'

As it happened, neither of them went to church. At nine o'clock, when Matthew had just rolled happily out of a dream and was thinking he might ring for his breakfast, there came a fusillade of knocks at the door, and Mrs. Nash's voice shouting — 'Matt, may I come in? Matt, let me in at once!'

She bounced in without permission (it was her house), the morning papers in her hands. There was a green pallor over the intaglio rosiness of her cheeks and her eyes were popping. 'Oh, Matt, Matt, what *have* you been doing?'

He sat up sharply, prickling with awareness of danger. He was still blurred with sleep; he could not see the page she was thrusting at him.

'It's all over the papers! Oh my poor boy, you'll have made the entire national press! Have you gone mad?'

His vision slowly adjusted itself. He was staring at one of the middle pages of the *Herald Tribune*, at a regrettably clear photograph of himself: Matthew Pryar, looking like a mad hare, embracing a spectacled girl in the middle of a wood. Beneath this was a considerable amount of letterpress, bearing the headline: BRITISH PROF SNATCHES SABINE.

Mrs. Nash flopped down on the edge of his bed, making him bounce. She was trembling. 'Tell me at once, Matt! *What have you been doing?*'

He had no chance to tell her just then, for she was called to the telephone, which was kept ringing steadily for the next twenty-five minutes, presumably by interested diners of the previous night. So he read the story.

The young men of Cobb had, it seemed, resented for a long time the absence of young women in anything like the immediate neighbourhood. In the hope of drawing public attention to their grievance, they had, as a rag, driven up in car-loads to Sabine Lake, snatched every girl they could see off the campus, and carried them forcibly, or chased them, down into Hamelin: where, after offering them Cokes and apologies, they had released them, and returned them respectfully to their college. That a prank of this order should have interested the *Times* and the *Tribune* would have been inconceivable, except for the mischief of some local photographer who, by happy chance, had captured Matthew precisely at the moment when he was hauling the girl off the pine-cones. He had hauled her with such good will, in fact, that at the moment when the shutter snapped she actually had her feet off the ground, thus giving the impression that Matthew was carrying her in a clumsy attempt at the fireman's lift. It was the kind of picture that is treasured among classical photographs of all time, since the days of Nicéphore Nièpce.

Shuddering, he forced himself to read what they said about him. 'Mr. Matthew Pryar, Visiting Professor at Cobb College, British expert on the work of Dorothy Merlin' (an asterisk for Dorothy here, and a footnote, since the writer did not expect anyone to have heard of her) 'is here seen lending more than moral support to the Roman rag.'

Matthew's face blazed, his head pounded. He lay down again, pressing his face into the pillow. If he could only go to sleep it would all turn out to be a bad dream. The telephone was still ringing away, the hall resounded with voices.

The English valet came in with a snowy breakfast tray; orange-juice, poached eggs, hothouse strawberries, flanked by a Peace rose in a crystal vase. 'I thought you might want it now, sir. And, sir, there are two gentlemen, reporters, who would like to speak to you, only Briskin told them, sir, that you were not available yet.'

'I shall never be available!' Matthew cried passionately, looking with horror at the tray. 'Get rid of them, Stevens, for God's sake, get rid of them.'

'Mrs. Nash is being pretty efficacious, sir.'

She must have been, for in a moment or so the noise died down, and after another cursory knock, she reappeared.

'Now, Matt, this may all be some dreadful mistake——'

'Of course it's a mistake!'

'— but owing to you, this house is besieged. I am on your side, I accept whatever you tell me, but it is not going to be *easy*, Matt. By this evening they will hear about it in San Francisco.'

'Pearl, I am over fifty!'

'What has that got to do with it, dear?'

'I don't rape Sabines, even in fun! I was just going for a walk, and that girl fell down, and I——'

'Yes, dear, now eat your eggs or they will be cold. You are going to need nourishment, I think, before today is out. Go away, you there!' This was a shout of fury, addressed to a face at the window. She opened it, crying after the retreating photographer, 'I'm setting the dogs loose!'

'Oh do,' said Matthew, now near to tears.

The telephone rang again. 'Does Mr. Pryar wish to take it, madam?' the butler asked her. 'It is a Dr. Dominick Morgan Barks.'

'Parke,' said Matthew. 'Oh, no, no. Tell him I'm at church. And please, I don't want to talk to anyone.'

'And you needn't!' said Mrs. Nash, melting. She patted him. 'I am quite sure the girl fell down, Matt dear. We are going to convince everyone of that. But believe me, they are going to take some convincing.'

Somehow he managed to eat some food, to rise, to bathe. The house was quieter since the telephone had been disconnected and. the six Dobermann pinschers were prowling the grounds. But this did not stop a flow of telegrams, pushed through the gates into the hands of the head groundsman, who was on guard there.

Matthew crept, more dead than alive, into the library, and opened them. From President Pickersgill: 'SHALL BE EXTREMELY OBLIGED IF YOU WILL GET IN TOUCH IMMEDIATELY.' From Dr. Parke: 'FAILED TO CONTACT YOU URGENT PLEASE CONTACT ME.' From Chuck Tiepolo: 'HOWSABOY EH QUERY CONGRATULATIONS ALL AT CENTRE.' From Edith Corall: 'MUST BE SOME MISTAKE WISH THERE WASN'T.'

It was the end of his hopes. How could he hope to get this story killed, to have his reputation so restored that any living soul could consider him a reasonable candidate for Dr. Parke's job? He forced himself to read the item again, hoping that perhaps it was libellous, but he very much doubted whether it was. In any case, the Americans had no libel laws to speak of, so far as he could tell.

Mrs. Nash joined him in a drink. She patted his hand from time to time, assuring him of her trust and her loyalty. More telegrams arrived, with invitations from broadcasting networks. A reporter who had found his way in was slightly bitten by one of the Dobermanns and had to be given an inconceivable bribe to make

82

nothing of his wound. This was not a money bribe: the only bribe he would accept was a short interview with Matthew. A starter on the local paper, he would have allowed himself to be bitten ten times as hard for the sake of an exclusive story. He would have lost a leg. He would have settled for rabies. Dead-pan, he took down Matthew's broken explanations, shook his hand warmly, refused a drink and a plaster for his leg, and ran for the first public call-box as hard as he could go.

The morning seemed unending.

'Could we manage a little lunch?' Mrs. Nash whispered, as to an invalid.

'No,' he said,' no, I don't think so. Oh, no.'

14. The Uses of Power

It was then that they heard, ringing across the garden, a voice open and clear as dawn, with a strong military rasp to it.

'All dogs lie down! Lie down at once. No bite-bites, you know I won't stand it! Pearl, darling! Call those bloodhounds off, or I shall smack-smack.'

Mrs. Nash, irradiated, all griefs forgotten, sprang to her feet. 'It's Jane! Matthew, it's Jane!'

She flung the french windows wide.

'Jane, we're in here! Hodgson, call off the dogs!'

Advancing upon them, impervious to the growls and rushes of the Dobermanns, was a small, fair woman whose gait was like the whipping of a foil. Triangular blue eyes wrinkled with amusement in a firm triangular face, hair like gold thread sparkled in the sun. She was perhaps ten years older than Matthew and looked at least as young. (Matthew, remember, looked no more than forty, if that.)

'I can't wait,' she shouted, as she approached, 'to meet your celebrity. I just dropped everything and came over.'

'Jane,' said Mrs. Nash emotionally, 'this is my dear old friend Matt Pryar, and not a word of it is true. Matt, this is Mrs. Merle.'

Mrs. Merle stepped over the sill and shook hands strongly, making Matthew's bones crack.

He found himself saying, in a nightmare attempt to be airy, 'It is quite marvellous that the dogs don't bite you. They have bitten a reporter.'

'Nonsense, I wouldn't dream of letting a dog bite me — Martini, please, Briskin. So you're Mr. Pryar! How splendid of you to cheer our lives up. I didn't like your girl, though. Why can't she wear contact lenses? They all do, nowadays.'

He told her he only hoped Mrs. Nash would forgive him for the hideous trouble he had caused her. He could never forgive himself. Nobody except Mrs. Nash was ever likely to forgive him. He was finished.

'You know,' said Mrs. Merle, 'you aren't in the least what I expected. Harry Dene's an old friend of mine — you know Harry?'

He said he did.

'He told me you were the most nonchalant man he'd ever met. Well? Go on, then! Be nonchalant!'

'I can't.'

Mrs. Nash retailed something of that morning of horror.

'Of course you can be nonchalant. You've got to.' Mrs. Merle waved for another Martini, crossed her delicate ankles and said, 'You'd better tell me the whole story.'

When he had done so, she frowned. 'You oughtn't to get into the habit of picking up people you don't know. There's no need to rush things, even if they are on the ground. They're probably quite all right there, just for the moment, while you're thinking, And then, with any luck, they may get up by themselves. Here, Mr. Pryar, the world hasn't come to an end! Deadly place, Cobb; if you'd come to me first I'd have told you not to go. *I* think you're a public benefactor to cheer things up for them.'

He had never felt so broken in his life. In normal circumstances he would have had only one thought, since he was a snob and knew it (there are far worse crimes than snobbery, crimes such as blackmail and cruelty to animals, and nobody ought to forget this), which would have been, to show himself to Mrs. Merle at his most lighthearted, his most urbane. Now he was scarcely even aware of cutting a poor figure.

'Others won't think so,' he said.

She inspected him, as if to see whether he had made proper use of his blanco and button-stick.

'Look here,' she said, and her rasp grew more pronounced, 'something's behind this. I know. I always do. Tell Jane-Jane.'

So he told her of his vague hopes at Cobb, and of the ruination of his chances.

'I see.' She rayed him with jewelled eyes, tapped with an enormous ruby ring on the edge of an ashtray. Had he been in his usual imaginative spirits he would have thought of her as something made by Fabergé, a pearl-encrusted egg, perhaps, containing a slightly alarming jack-in-a-box. 'Now then, Mr. Pryar! Have another drink-drink and let's talk sense.'

Briskin gloomily announced lunch and an emissary from the Hank Black Show, who had flown up from New York by helicopter.

'He must go away,' Mrs. Merle said steadily, 'and lunch sounds excellent. I'm hungry.'

Somehow, under her minatory gaze, Matthew was impelled to eat, and he felt the better for it.

'I think it would be a good thing, Pearl dear, if you reconnected the telephone. I don't like to feel out of touch with my hospital. And if anyone is troublesome, I don't object to answering it.'

Within fifteen minutes it had rung ten times. Mrs. Merle had an extension placed at her elbow. On each occasion she answered with the words, 'Mrs. Calvin Merle speaking. No, Mr. Pryar is not here. Please don't call again.' Somehow, possibly by supernatural means, she succeeded in discouraging other callers. For a long while the instrument was quiet.

'Sense,' she said at last. 'Now, Pearl, you have been absolutely wonderful but I think I'll take this matter in hand myself.'

'If only you would!'

'I've said I will. Mr. Pryar, when you've had coffee I think you should lie down. Pearl will give you a tablet. Then you will have a good sleep,' she added mesmerically. Matthew did not believe her. 'Pearl, may I stay all afternoon, darling? This is going to take some time.'

Matthew slept at once. He awoke in the early dusk, to absolute quiet. Beyond the window, a new moon and three stars shone peacefully down upon him. The air smelled sweetly of the breeding earth.

He washed himself, changed his shirt and tie and went into the library, where he found the two women sitting comfortably at tea.

'Now you are not to worry any more, Matthew,' said Mrs. Merle, 'for I am going to call you Matthew — and one day, if you show a little more backbone, I may even call you Matt-Matt. Everything is arranged and your troubles are over, though Pearl must not let you go back to Cobb until Tuesday morning. I have dealt with the press and the networks. Everyone has been threatened with libel suits. And they will welcome you back at Cobb with open arms, because although they have all the money they need, they still imagine they need more. Colleges always do. Now they will be able to build an extension to some hideous dormitory block and call it after me — I thought it as well that they should not call it after you, so I didn't make the suggestion. Pearl will tell you all about it. Pearl, dear, I must run now, I'm late already. Lovely tea-tea, darling, lovely everything. I've had a perfectly wonderful time, I don't know when I've enjoyed myself so much!'

She would not wait for Matthew's questions, nor for his thanks. She was all of a rush. They could hardly keep pace with her to the door. He felt almost desperate, knowing so little, being grateful for so much — that is, if she really had saved him. But ever since her feat of making him go to sleep simply by telling him he would, he could distrust her in nothing. He looked at her wonderingly, and then, to his own surprise, kissed her.

'My God,' she cried, 'he's recovered! Bless you, Matt, and don't worry — No, Pearl, I want to walk. Good for me. You're all so lazy around here! How very nice of him to kiss me, isn't it? Perhaps Harry Dene knows him better than I thought. Goodbye, darlings, and have a wonderful evening. — Oh, by the by, Pearl, I cancelled your dinner guests. I thought it was for the best. I do hope you don't mind.'

She was off, with her long whipping stride, calling her clear farewells like the Last Post across the dark and dew of the gardens.

15. The Return of the Native

Though the students, whom Matthew at last had ample cause to notice, welcomed him with 'Hi, sir!' prettily enough, it could not be said that they were laughing behind their hands. Fresh open grins adorned and brightened all young faces, creating a garland of smiles to wreathe the whole campus. From this he shrank. But he was greeted at his house within ten minutes of his return by the President and Dr. Parke, eager to assure him of their regret for the unfortunate incident which had befallen, and of their determined fellowship and support. At least, Matthew supposed the eagerness to be on both their parts, though Dr. Parke did all the talking while the President smiled shyly and wintrily behind his handkerchief, as if he had lost a tooth. The culprit, they said, had been discovered and expelled: he was, in fact, the photographer of the college newspaper who, his mind overset by such a scoop, had communicated it to the central news agency. (Mr. Pryar must not worry about him too much, since it was believed that *Life* had offered him a job.) Six other young men, ringleaders in the raid, had been suspended for the remainder of the semester. Peace had been made with the infuriated Principal of Sabine Lake. And, Dr. Parke confided, the college had just been made recipient of a splendid gift, a gift from a sympathiser who wished her name to remain anonymous, at least, for the moment. 'I mustn't even tell you, Matthew,' he cried happily,' but it is from a lady who is very eminent indeed.'

Matthew suggested Elizabeth Taylor.

'No, no, no, no! Someone quite different. But I must be discreet, my dear boy. It is within the terms of the agreement.'

'. . . regret the inconvenience to yourself.' the President mumbled. 'Sure you won't have any more. You've seen the morning papers, I guess. Apologies all round.'

They excused themselves and went away.

Matthew thought he had better look in at the Centre to see if there were any letters for him. Tacked up on a wall of his room he found a huge sheet of brown paper on which was chalked, in scarlet letters: WELCOME HOME, YOU OLD RAPIST! This was signed in a corner, 'Love from Chuck and Edith.' On his desk were many cablegrams and these depressed him: they were from English friends and acquaintances who had not yet learned of his exculpation. The topmost was from Dorothy.

'HOW ABSOLUTELY REVOLTING DONT KNOW HOW YOU CAN STOP EVERYONE LONDON OUTRAGED STOP PLEASE CABLE BY RETURN YOUR PROGRESS BOOK ON ME.'

She had not added 'love'.

He scrumpled this up and threw it away. He had no time to waste on Dorothy. An idea had come to him. Thoughtfully he asked for the number of Dr. Parke.

'Yes, my dear Matthew? What can I do to make your stay here smoother or more pleasant? As I said before, I do very much regret——'

'I was thinking about that splendid donation.'

'Yes, indeed! And I believe you were teasing me when you suggested Elizabeth Taylor. A little bird tells me that you may be in the secret yourself.'

'May I ask what use it's going to be put to, or is that cheek on the part of an outsider?'

'An outsider? Don't let me hear you say such a thing again! Of course you may ask. But the fact is, it may be months before we reach a decision. New dormitories, perhaps — an extension to the library — who can say? The President never lets himself be hurried.'

'I thought: perhaps an inn.'

'A sin? I don't quite get you.'

'An inn, I-N-N, Dr. Parke. Don't you think it would be an enormous attraction?'

'And well you may be right!' Dr. Parke's voice leaped with enthusiasm and so, for a deluded second, did Matthew's heart. 'But have you considered that Cobb *needs* no extra attraction? We might attract quite the wrong people, you know, sightseers, kibitzers — oh no, I don't think that would do at all!'

'I see,' said Matthew, and after expressing some half-hearted courtesy, hung up.

He was not further cheered by opening other cablegrams. From Dorothy's disagreeable husband: 'ENVY YOUR PERENNIAL YOUTH NOT TO WORRY WILL ALL BLOW OVER IN FIVE YEARS COSMO.' From Duncan Moss: 'IMPLORE YOU AND POPSY SIT FOR ME AM BETTER PHOTOGRAPHER LOVE.' From Mildred Duchess of Shropshire: 'ADVISE STAY IN U.S. TILL ENGLAND FORGETS ARE YOU QUITE MAD WITH LOYAL LOVE MILLIE.'

But, he said to himself, those were sent before I was cleared. He looked at his watch. I should just about be exculpated by now in the U.K.

Seeing the time made him realise that he was hungry. It was twenty-past one: if he made good speed he could just snatch a meal at the Boosie House. He raced across the campus, light as a boy, and up the lovely stairs. He was greeted at the door of the Pump Room by Mrs. Untermeyer, who had an uncommonly *louche* smile for him. 'Oh, Mr. Pryar, I'm so sorry! I'm afraid the dining-room is pre-empted——'

'Naturally,' said Matthew. 'By geometers.'

'Geographers,' she corrected him. 'But the cafeteria's still open.'

It was. It was crowded with students wolfing hamburgers. When Matthew entered, they rose to their feet as one man and they cheered him. Tightening his courage, he acknowledged the greeting with a smile and a wave of the hand as nonchalant as Mrs. Merle could have wished, gave a slight bow, and seated himself. There was no need for him to wait in the queue. Eager lads took his order, eager lads brought him the depressing result. They watched him in admiration while he ate, though no one addressed him directly until he was on his second cup of coffee, when a young man stepped forward and offered him, with grace and ceremony, the dining facilities of his fraternity house upon any evening of the week for so long as Matthew should be at Cobb. He was succeeded by another student, and then another, till not a fraternity remained unrepresented.

'The food is better, sir, than here,' said a stiff-spined, stiff-haired, rather fat boy called Jellinek, 'and we are permitted a little liquor.'

In this manner, one of Matthew's worst problems was solved. He would no longer go hungry. He might now apply his mind to more important things.

16. House-Guests

'O.k.,' said Tom Helliwell, 'no one's going to mention it. It doesn't matter a damn. Strictly for the birds.' This was the first thing he said as he got out of his car to be welcomed by Matthew.

'Well, are you feeling happier about things now?' He peered into the khaki dust of the hall. 'Have you really found your feet? They say an old lady lived here, did her exercises at ninety, died of them, in fact.'

'I have found my feet upstairs,' Matthew replied, 'but not down here. And I think it would be a little false not to refer to my recent notoriety. We shall only be conscious of it in the background of our thoughts. Let me have your bags.'

He took Tom into the bedroom next to his own. Anderson's relation had made it quite decent, though it still looked as if it might be haunted. 'When you're through unpacking, we might run up to Monkshill and have some dinner. That is, if you will run us up,' he added punctiliously.

Tom soon emerged from bedroom and bathroom, smart in various tones of tan and oatmeal, with silvery tie. Matthew had a drink ready.

'Well, yes, Matt, I'd say you were nicely settled here. Might be in your own home. — Have you seen the girl since?'

'Of course I haven't seen her.'

'I suppose she's not too photogenic?'

'I didn't look.'

'Too bad she wasn't more photogenic. On the homely side, I thought. But that may be the photograph.'

'I did not observe this girl,' Matthew said with a trace of heat, 'It was all over in a second.'

'They didn't get her name, did they?'

'I haven't the slightest idea. All I could concentrate on was mine.'

'Too bad. I must say I'd rather have liked——' Tom gave a soft, lubricious smile, a reminiscence of something which had not happened yet.

'You said she was homely.'

'But, Matt, I like them homely. I always have. I adore the dogs — they have unsuspected depths.'

'I am out of mine. Where do dogs come in?'

'Plain girls. The ones who get left, out of the party. Some of them turn out to be raging beauties, when you get them at close quarters. Also, they know the meaning of gratitude. Are you sure she never told you her name?'

'Look here, Tom, you said we weren't going to talk about it.'

'You insisted that we should.'

Then I really think, my dear fellow, that I was at fault, Let's not.'

'O.K., let's not.'

So they didn't, not for a full hour; but the moment they were sitting over Martinis in the inn at Monkshill, Tom reverted to the subject and Matthew came out with the whole story of his distressful week-end.

Tom was not only entertained, but impressed. 'Well, you had the luck on your side. Mrs. Merle! What people you know! And she stayed all afternoon, did she? She's never given Pearl more than fifteen minutes in her life.'

Matthew told him about the gift to Cobb, and made some light, objective-sounding propaganda for the inn.

'They won't go for it,' said Tom, 'they won't. Not a hope in hell.'

'Why not?'

'Too many don't drink.'

'You mean they're teetotallers?'

'Yes.'

This, though it should not have been, was an eye-opener for Matthew. 'I know the President is. But Parke drinks.'

'Drinks? Have you ever known him take more Scotch than would colour the water? He hates it. He only lets you give him a teaspoonful because he's such a dear old man. He doesn't like to hurt feelings. Besides——' Tom ran off a list of Faculty members who, not given to toping even so much as Dr. Parke, rejected with frozen bonhomie alcohol in any form. 'So you're up against a blank wall, Matt. They'll give you all kinds of reasons for stopping the inn project, but you can take it from me that's the real one.'

Among Matthew's few but useful gifts was the capacity to cut his losses. He knew instinctively, and also by hindsight observation, that what Tom said was true. It occurred to him that in all affairs of men, when many reasons were given for not doing a thing, the sole genuine reason was the one never mentioned at all. The greater the number of reasons, the greater and more concentrated the chicanery. From that moment he thrust the inn idea out of his immediate objectives. He would waste no more time on it. He had other things to do.

Up to now, he felt, he had not done so badly. He had solved, more or less, the problem of domestic help, the problem of food, and the mystery of inn-resistance — which was how he put it to himself: all this in a little under three weeks. It was not bad going. Now he could devote himself entirely to the business of getting himself a splendid and lasting job, a job which would keep him out of Dorothy's way for years, incidentally, though such incidentals were trifling in comparison with the real gains: i.e., a hefty salary, and the chance to prove the administrative genius he had only recently discovered within himself. He smiled, thinking back. Buds should break. Streams should flow. Mrs. Merle should pay. So should Mrs. Nash. There would, of course, be an inn in the end, but it wouldn't sound like one: it should be called the Matthew Pryar Memorial House.

'Did you know that Dr. Parke means to give up soon?' he asked Tom, as if idly.

Tom said comfortably, 'That's an old one.'

'No. I assure you, he means it now.'

'Oh, for Chrissake!' Tom was a picture of polished perturbation. 'He can't do that. I don't know how we'd get along without the old boy. He practically *is* Cobb — you can't think of it without him! Damn it, he's a father-image!'

'Nevertheless,' said Matthew, 'dreadful as the event would be, I do think you ought to be considering the future.' He added, 'Not that it's any business of mine, of course.'

They were eating deep-dish chicken pie, frail in flavour, preposterous in quantity.

'It's no good,' Tom said, 'I can't see it. Let's say I can't face it.'

'If you had to face it, would you be likely to turn to an outsider? In England we often advertise these jobs, even when we know perfectly well who is going to get them.'

'It wouldn't be the same, not without dear old Dr. Parke.'

'But, Tom, he might even die some time. Or get into a car smash. His driving is quite frightful. What then?'

'Then,' said Tom, 'the rush would be on. But let's not cross our bridges till we come to them.'

'Say a younger man, preferably *not* a scholar, who has his whole time free for administration——'

'It's no go,' said Tom. 'I tell you, I just can't see it.' But his face cleared somewhat of grief, and took on a tinge of thought.

Matthew said no more, fancying he had at last planted a seed. It wouldn't need watering for a bit, but he would be ready with the garden spray when, it did. He was so absorbed in his thoughts that he finished the whole pie without noticing it, and was made aware of the fact only by the first bloated twinge of indigestion. He turned the talk to neutral subjects, allowing Tom to speak at length of women. They drank some more Scotch and did not start back to Piltdown till nearly half-past eleven.

The campus clock was chiming midnight in its hesitant, milk-and-water way, as they drew up at Matthew's house. On the step sat a small smudgy figure, patiently waiting.

'Why, hullo there, J.L.,' said Tom, 'what on earth are you doing here at this time of night?'

J. L. Walters got up stiffly from his vigil. He looked extremely cold.

'Mr. Walters,' said Matthew compassionately, 'have you been waiting long? We were up at Monkshill——'

'About an hour and a half.'

'My dear chap, I'm desperately sorry. But what for?'

'I understood from Mrs. Pickersgill that you were kindly putting me up for a couple of nights.'

Matthew was stricken with horror. Had this been the arrangement? Could he have misheard, misunderstood? He was damned sure he hadn't, 'But I couldn't be more distressed. I myself understood that you were staying with the President, and that Tom was staying here——'

'So did I,' said J. L. Walters, 'but she said not. I got to the President's house at ten-thirty and of course they were all in bed. Mrs. Pickersgill came down in her robe and said you were expecting me. So I walked here. One and a half hours ago,' he added, with a top-dressing of righteous grievance and an overtone of savagery.

Tom did not seem to be put out. Awakening Matthew from paralysis, demanding his key, he let them all into the house. 'You've got plenty of room here, Matt. There must be at least four other bedrooms J. L. can choose from.'

'The beds aren't made up.'

'Well, then, he can have mine. I'm O.K. on the couch.'

Matthew, all hope gone, said that would not do at all. J.L. could have his room, he would sleep on the couch himself. He added, to save embarrassment — for his social sense was once more alive and operating — that he often slept there, simply because he liked it.

'Then that's all right,' said Walters. He refused a drink and asked if there was anything to eat.

'I don't really know——' Matthew began.

Walters, who seemed to be familiar with the house, made straight for the kitchen and turned up the lights. They went on reluctantly, as strip-lights do, first a wan brown twilight, then a hellish violet glow, and then a steady glare. He made for the refrigerator and looked inside. There was a tin of corned beef. There were six eggs, intended for breakfast. There was bacon, bread and butter.

'Don't you bother,' he said to Matthew, who had not stirred hand or foot, 'I'm used to fending for myself.'

They stood around, dropping with sleep (for Tom had travelled from Boston by road that day), while Walters, in an efficient but leisurely way, prepared a hearty meal, consisting of four eggs, half the bacon and a good slice of the corned beef. He also ate a great deal of bread and butter.

'Half a loaf really isn't much better than no bread, when you come to think of it,' Matthew whispered to Tom, who was too drowsy to be amused.

Walters was a very slow eater, chewing each mouthful in the manner prescribed by Gladstone. (To while away the time, Tom and Matthew drank more whisky.) When he had finished, he insisted on washing up.

'But I have a woman coming in——'

'Never put off till tomorrow. This will only take me a second.'

Very slowly indeed Walters scraped the plates and stacked them in the dishwasher. The machine began to purr, whine and splash.

'I'm sure you can leave them now,' Matthew said. 'They'll be looking wonderful in the morning. This really is a magnificent device, I do assure you.' Though he had never seen it working.

J.L. said it was never his habit to leave machinery unattended. Neglect a small machine, and you might play hell with a big one. It was the same as learning never to point a stick: if you pointed sticks, one day you would find yourself pointing a gun. He was adamant. Neither Tom nor Matthew could move him.

When the dishes were done, when he had neatly replaced them in the cupboard, it was twenty minutes to two.

'Well,' he said, looking slightly more alive than usual, 'time to turn in. I may have a cold coming.'

He had forgotten to pack handkerchiefs and pyjamas, so he borrowed both from Matthew.

17. A Gentleman May Conceivably
be a Traitor

At half-past seven, Matthew was aroused from his hideous sleep on the couch by Anderson's sister-in-law, who turned out to be a native of Brixton, England, but with whom he was unable to establish any national *rapport*. No, she said, she couldn't make a breakfast for three gentlemen out of that lot (she pointed scornfully into the Frigidaire); she couldn't get blood out of a stone, and she wasn't going to let herself down by trying.

'I got standards, Mr. Pryar. Two gents, just about. Three, not on your tintype. You ought to have thought about that earlier, see?'

'But Mr. Walters was quite unexpected——'

'That's your pidgin. All I see is what's before me eyes.'

'Mrs. Anderson, we are fellow-countrymen——'

'Not now, we're not. I'm an American citizen, and when you go to Rome, do as Rome does. You'd better hop along to the Boosie, and I'll feed your two as best I may. Not that they'll make themselves sick on what they've left.'

So Matthew breakfasted in the cafeteria while Tom and J. L. Walters (in dressing-gowns, presumably, eased and comforted) ate up what was left of the eggs and bacon in the dining-room. By the time he returned they had gone off to their committee work, so he walked over to the Centre, determined to make a start on Dorothy at last.

It was quiet and comforting in his splendid office, conducive to endeavour. Matthew, gritting his teeth, took Dorothy's collected works from a drawer, and because he felt very tired thought he might start on a middle section entitled, *Light Thoughts*. (An appendix reference here, so that the more obtuse readers could appreciate the link-up with Young's *Night Thoughts*.)

Six of these pieces were intended, overtly at least, to give pleasure to children, and Dorothy, little tease that she was, had thrown the whole of her more frivolous nature into them. This was, indeed, not very much; but such as it was, she had thrown it.

He stared, attempted to concentrate upon the first; which was called, *Objurgation to Sir Mischief*.

'Don't bother — Mother
or lather — Father
if you'd rather —
I'll give you a plum.'

Beyond noting that she had taken a hint or two from Miss Dickinson's idiosyncratic punctuation, this told him nothing.

Rising from his desk, he walked up and down the room repeating, through clenched teeth, since people believe that by uttering through clenched teeth while in solitude they may somehow convey some lasting message to the brain:

'Don't bother —
Mother or lather — Father ...'

He did not like it. He could not stand it. For the first time in his life he was aware, not only of Dorothy's limitations, but of her staggering absurdity: and when a scholar becomes fully seized of the absurdity of his subject, it is all up with him.

How much longer he would have prowled his elegant and workmanlike room, muttering Dorothy's tripe, can never be guessed: for he was interrupted by Doug Ruddock, eager, Matthew quite wrongly assumed, to talk about Sabines.

It was not that at all.

'Now you don't altogether believe me, Matt, do you? But just listen to this.

"How many times these low feet staggered —
Only the soldered mouth can tell——"

'Staggering again, see? Or this one:

"Her pretty speech — like drunken men —
Did stagger pitiful——"

'Or get the significance of this:

"And Saints — to windows run —
To see the little Tippler
From Manzanilla come!"

'Did I tell you it was sherry? Well, it wasn't. It was *rum*!'

'Manzanilla is sherry,' said Matthew, who was on the whole relieved.

'I'm using Thomas H. Johnson, Belknap Press. He says she associated Manzanillo, city on the south coast of Cuba, with the export of rum. And here's Emily and the boozing bees again —

"We — Bee and I — live by the quaffing —
'Tisn't *all* Hock with us —
Life has its Ale——"

'How the hell can you doubt it, boy?'

'Oh, I don't, I don't,' said Matthew, 'that is, if you don't. But, Doug, I too have work in hand.'

'Your Merlin. Better you than me. Well, if you don't want me I'll go. See you another time.'

'I'd loathe you to think that I didn't want you——'

'Thousands don't. Including Mrs. Ruddock, back in Utah. Never mind. Maybe when you're less busy.'

He had gone, leaving Matthew thoughtful.

The trouble was that any interruption, once he had ground his mind down to Dorothy, instantly reduced such attractions as she might have had to the status of last night's supper served up cold for breakfast to some recalcitrant Edwardian child. He was unable to return to her.

He went to look out of the window. Across the campus darker clouds were gathering and the twigs whipped on a keen new wind. Snow was on its way again which, if he knew this part of the world at all, would last when it fell all winter long. Above the clouds the sky was a somewhat hectic blue, the blue of a dubious turquoise with too much green in it. The young men scurrying to their classes had pulled their woolly caps down over their ears.

And damn it, Matthew thought, I haven't brought a greatcoat.

He arrived chilled at the Boosie House expecting to feed his guests there: but they were locked away with other Trustees in an upper room where, he thought for one fanciful second, they would undoubtedly be getting better food. A second, more realistic thought, assured him that this was unlikely, since the Boosie House had only one *chef de cuisine*.

After his meal he went home to collect his coat, and then back to his office where, joylessly, he contemplated another of Dorothy's *Light Thoughts*, which read as follows:

'Jollity,
Solidarity
    Makes We —
    You and Me —
    US:
        Baby, see!'

— after which he shut her poems into a drawer and decided that she must wait.

Ruddock, he thought. Dr. Parke was extremely biased in that direction. 'Lustre to Cobb', indeed! He wondered what they would all think if the drift of Doug's Dickinson researches were made known. Supposing someone of low moral fibre were to reveal it — as, of course, nobody would. What would Parke think then? Of course, it was hardly cricket in the circumstances for Ruddock to be taking Cobb's money. He must realise, as keenly as anyone else, the distress his activities must eventually cause. In a way, it was a pity Parke didn't know: but — Matthew came back to this — only someone of low moral fibre would dream of telling him. If the book appeared before Parke's successor had been appointed, that would be the end of Ruddock: but from what Matthew had learned about scholars, it was not usual for books to appear until a decade or more after their inception. Doug might, then, be chosen in all innocence. Had he, Matthew, a duty in all this? Cobb had been generous to him according to its peculiar lights, had given him this delectable room to work in, was paying him a pretty stiff fee. Had he, therefore, an obligation of loyalty to Cobb? It was not inconceivable. Had he an obligation of loyalty to Ruddock? Naturally. The drunken bees had been offered as a confidence between gentlemen.

Matthew saw himself upon the horns of a dilemma.

Plainly, he couldn't breathe a word to Parke: that was just not on. Yet there could be no blinking the fact that Doug, under his very nose, was preparing a savage blow for his mild benefactor. How would he, Matthew, feel when that blow fell, knowing that he might have prevented it? How could he look Dr. Parke straight in those dulcet blue eyes? How could he face that poor old Laodicean, Pickersgill?

It did not occur to him that, if such a time came, he need face neither, he could simply bow out and return to England. He could think of nothing but those distressful faces, one elderly, small and childlike, the other hunted and pale.

'All the same, it's nothing to do with me,' Matthew said sturdily, and aloud.

His heart was eased. He went off for a brisk cold walk over earth which sprang like a ballroom floor.

He had not passed beyond the limits of the campus when the two monstrous sisters, Beata and Trilby, descended upon him.

'Ah, you take exercise!' Beata exclaimed. 'That I am truly glad to see. Most of the Fellows, they make their offices ugly with smoke, they grow pale, they grow weak, their eyes redden. I think the sight of them is horrid. My sister and I, we walk seven miles a day. It is so.'

'And now we have walked our seven miles,' said Trilby, who seemed to be by far the nicer of the two, 'so I must return to my husband. If I am late, one tiny second late, he worries sincerely about me. He thinks I may meet bad men in the woods.'

Matthew wondered what chance a bad man would have against a back-hander from Mrs. Pickersgill.

'Pooh, he is neurotic,' said Beata. 'Are you walking further, Mr. Pryar? Because I am not in the faintest weary, and I will go with you.'

'As a matter of fact,' said Matthew, 'I was just thinking of going home.'

'But your home is not in this direction.'

'A short *détour*, that's all.'

'I think you are not meaning to go home. Goodbye, Trilby. I will walk Mr. Pryar to the ponds.'

She spoke as if she meant to walk a dog, and indeed, that was what he felt like, striding along as mesomorphically as he was able, but yet failing quite to keep up with her. He could just about catch the line of her Valkyrie profile, as she chattered away to him.

'I think you were full of complaints when you visited us, Mr. Pryar, but I think you are not so complaining now. Not now Dominick has explained to you.'

(What had Dominick explained?)

'We are a truly happy family at Cobb, Mr. Pryar, all in love and friendship. To complain is quite unusual. Nobody does. So you will not. I think there is a girl you like, I saw her in a newspaper. Therefore you will settle down.'

'I did not know that girl from Adam——'

Beata decided to jest, which was terrifying. She paused for a moment to turn her great dark handsome face upon him. 'A bow is as good as a blink to a blind horse, Mr. Pryar. I do not intrude. I do not ask to know. Things sexual are good and I am for them.'

She plunged on, Matthew at her heels, through slopes of silver birch, towards the icy shine of the waters.

'I do wish you wouldn't go quite so fast,' he protested, driven to it.

'We slow down, we get cold. To be brisk is best. I cannot believe you truly like the poetry of Dorothy Merlin. Before, I had not heard of her. Now I wish I had not,'

He tried to make some sort of case for Dorothy, for her peculiar distinction, her peculiar place in English letters.

'She makes fuss about having babies, pooh! She is a coward, I think. I myself have had five, all over ten pounds. Their heads were very big, but I did not scream, not once. The screams of others could be heard the whole hospital over.'

Matthew, who loathed obstetric details, flinched.

'If they had taken after Dominick they would have been tiny babies. But no. It is true we may trust the genes.'

He suggested that they must be splendid specimens by now.

'One in army, one in navy, one in marines, one at Princeton, one at Sorbonne,' she informed him rapidly. 'Pooh! There is nothing to babies.'

They had reached the water's edge. Here, blessedly, she allowed him to pause. A lacing of emerald ice was forming itself along the margins of the pond, infinitely delicate now, but it would be powerful enough to skate on within a week. One of the crews was out for the last practice of the year; the voice of the coach, following in a motor launch, rang out incomprehensibly through the megaphone.

'I cannot ask you to tea,' said Beata, 'because when Dominick returns he will be exhausted as a tiny child. And when he is exhausted so, he does not relish strangers.'

'Oh, I couldn't come anyway. But it was nice of you to think of it.'

'He is always exhausted by deliberations. I shall myself be glad when he has withdrawn himself from the burly, and is back with Björnsen.'

Matthew said he was so sure she was right.

He had not expected her to elaborate upon the deliberations, since he was of the common and mistaken opinion that stone-faced women are necessarily discreet ones. He was quite wrong.

'Today he try to retire. They will say No, no, and not accept just as usual. But he is sincere. Without him doubtless the Centre will fall to little pieces. But is he to be a human sacrifice?' She glared at Matthew, as if he were solely responsible for the retention of her husband in his office.

'You are so entirely right,' he said. 'I'm most deeply convinced that he shouldn't be.'

'But after Dominick — who?'

This did not seem merely rhetorical.

'It's a great burden for a scholar,' Matthew said eagerly. 'Don't you think a younger man, with few scholastic pressures and far more time to give——'

'*They*,' she said darkly, 'will doubtless want that Ruddock. I do not say that we do, Dominick and I. Tell me, Mr. Pryar, what is your opinion of Dr. Ruddock?'

'He's an excellent chap, from what I know of him.'

'And his work? His monument to that strange, great Emily Dickinson of whom Dominick is so truly fond?'

To his horror, Matthew found himself saying it. 'Well, it may turn out a trifle odd.'

She was on to this at once. 'Odd?'

'Let's say original.'

'How, original? I do not think a work of scholarship should be so very original.'

'I didn't mean flashy, you know.'

'You said odd. It was the word.'

She towered over him, hands deep in her tweed pockets, as if she could just manage, by the exercise of restraint, to keep them there.

'Some *unique* theories, perhaps. Not that I *know*,' Matthew answered desperately.

'Ah, but pooh! You do, I think, know. And what do you mean, is unique? Dominick's work is never unique. Only truly sound. Come, Mr. Pryar! Do not attempt to draw the wool.'

'Well, I think he thinks there might be an explanation.'

'For what?'

'Well, she shut herself up a good bit.'

'And why does he think she so did?'

'Look here, Mrs. Parke,' Matthew said, 'you mustn't press me——'
He was really frightened by now.

'Nonsense. It will go no further than ourselves. And Dominick.'

'There's nothing to it, I assure you.'

'What,' said Beata, moving in, so that he found himself backing
insensibly towards the water, 'has Dr. Ruddock found which is
unique?'

'Look, I can't say, honestly I can't.'

She gazed thoughtfully out at the crew, slitting the waters with
their thin, varnished knife. 'So she was perhaps lunatic, he thinks.
Psychotic. Or perhaps it was the drink.'

Matthew started violently.

'Ah, that is it, then? Dr. Ruddock supposes that she was given
to what is called a bottle? Oh, how shameful!'

'Mrs. Parke, I never said so!'

'But you have flushed, no? You are as red as a cherry, I think.'

'I did not say so. I don't know anything about it.'

He was a gentleman; he had not said so. But he was terrified
now that she might believe he had.

'So that is it. Dominick must know. He must not be hoodman
blind.'

'Mrs. Parke, you are going to get everyone into a desperate
amount of trouble if you go around saying——'

Her eye flashed lightning. 'Go *around*? I do not "go *around*, as
you say.'

'No. I beg your pardon. But——'

'Oh, shameful, shameful!'

'Listen, I know *nothing* about Dr. Ruddock's theories, nothing
whatsoever——'

'So. That is the way you will have it. Very well.'

She turned abruptly and strode off in the direction of the campus,
Matthew panting after her.

'I do beg you, Mrs. Parke——'

'Dorothy Merlin is entirely no good, I think. She is a

mouse-woman, without spirit. I do not admire mouse-women.'

He was too miserable to defend Dorothy against one of the very few charges that might rightly be regarded as untrue, not to say insane. He plodded along over the crackling leaves, silent, heavy of heart. He pushed down the alien creature who lay in the depths of his being with a grin on its face, with an ungentlemanly little mouth framing the words: 'Done it!'

18. An Englishman's Bath

Chilled to the bone and, in the conscious sector of himself, ill at ease, Matthew went home, went straight up to his bedroom, undressed, and decided to soak in hot water for half an hour or more. The house was quiet.

He walked into his bathroom, and into a hot fog.

When he had adjusted his eyes to this, he saw J. L. Walters occupying his bath, floating at ease in water which appeared slightly scummy. He had a newspaper in his hands and his glasses were on his nose.

'That you, Mr. Pryar? I can't see.'

'Excuse me——' Matthew began.

'Oh, don't go away. Hope you don't mind me taking a bath.'

'Indeed, no.' (Though Matthew was furious, outraged in some profound part of his entire entity.)

'I don't mind, believe you me. All the same, is what I say.'

'What is all the same?'

'You and me. Mankind.'

In fact, J. L. Walters would have no need for *pudeur*, since fug and scum effectively concealed all but the white smudge of his contented face.

'All the same——' Matthew began again.

'Yes, I said we were all the same. Often think of that. Oh, do you want to get in here? I'm almost through. By the way, it's true about dear old Parke. He really is retiring.'

Matthew, about to retreat in fury, thought the better of it. 'Really?'

'Sure!'

'Any plans for a successor?'

'Well, I suppose it wouldn't hurt if I told you, you being British and out of it. Still, better not. It's all hush-hush at present.'

Matthew was filled with loathing. If there was one place where strangers should never be found, to shock, to dismay, it was in one's own bath in one's own house. He knew the invasion not merely of material but of spiritual privacy. A bright little picture flitted through his mind, of George Joseph Smith jerking up the heels of his third or fourth bride and putting her head conclusively under the water.

'I know you like poetry, Mr. Pryar. I like the verses they put in the *New York Times* — it's wonderful to me where they get them from. There's a swell one here about October and the dying year.'

'If you will excuse me——'

'Ten minutes,' said J. L. Walters, 'that's all. I can't get out right now, I have to let the water cool down. If you really want to bring on a coronary, the best way is to jump out when you're still hot.'

Now that the steam was thinning, dispersed by the opening of the bathroom door, Matthew could see rather more of his recumbent guest, green-white as the chincherinchee flowers of South Africa, and what he saw was far from pleasing. The effect was not unlike an archipelago: a flat, faintly mounded island for the chest, a round one for the stomach, two small peaked ones for the knees, two tiny red ones for the big toes. A modest man, he would all too gladly have backed out, had curiosity not got the better of him.

'I suppose there must be at least half a dozen candidates.' It comforted him to think that he, at any rate, was decently clad, in a dressing-gown of crimson poplin with crimson and white spotted cravat.

'Say three,' said J.L., 'the rest are outsiders.'

'Since I'm an outsider, it's of purely academic interest to me. So do,' Matthew added with a kind of alien winsomeness which dismayed him the moment he heard his own voice, 'give me the "dope".'

'Ah now! Ah now! Better not. *In camera*, you know.'

At that moment the door burst open and in came Tom, wearing cashmere robe and orange leather slippers. 'For Chrissake, what——Oh, sorry, Matt. Didn't know you were here. I'll wait. Who's that — why, J.L., you old coot, how did you get back before me?'

Since J. L. Walters had refreshed his bath from the hot tap, the steam had thickened again.

'It is you, J.L.?'

'It is indeed,' said Matthew suavely, 'and you are correct in recognising me. We are all in here. Mr. Walters is not yet ready to emerge.'

'He'll emerge,' said Tom, and advanced upon his fellow trustee with a menace George Joseph Smith could hardly have equalled. Had there been a harmonium in the house, Matthew would have gone straight off and played *Abide With Me* on it.

'Here, lay off!' J.L. gave a scream, and leaped up. Matthew dodged out of the room. He went to one of the other bathrooms (he had forgotten its existence) and locked himself in there, only to find there was no towel, no soap, nothing. He banged out again, back to where the other two were now arguing in raucous, bellicose, friendly voices. He knocked.

'Tom! Hand me out a towel.'

Voice through the door: 'They're all wringing wet.'

'I don't care.'

'They're sodden. There ought to be some more in the linen closet.'

'I do not know where the linen-closet is.'

'Right-hand side of the back stairs,' J.L. squealed, 'you'll find one there.'

But Matthew could not locate such a cupboard. In despair, and also in a fit of ingenuity, he tore the counterpane from J. L. Walters' bed (the bed which had been his own), and made off with it. It was candlewick. It would be a decent drying agent.

He stayed in the third spare bathroom nearly as long as J. L. Walters in the master-bathroom, lying in the hot water and coming as near to the emotion of hate as he had ever done. Matthew was simply not used to invasions; in his London chambers, in St. James's Street, invasions were not allowed to occur. He felt hemmed in, besieged from all sides. It might have been different had he been used even to women visitors; women are natural invaders, and one resents them no more for what is integral to their make-up than one resents a cat for catching birds. Slowly, steadily, women make the habit of invasion more or less acceptable. Matthew, however, always went out for his girls, to their homes, a welcome invader himself. He inevitably told them (and to their amazement they believed it) that it was a condition of his lease that no women should enter his chambers.

He was, moreover, an exceedingly modest man. During his few adventures in love, he had preferred to have the lights out. This was not because he himself was not agreeably formed, tolerably broad across the shoulders, narrow in the hips, with buttocks hard and square as two tin loaves: he just did not think women were very pretty to look at, and it made him flush slightly when he did look.

But he would have preferred his house at Hamelin full of women, women crowding like Burne-Jones girls all over the stairs, than having it full of Tom and J. L. Walters. For one frantic minute he wondered whether he could pluck up courage to come out of the bathroom at all till they had gone.

However, this would not be for quite another twenty-four hours, perhaps more. He dried himself in a wealth of candlewick, put on his dressing-gown again and returned to his bedroom. He could not get in because it now belonged to J. L. Walters, who was dressing at a snail's pace and humming little bits from *La Bohème*.

'All right, Mr. Pryar, shan't be long. Won't keep you a minute.'

Matthew sat down at the stairhead, looking down into the murk. He folded the bedspread over his knees.

The bell rang and Edith bounced in, tam-o'-shanter alight, her pouter-pigeon breasts straining under a jolly yellow sweater. 'Matt! Matt! What on earth are you doing up there? Why are you wrapped in a blanket? Can I come up?'

She sounded quite her old self: and she was smoking one of her baby pipes, with cherry-wood bowl and amber stem.

'Of course come up,' Matthew said, 'I am turned out of my rooms.'

She ran to him, gave him a smacking kiss. 'Oh, Matt, guess what! — I say, you do look strange.'

'I am afraid I do. But I can't guess what.'

'I'm going home! Back to Cambridge, *England*! Look, do let's go and sit down, not in the hall. Matt, good sometimes comes out of evil.' Though she shuddered briefly.

'Tell me, dear Edith,' Matthew said. He led the way into the living-room.

It appeared that, only this morning, Hefflinger's Hannah had got loose, and had been found in the corridor of the Centre, just outside Edith's door, being moused by Ruddock's cat. Edith, happily, had not seen this, or she would certainly have fainted: but Chuck had come to tell her all about it, with graphic descriptions. 'So then I suddenly thought, *why should I bear it?* What was keeping me here? So I got hold of Pat Ehrlinger, and she got me reservations for the morning jet, and I'm off! Of course, I'll have to lose half my fee, but what does it matter? No more filthy Hannah, no more Romeo, no more Hefflinger, no more Cobb — oh, dear, but no more Matthew! You are the one person I shall miss. Darling, don't rape any more Sabines, you'll never get away with it next time.

" 'Et aqill fan entre lor aital agrei:
L'us es compains gens a for mandacarrei,
E meno trop major nauza que la mainada del rei.' "

'Edith, I will not stand it!'

'It's as plain as piecrust, if you'd only listen properly. It means that scoundrels keep the citadel, ramping around like the king's guard, while some strutting brute like you tries to lay the hapless maiden. Please don't lay any maidens from now on, you will only get into hot water.'

Reminded of hot water, Matthew raised his voice. 'Tom! Are you through there?'

But Tom had burst out singing. From the bathroom came *Carmen*, from the bedroom *Bohème*.

'Look,' said Edith, 'leave the beasts alone. I don't know what

112

they're doing, but leave them to it. We can go along to my place for a drink. To celebrate.'

'I can't. I'm not dressed.'

'Why not?'

He explained.

Edith's mouth tightened, her formidable, Cambridge mouth. 'I'll see about that.'

She went straight to the best bedroom, gave a cursory bang, and walked right in. 'Excuse me. Mr. Pryar is waiting to dress.'

Matthew, peering behind her, could just see Walters pottering, in vest and drawers. He looked horrified.

'I know you don't know me. Let me introduce myself. I am Edith Corall, Fellow of Madingley College, mediaeval history.'

'J. L. Walters. I must apologise——'

'How do you do, Mr. Walters, will you be long? If so, I will take Matthew's clothes with me.'

'No, no, I assure you——'

'I'll time you,' Edith said, 'four minutes dead. I'll give you a count down.' She shut the door on him. 'Matt, there is now *nothing* I cannot do. Darling Matt, I am going home, home, home! It will be wet and muggy in Petty Cury, with no snow, and the world will sing with bicycle bells. Oh, Matt!'

He embraced her, feeling both affectionate and jealous. She was going home. In England she would resume the whole of her parrakeet glory, and he would stay here, poor Matthew, wrestling with Dorothy. He thought:

'Don't bother — Mother
or lather — Father . . .'

'Three!' cried Edith in a stentorian voice.

He was startled. 'What do you mean, "three"?'

'I was giving him the count down. Dear Matthew, I would not endure strangers in my house, my bathroom, my bedroom, so it stands to reason that I shall not endure such a thing on behalf of my friends. — Two!'

The house shuddered. The ancient ghost bent and touched her toes.

'Furthermore, Matt, I do not like to think of you here, subject to people like Hefflinger——'

Here her voice paled.

'I don't mind *araneae*, perhaps I should, but I honestly don't. Or much.'

'— half-starved——'

'I have the *entrée* to all the fraternity houses.'

'That's as maybe,' Edith retorted, like a policeman. 'ONE!'

J. L. Walters shot out of the bedroom, fully clothed. Tom Helliwell sidled, in his robe, out of the bathroom and into his own quarters.

'You see,' Edith explained to Matthew, 'it is just a matter of confidence. One has to *believe* that man will finish dressing, and that the other will get out of the bath. If your belief is sincere, then they will justify it.'

She looked around her, as if to see whether she had neglected any other means whereby she might demonstrate the power of faith. Satisfied that no stone was left unturned, she embraced Matthew again. 'Good-bye, dear. I shall be leaving early tomorrow. I did want you to come round to my rooms, but those men have made me so late, and I have so much packing to do.'

He could hardly believe that she was really going.

'Edith——'

'No, I don't like prolonged farewells. We shall meet again in absolutely wonderful and soothing circumstances, dining, I dare say, with the Provost of King's.'

She was gone.

J. L. Walters was present, and Tom Helliwell.

'Shall we go to Monkshill?' Tom asked. 'We'd better, if we're going to get anything to eat. J. L. can drive.'

He sounded sheepish.

When they were waiting for J. L. Walters to warm up the car, Tom said, 'I suppose you wouldn't like the job for yourself, Matt? In fact, from the way you were talking, I had just a dim idea that you might.'

19. Earning One's Keep

'Wrong they may be, wrong they probably are,' said Chuck Tiepolo, dramatically appearing in Matthew's office just as the latter had dragged Dorothy wearily once more from the drawer, 'but they are dead sure I am the right guy to approach you. Me, I don't see it. But they do. They think you ought to give a lecture.'

'Who,' said Matthew, terrified, 'is they?'

It was true that he had once toyed with the idea of lecturing, imagining himself treating a large audience to a perfect fusion of scholarship and urbane demagogy. To be confronted with the real possibility, especially in view of the very slender interest his subject had evoked, was quite a different matter.

'The Parkes. Pickersgills. Who else counts around here?'

'I have never lectured in my life.'

'Got to earn your keep, boy.'

'But what should I lecture about? Merlin?'

'If you were me, you'd lecture about Rape and Its Role in the Community. But that's more in my line than yours, despite your recent field-work.'

'No one would come to listen,' Matthew said despondently. Among other things, he was feeling rather miserable because Edith had gone.

'They'd dig it,' said Chuck, 'don't you worry on that score.'

'No, I couldn't lecture.'

'Well, they think you owe it to them.'

'Do you think any of us owe them all that much?' Matthew asked, baited into this mild protest.

'I don't know, boy. I'm only telling you how *they* think.'

'I will not lecture. I swear to you, Chuck, I would if I could, but I am entirely incapable of doing any such thing.'

'I thought you addressed the protest meeting O.K., the other night. You Britishers are always good on your feet.'

'That was different'

'Well, anyway, let's talk it over *en route.*'

'To where?'

'My supplies have run out. I imagine yours have. I thought you might need transportation.'

'Piltdown?'

'Just going now.'

Matthew said he would come. His larder was bare.

He waited outside the Centre for Chuck to bring the car round. While he was standing there, J. L. Walters came smudgily by, to say farewell. Matthew, exacerbated by terror of lecturing and reminded suddenly of Walters' horrific appearance in his bath, turned nasty — nasty for him, of course, which would not have been nasty by the standards of Tiepolo or Ruddock. He hated this faint little lawyer who had borrowed his money, his handkerchiefs, his pyjamas.

'I'm so awfully sorry to bother you, Mr. Walters, but I've got to get in some food today and the bank's closed. I wonder if you could possibly let me have that five dollars?'

J.L., who had been about to move from one foot to the other in the normal course of walking, stood poised for a fraction of a second on one foot only.

'Five dollars?'

'At Mrs. Nash's. You remember.'

J.L., standing firm again, shook his head. 'But if you say so, O.K. That is, if I've got it.'

'I wouldn't want to cause the slightest inconvenience——'

Walters raked out at a snail's pace from his pocket two grimy dollar bills, three fifty-cent pieces, five quarters, two dimes and five pennies. He counted these carefully over in his own palm, then poured them into Matthew's.

'Thank you so very much. But are you quite sure——'

'I'll send the pyjamas back to you. I'm going to Montpelier for the night, and I hate sleeping raw. Well, glad to have known you.' J.L.'s dull gaze fastened upon Matthew's face, as if seeking to implant it in his memory.

'Oh, we shall meet again. I say, Mr. Walters, if you'd really rather leave the money for a bit——'

But J.L. had gone, with curious rapidity.

Chuck came roaring up in a horrible open car, painted yellow. 'Hop in.'

'I ought to get a hat——'

'Look in the glove-compartment.'

Matthew looked, and found a red woollen ski-cap. Cold defeating self-consciousness, he pulled it well down over his ears.

'Helliwell gone?' Chuck asked.

'He goes tonight.'

'I don't dig that queer.'

'——?'

'Queer.'

'Oh, but I do assure you he isn't. Far from it,' Matthew added fervently.

'Don't kid me, boy. I've got eyes.'

No further mention was made of the lecture until they had bought various necessities and dainties from Mr. Balyai, had had a drink and a sandwich at Joe's Tavern, and were on their way back.

'So I said, I thought you might lecture on Merlin next Thursday, in the Pump Room, eight o'clock.'

'No, Chuck.'

'I don't know whether I can get you out of it.'

This sounded promising, and Matthew leaped at it. 'But you could try?'

Chuck shook his big, coarse, smoky head. His lower lip Stuck out. 'Make me unpopular.'

'Oh, surely not!'

'Hell, I have to earn my own keep.'

He was silent for a while, as if brooding rather hopelessly upon some way of easing Matthew's problem. Then, decisively, he shook his head again.

'Merlin will go down O.K. The boys will get a laugh if you read her stuff to them. They'll be crazy for you. You're the national hero, anyway.'

Matthew did not fancy the vision of himself reading *Joyful Matrix* or *Light Thoughts* in the Pump Room, to an audience of happy, healthy youths in the final stages of hysteria.

'Don't bother — Mother
Or lather — Father——'

Oh, God, no! He could not bear it. He had long since discovered that the apparent humourlessness of the American young is a delusion. In the company of their elders they pursue a line of purely formal, verbal comedy, so predictable that it has long since become meaningless. Among themselves, they are burning up with brutal irony, original in their cruel sarcasms, verbally ingenious, arcane in inspiration. He was simply not going to risk this humour being exercised upon himself, even behind his back.

'Look, Chuck——'

'Oh, I know!' Chuck turned his eyes up to heaven as if in rebuke to God for giving him so poor a memory. 'I was going to ask you. They're behindhand with our cheques — do you realise that? And I'm broke. Could you let me have fifty bucks till pay day?'

Now Matthew, though well-heeled by the standards of most people, had in fact run himself a little short. He, too, did not fancy living on a shoestring till Cobb paid him. 'I'm so sorry; of course I'd love to, but I don't see how I can manage it. If a ten would be of any use?'

Chuck shook his head again. 'Thanks. But my girl's coming for the week-end, and a ten wouldn't set me anywhere.'

He swung the car round in front of Matthew's house. Matthew, shivering, dropped the ski-cap back into the glove-compartment and alighted.

'I'll tell them it's O.K. about Merlin, then,' Chuck sang after him. 'I don't think I could have got you out of it, anyway. It would hardly have been worth the try.'

Matthew stared, incredulous. Could this be as he thought? He said, 'If I can manage fifty, I'll drop it in on you tomorrow morning.'

'You're a good guy. But I sure hate to trouble you——'

'I think I might manage.'

'I guess,' Chuck said, 'that you might like twenty-four hours to think about that lecture. I won't tell them you've accepted just yet. Not till tomorrow lunch-time.'

His satanic face was split by a huge thick-lipped grin. He let out the clutch, waved his hand, and roared off.

Matthew stood deep in thought. It seemed to him inconceivable that Tiepolo was resorting to blackmail. It also seemed to him inconceivable that the conversation about the fifty dollars could mean anything else. For a moment he was disposed not to yield to it: he would bite on the bullet, and lecture on Dorothy. Once you start paying blackmail money you never know where it will ... Oh yes, he did know. It must end, after this single demand, for Chuck would not be able to threaten him with a whole series of lectures. He did not imagine that the money would ever be returned; and fifty dollars was a fair sum to give away. Also, he would be genuinely hard up that evening, and he owed Tom Helliwell dinner. It was very difficult.

It was made a little less so by Tom's announcement that he would have to get off right away, as he had a date in Concord. 'So sorry, Matt. I hate to leave you.'

Fifty dollars: and then no more fear of those bright, attentive faces. He decided to pay up.

'No decision reached,' Tom said, as he packed his bags, 'I can tell you that much. About Parke's successor, I mean. *Did* you ever think about it, by the way?'

'Only idly. They'd never look at an outsider, far less an English one.'

'Oh, I don't know.'

'And the competition must be strong.'

'I'd like to tell you who the competitors are, but I guess I'd better not.'

Tom smiled with his bright blue eyes.

'Who counts on the board?'

'Well, Parke, of course. Van Eyck somewhat.'

'And you,' Matthew said with quiet confidence, meaning his friend to think him no fool.

Tom knotted a pale blue tie with a golden stripe in it. 'Good God, no. I'm the youngest and newest. I'm only the office boy.'

Matthew laughed, in gentle disbelief.

'I was put on the board only because my old man gave them a lot of money thirty years ago. No. The man with the real pull is J. L. Walters.'

This was so startling that Matthew sat down on the bed.

'Walters? Why?'

'I thought you knew! He's as rich as Crœsus. Richer than Pearl Nash. Rich as Jane Merle, or nearly. So they say. You want to keep on the right side of J.L., you know.'

'But you said he never uttered, you said he was a corporation lawyer——'

'So he is, old man.'

'You said he was dim——'

'Well, he is that.'

'You didn't tell me he was rich——'

'Well, why else should he be around? That went without saying.'

'How does he show his influence if he never utters?'

'I said I'd only heard him utter twice. On both occasions he told the trustees precisely what he wanted, and he got it. What in this world are you so worried about?'

'Tom,' said Matthew with despairing dignity, 'I asked him for my five dollars back.'

'Then I am afraid,' said Tom, 'that if you had any expectations, that will have torn it.'

With a tremendous effort, Matthew pulled himself together. 'No, of course I hadn't. Sure you haven't forgotten anything? Razor? Toothbrush?' He wandered out into the bathroom as if in search of these things. Closing the door, he sat down on the lavatory seat and shut his eyes. For five disastrous dollars he had wrecked his chances. Had he had the faintest idea of J. L. Walters' power, he would have given him not only the dollars, but a year's supply of handkerchiefs, a dozen pairs of silk pyjamas and a year's subscription to *Horizon*.

'I've got everything,' Tom shouted.

Matthew did not want to come out. The bathroom, with its mural dolphins, its shower-curtains made of emerald plastic, was an aquatic retreat from the world which had so violently upset him. He had never really quite believed, until this moment, that he desired, above all things, to become Director of the Centre for Visiting Fellows. It had been a fantasy designed to flatter the new-born discovery of his powers of administration — no more than that. Now, thanks to his own idiocy, it was a fancy no longer.

He tried to think clearly. Suppose he hadn't made a mistake. Suppose he had been chosen. It would have meant living in America for the best part of his time, and at Hamelin, of all god-forsaken places. What was he running away from? 'Dorothy,' a voice suggested; but the voice was quite wrong, as inner voices often are. Any person of reasonable guile could escape from Dorothy, even in England. Then from what?

From his public *persona*, which was beginning to bore him: the *persona* of the young-man-about-town, the week-end guest at the great houses, the fill-in at all the great tables, when some male guest had let the hostess down, the eligible bachelor who had always to pretend (for ah, how many weary years!) that it would be possible for somebody to catch him. He didn't want to be pursued by obtuse women any longer, he didn't want to pose as the gallant idler, he wanted to be of use in the world. Not only as a gentleman: as a scholar. An administrator. That was what he wished to be. Here, he could make a life fit for himself and others, and every month he would take a week off in New York. When he wanted a nice, quiet, decently-bred woman, a *femme de trente ans bien élevée*, he would go and find her on Friday and leave her (busy man that he was) on Monday.

'Matt,' Tom shouted,' I've got to be going. Are you all right in there? I thought you were looking a little pale.'

Matthew came out. 'No, I'm fine.'

He expressed his pleasure at the visit, and they parted with jovial cries.

Then, as he was too late to dine at a fraternity house, he returned to night and silence, to Scotch, *moules marinières*, and a rather fatty cooked ham. After this meal he thought he would watch television, but the picture went jumping about like a lunatic in the most manic phase, and when Matthew tried to adjust the set the knob came away in his hand. Therefore he could neither see properly, hear properly or, worse still, turn the damned thing off. He spent a noisy and miserable night.

20. Sober after 1870

So depressed was Matthew that next morning, having telephoned a television repairman, and having left five ten-dollar bills in Tiepolo's office, he went to his own room and wrote two hundred and fifty words about Dorothy.

His instinct that the snow, when it came again, would be permanent, was amply justified. Four inches had fallen during the night and the sky looked hard as iron. Winter had come, with Thanksgiving a fortnight away. He wondered for a moment how he was to avoid the horrors of pumpkin pie, then bent himself again to his labours.

At mid-day Ruddock, bearing the cat, tiptoed in. 'Got a moment to spare?'

Matthew threw down his pen, hoping to give the impression that he was displeased by the interruption: in fact, it was welcome.

'You ought to use a typewriter, Matt. It looks creepy to see you writing with that thing. Like seeing someone scratch on stone with a flint.'

Ruddock sat down in the peacock chair. The cat, vain of his orange beauty, draped himself over the back, tail waving like a palmleaf wielded by Iras or Charmian over the heated mistress. 'Silly to say they only wag their tails when they're angry. The time you want to watch him is when he's having a good purr.'

'I can't type. Anyway, I don't like the noise. What did you want, Doug? Is there anything I can do?'

'Maybe,' Ruddock rejoined, his flat face buttered over with a look of infinite self-satisfaction, 'it's something I can do for you. At least, I can let you in on the ground floor of a literary discovery.'

'Miss Dickinson.' Matthew's conscience stirred sickishly.

'Who else? Now: you know how rough her jags must have been.'

'So you say.'

'Oh, for Pete's sake! Listen —

> "I stepped from Plank to Plank
> A slow and cautious way . . ."

Do you imagine that's not drawn from direct experience? I tell you, there were times when she could hardly manage to get down the yard.

> "I knew not but the next
> Would be my final inch —
> his gave me that precarious gait
> Some call Experience!"

Not what most of us call it, though. God, Matt, how little idea she had of disguise! It makes one feel quite sorry. Still, that's not the point. I'm coming to the point.'

The cat leaped down, rushed to the window and began to dance at the snowflakes.

'Oh do,' said Matthew.

'*She sobered up*. Quite suddenly. What do we find in 1870?

> "Partake as doth the Bee
> Abstemiously."

That's a right-about turn, isn't it? When do you think of the will-power of that woman! No Alcoholics Anonymous in those days, no cures, no psychiatrists. No, she had to fight it through alone, shuddering in her white dress behind the closed shutters, sweating-sick with withdrawal-symptoms——What a triumph!

> "Who never wanted — maddest Joy
> Remains to him unknown —

The banquet of Abstemiousness
Defaces that of wine —"

Marvellous! I tell you, I could go on my knees to that girl. She stuck it out, till she had a bad relapse in 1884. "A Drunkard cannot meet a Cork Without a Revery" — see? And she goes on: "This January Day — Jamaicas of Remembrance stir — that send me reeling in——" For most people, it would have been the one fatal drink, to ruin all that wonderful work of the will. The cold winter sun perhaps shining right on to the rum bottle ... a moment's temptation — and bang! Not Emily, though. She started all over again, I mean, started the long uphill climb again. A hint of backsliding in 1885——'

'Look, Doug,' Matthew said, 'you oughtn't to tell me all this. I'm sure you shouldn't. I mean, it's a great deal of trust to repose in me. Supposing I let the idea out, by purest accident——'

The cat continued to dance, star of the snowy ballet, with a million Wilis whirling behind him.

'I know how to pick my man,' Ruddock said comfortably. 'It's a matter of insight, and that, I flatter myself, I'm not short on. By the way, wouldn't it be useful to you if you could catch Merlin out in something? Give your book some popular interest. Do her good in the long run, too. Have a good close look at her image-clusters, why don't you?' A shadow fell across his face. 'Still, I suppose there might be libel to consider. Too bad she's still alive, really. It does make a difference.'

Matthew thanked him for the suggestion, while rejecting it. He was feeling horribly ill at ease. He hardly listened while Ruddock chattered on, happily, triumphantly quoting, a soft shine in his frog's eyes. He believed he could not go on living with himself if he did not confess his involuntary (was it?) betrayal. He had, when in London, attended High Anglican services with some regularity, had indulged in a '*con*fessor' (accent on the first syllable), and dined that confessor at Pratt's from time to time. In a shine of brass and daffodils, a scent of spring and incense, he had expounded his sins and had been relieved to the heart that Father Fawkes never took any of them very seriously. Pride, snobbery, a little deceit, a minute quantity of fornication, some fairly extensive social lying: they had been painful to confess, because they all seemed so silly. He would sometimes have preferred to be a great sinner, and cut a dash. Now he believed he was a great sinner: and he did not like the sensation at all.

'Look, Doug,' he said desperately, 'I did let it slip to someone the other day that you might be on to something quite new——'

'Well, that's O.K., boy, so long as you didn't say what.'

'I didn't,' Matthew said truthfully, and with the knowledge that this truth was somehow a lie.

'Then what are you worrying about? Listen, this is a good regret-piece — that's what I'm calling them, "regret-pieces."

"Had I known that the first was last
I should have kept it longer.
Had I known that the last was first——" '

Ruddock's eyes protruded, he seemed to be strangling with excitement.

' "I should have drunk it stronger!" '

A knock on the door. Who but old Dr. Parke, gently inserting his trim and tiny self?

'Ah, Matthew! Ah, Douglas! Douglas, I was looking for you but you were not in your room. Then I thought I heard your voice, so I peeked in. May I have a word with you? Will you be in your room again shortly?'

'Coming now.' Ruddock rose. The cat, seeing preparation for departure, forsook the ballet, plunged between his legs and skidded out on all claws into the corridor.

There was a roar. 'Get out of here, you!' — and a terrible sound, something between a growl and a miaow.

'Chuck!' Ruddock had raced after his pet. 'If you damned well hurt my cat, I'll——'

'Hurt your cat! That filthy animal nearly had me on my face. Why can't you control him? Put him on a lead, stick him in a cage, get him out of my way!'

'Gentlemen, gentlemen!' Dr. Parke was very soft in the doorway. 'Don't say such things! You will only regret it, Dr. Tiepolo. And Douglas, I am quite sure he did not touch your cat.'

Matthew, in relief, heard the battle dying away, heard the door of Ruddock's room bang to, heard Chuck swearing as he ran downstairs. But, of course, this was only a respite, in which he might have a chance to think. He dreaded to imagine what Dr. Parke was saying to the Emily Dickinson Fellow. He decided to go early to lunch. Packing his papers away, he wrapped up warmly, put on his rubbers, crunched and squeaked across lustreless snow to the Boosie House. Luncheon was available in the Pump Room that day. He ordered clam chowder, turkey hash and Boston cream pie.

He had only begun to eat when Chuck joined him. 'Mind if I sit down? Oh, thanks for the fifty.'

'Not at all, my dear fellow.'

'That damned cat nearly killed me.'

'I am so glad you escaped.'

Chuck looked up with acetylene stare from beneath his moustache-like brows. 'You wouldn't be fooling, Matt, would you?'

'But of course I am glad you escaped! He is a really splendid cat, but he could conceivably be the cause of an accident.'

'No,' Chuck brooded, 'I don't see that in you. Irony, I mean.'

'And you are perfectly right.'

'I told them you'd probably give your Merlin lecture a week from Friday.'

Matthew froze. With an immense effort of will he replied, 'Possibly I shall.'

The whole of Chuck's head seemed to smoke, as if rearing out of some Dantesque bog. 'Then that's fine, isn't it? If you'll give me your title, I'll get it along to the printers. I tell you, it'll be a riot. All the boys will come.'

'I would prefer,' said Matthew, 'not to lecture to an empty room.'

'Man, I can assure you you won't.' Chuck bored enthusiastically into his own hash and a panchromatic salad. 'They'll be on the window-sills.'

The meal continued for some time in silence.

'If,' Chuck said, 'though it's a shame to ask you, you could let me have another fifty on Saturday, I'd give you it all back next week.'

'I haven't got another fifty,' Matthew said steadfastly.

'Sorry, sorry. Don't give it another thought.'

'I promise I won't.'

'Good. Well, then, let's have your title.'

'*Merlin and Magic*,' Matthew replied, on the spur of the moment. In for a penny, in for a pound.

'Swell. They'll certainly dig that. So will I. Be there to support you.'

He stood up. 'Well, I must get going. 'We'll just get the bills done in time, I guess.'

It is one thing to be brave on the spur of the moment, when confronting a blackmailer: another to be resolute when the sinister figure has withdrawn. Matthew sat stunned over his coffee, the cream pie untasted. He jumped to see Dr. Parke beaming down on him.

'My dear Matt! I have a favour to beg.'

'Anything I can do——'

'Your very brilliant and charming compatriot, Miss Groby, seems to be far from well. Miss Ehrlinger found her on the floor of her room and took her back to her apartment. I should not have called upon you if Dr. Corall had not left us, but if you would be so kind as to visit Miss Groby——'

Matthew said he would go right away. It seemed like yet another reprieve.

'Ah, I knew you would! Please see that she lacks for no comfort. Oh, by the bye: could I have a word with you later in the day?' (This was whispered.) 'I am a little disquieted by something concerning your very talented and admirable colleague, Dr. Ruddock. Perhaps we might have a little chat some time.'

21. Maud Abroad

Miss Groby lay in bed in her two-room apartment, the blankets up to her chin. Above them her small, woebegone face looked like the face of a marmoset whose stomach had gone back on it. Medusa hair, seeming to have no connection with the head, but rather to be laid as a shawl beneath it, streamed wildly over the pillow. 'Oh, Mr. Pryar, oh, Mr. Pryar!'

He asked her what he could do for her. He would do anything, anything. She might rely on him.

Tears welled to her large vague eyes.

'Oh, Mr. Pryar, I have sadly overdone things!'

'You work far too hard, I know,' he said comfortingly.

'Oh no, dear, that's not it at all, I do no work whatsoever. And I'm so ashamed.'

'I've been off work myself lately. We all have our fallow patches. Why be ashamed of that?'

'I am not ashamed of that, but of the Scotch whisky. Mr. Pryar, it never suits me to be abroad. In England I lead a decent life, truly I do. I am entirely abstemious, I am a churchgoer. But when I am abroad I get so lonely, and I miss Henrietta Barley, who lives with me, even though she has a very rough side to her tongue, and then things go so wrong. When I was at the University of Strasbourg it was *vin ordinaire* — so cheap, Mr. Pryar, and so comforting! At Liège, it was more difficult, but there was a good beer, only it was necessary to drink so much of it. Oh, I do wish Henrietta was here, though she would berate me terribly!'

Matthew did not know what to say to all this. He made cheerful, future-directed noises.

'And now, after the dreadful happenings of this morning, and Dr. Tiepolo laughing — I heard him, though they thought I was unconscious——'

'You couldn't have heard him. He was over at the Boosie House with me.'

'Well, it was one of the others. After this, I must *not* drink any more Scotch whisky, and without it what can I do? People will despise me.'

The tears rolled down like yellowing pearls from broken strings. Embarrassed, Matthew watched for a moment: then took out his handkerchief and patted her dry.

'Thank you, dear. That's much nicer.'

He asked if she had eaten anything.

'I don't think I could. And I am not at all sure whether there is anything in the refrigerator.'

He went to look. There was a stale piece of bread and a bottle of milk. The milk was sour.

'Dear Dr. Corall used to be kind. She used to lend me food, if I forgot. It is all so terrible, now Dr. Corall has gone!'

'I'll go back to my place and find you something. My milk's fresh, anyway.'

But she detained him. 'Oh no, no! Do stay with me. Just stay with me.'

'Oughtn't you to have a nurse?'

'No, no. That would be weakling. Henrietta would say it was *corrupt*. She can be so tart, dear, yet she is very kind at bottom.'

They seemed to have come to an impasse.

'It is strange that I should not have felt at all sick,' said Miss Groby. 'Very strange. When I recovered my senses I felt terrible, but no, not at all sick. And I have to tell myself, "No, you must *not* drink Scotch whisky".'

'Where is it?'

She pointed to a drawer in her desk.

Matthew got the bottle and poured two fingers.

'You also, Mr. Pryar. Do please join me.'

She sat up in bed.

'If you would reach me my little purple cardigan — thank you. Do you really think I should?'

'I don't know what else, at this moment, to suggest.'

She shuddered at the first sip, then brightened; but the glow soon faded. 'And there is this terrible week-end coming. Oh, I don't know what I shall do!'

Matthew reflected. He himself was planning to go to a rich friend in Portland, Maine; yet he could not bear the idea of leaving Miss Groby all alone. His mind flitted around in a dazzle of hopeless ideas like a bird in the bemusing branches of a spring tree: then the bird alit on a branch firm enough to bear it. 'May I use your telephone?' Fortunately it was in the other room. He asked for the number of Mrs. Nash. He was not too sensitive about seeking her help. Americans, as he well knew, are not only hospitable in emergency but radiant: the most lavishly helpful people in the world, accepting the burden of nuisances as if they were bunches of hothouse flowers, all the more delightful because unexpected. Matthew knew nobody in England who could come within touching distance of such open-heartedness. Americans, he thought, missed the lost frontiers, were secretly hungry for challenge and hardship. They lacked sufficient exercise for their generosity, which was as built-in as the passion for games-playing in the souls of Fijians: if they could not save the world, they would settle cheerfully for its Maud Grobys.

'Is that you, Pearl?'

'No, I'm afraid Mrs. Nash is out. Would you please leave a message?'

'Is that her secretary?'

'No. What is your name, please?'

'Matthew Pryar.'

The chilly tone changed to something quite different.

'Why, Matt-Matt! How wonderful to hear your voice. This is Jane Merle.'

'Mrs. Merle! What are you doing playing secretary, if I may ask?'

'Oh, my dear, it's pure chance. I just dropped up here to scribble a note, and then the telephone rang at my elbow and of course Briskin came flying, but I simply had to answer it. I'm never allowed to answer my own, you see.'

'Why not?'

'Because it would certainly be a madman asking me to finance a wonderful new space-ship or some marvellous bomb-bomb.'

'Bon-bon?'

'Bomb. MB on the end.'

'Oh. I say, it was superb of you to get me out of my difficulties!'

'It was fun to do it. Are you by chance in difficulties now?'

He looked cautiously through the open door of the bedroom: so far as he could see, Miss Groby had fallen into a peaceful sleep. He told Mrs. Merle all about her, emphasising her scholarly eminence and her distressful condition. 'So I was wondering whether Pearl would be tremendously sacrificing and have her for the week-end. I've got to go to Portland myself, but I'd put her on the plane.'

'So the old lady was smashed,' Mrs. Merle said thoughtfully. 'I see. Well, Pearl won't be here, so that's no good. But I think I can help.'

'My dear Mrs. Merle——'

'Jane.'

'My very dear, good Jane, you have helped enough already.' (Though his heart rose up.)

'I am going to be almost on your doorstep. I shall be in Concord, visiting my nephew at St. Paul's and staying with my sister, who lives quite near the school. I am driving up. I shall pick up your poor Miss Groby on Friday evening, take her off with me, and send her back — I shall stay on for a week or so myself — on Monday afternoon. Only you must assure me that she is not likely to be violent.'

Matthew, overwhelmed, went through all the motions of rejecting such goodness. He assured Mrs. Merle that Miss Groby was far from violent or even noisy: either she was gentle, or she passed out.

'Then that's all right. If I think it necessary, I'll get a nurse.'

'I honestly can't let you take her on!'

Mrs. Merle rasped at him in full military tones. 'What's it to do with you? You're not suffering. Miss Groby apparently is. Oh — one other thing. I cannot promise to restrain her drinking. As a stranger to her, that would be impertinent.'

Matthew said that of course this would be unnecessary. Miss Groby only had this trouble when abroad, and did not appear in danger of true alcoholism.

'Why, do we drive her to it?'

'No. But she misses her companion, a Miss Barley.'

'Then I shall ask Jocelyn to produce a Slavonic scholar or two to comfort her.'

'But could she?'

'Certainly. The only thing is to know where to look. So it's all arranged. Just give me the address. Oh, Matthew, you wouldn't rather come to my sister's than go to Portland?'

He only wished he could, he said, but he was committed.

'Who are you staying with?'

He told her.

'Old Sarah Crewe,' said Mrs. Merle thoughtfully. 'Well, if you can bear it it's your funeral. I might see you, possibly. Goodbye.'

She had rung off before he could thank her again.

Returning to sit by Miss Groby, he pondered the American miracle. There were times when it seemed that you only had to say 'Open Sesame' for the door to fly back upon a cave full of bounties. Why, then, were things so very unlike this at Cobb? 'Un-American activities,' he said aloud to himself.

Miss Groby's eyes flew open, wide and terrified.

'Oh, my dear Mr. Pryar, please don't say that!'

'Say what?'

'What you said. I am always so afraid I shall be brought before the Committee.'

'Why? Are you trying to overthrow the Constitution? I am quite sure you aren't. I am utterly and totally convinced of it.'

'Because I am so interested in the Russians. You know one dares hardly *speak* the word.'

'Terribly old Russians.'

'But,' she whispered, 'I am not even prepared to dislike *all* the new ones. What do you think of that? I had a very pleasant time in Moscow, with some most agreeable academicians. And in Leningrad, too.'

'Did you,' Matthew said tentatively, 'have any trouble with vodka?'

'No, dear. That was the curious thing. I am afraid that might be thought a *suspicious* circumstance if it were known in the United States.'

'We won't tell them. Miss Groby, I have arranged a really splendid week-end for you, so you will be well enough to go, won't you?'

He told her all about it. She demurred at first. She was too weak to leave her bed, she was frightened of strangers, she had no clothes good enough for a stay with rich people; if they dressed for dinner she had only an old black skirt and a bridge-coat. 'My niece made it for me and the cut is quite professional, but brocade does get a little tarnished, and though I do cut off the loose threads, I fear it wouldn't look very smart in a good light.'

'Nonsense,' said Matthew. 'Besides, they are going to find Slavonic scholars for you.'

'Who?' She glittered with eagerness. 'Collier? Zondenbok? Skattmester?'

'Are they the tops?'

'Oh yes!'

'Then at least two of them, you may be sure, will be there.'

'Mr. Pryar,' said Miss Groby, 'I think another very small drink — a tiny one! — might help me. And then if you will heat my milk, which may be sour but is in no way impaired so far as nutriment is concerned, I shall pour the Scotch whisky in.'

'I think,' said Matthew, having successfully found a glass, a saucepan, and turned on the hotplate, 'that you are soon going to feel much better about abroad.'

22. Saved by the Bell

On Sunday morning Mrs. Merle, looking beautiful and remarkably small in sky-blue Irish tweeds with little round cap to match, drove to Portland, filched Matthew masterfully from his hostess, and took him to her sister's house near Concord, where, in a covered and centrally-heated court, they found Miss Groby playing a tremulous but by no means ineffectual game of croquet.

She looked far better. She was flushed not so much by drink as by the excitement of her visit, and by the fact that Dr. Skattmester was partnering her against Jocelyn Briggs and Professor Zondenbok.

'You see,' said Mrs. Merle, 'she only needed someone to take a little notice of her. That's what most people want when you get right down to it.'

They all spent a happy afternoon. Mrs. Briggs went out riding. Miss Groby talked rather bossily with the experts about the degeneration of the old Church Slavonic tense-system in the literary language of the fourteenth century, and it was obvious that both deferred to her. Mrs. Merle and Matthew talked gaily about all the earls they knew — snobbishly on Matthew's part, not so on Mrs. Merle's, whose cousins they nearly all happened to be. Matthew felt that he and she were truly *en rapport*.

'Well,' she said, as she drove him back again, 'you have done your good deed, and Miss Groby is in tearing spirits, and you needn't worry any more. Let me know if you want to go to New York in about a fortnight's time, and I'll drive you there. It takes about seven hours, but one can lunch on the way.'

He thanked her fervently, begged her to renew his thanks to her sister.

'Joss doesn't mind. She has a heart of gold, besides everything else of the same material.' Seeing him smile, she added, 'Oh, I'm simply a pauper beside Joss-Joss. Our father much preferred her, she had a better seat on a horse.'

They parted with mutual expressions of self-esteem.

After such pleasures, it was hard to drop in for his mail at the college shop and find an enormous poster pinned to the door, announcing that on Thursday evening at 8 p.m. in the Pump Room, Dr. Matthew Pryar would lecture on *Merlin and Magic*. It was added in brackets who he was and who Dorothy was.

This struck a chill to his heart. Somehow he had either never fancied things would get so far, or had supposed he would be able to escape. He could see no escape now. Huge boys with snow-bright faces stopped on their way to classes to assure him, with the air of people assuring their Christian friends that they would all be in ring-side seats at the Colosseum when the curtain went up, that they wouldn't miss his talk for all the rice in China. He was not consoled.

He went, depressed, to his office, where he found Doug Ruddock waiting, white-faced, mutely stroking the cat.

'Hullo, Doug,' he said uneasily.

No reply.

'Anything I can do?'

'Is there anything you might have done already? Just ask yourself that, Pryar.'

'I honestly don't know what——'

'Just ask yourself. Think a minute.'

'I assure you I didn't mention to Mrs. Parke——'

'If I'd done that, I wouldn't either. Especially to a woman.'

Matthew was bewildered. 'Why not to a woman?'

'Because they hate that sort of thing. They feel different about dumb animals.'

'My dear Doug, that is an absurd thing to call yourself. I——'

'I wasn't talking about myself. Don't try to be smart.'

'All I said to her, and it slipped out, was about being on to something new. After all, everyone here is after that. I mean, research and everything.'

'You must have done some research, I'll say. Thought you'd just make him ill, but not kill him, is that it?'

'Kill whom?'

The cat growled; it was being hugged too tight. As Ruddock did not heed it, it ripped itself out of his arms, clawed at his neck and sprang away, to continue growling from a point of vantage under Matthew's desk.

'Leaving a saucer of milk where he could see it, with your door open——'

'Look here, Doug, you must believe me, I am simply *not* understanding a word of this.'

'— the saucer just inside, so in he goes: and damned lucky I was behind him, because I thought it looked queer.'

'The milk did?'

'You know goddamned well it did! But you didn't know I'd take it to the medical school, did you, and get it analysed? And you didn't know I'd find out.'

'Dear lord,' said Matthew, 'what did you find out?'

'Ask Dr. Peters what he found! Goddamned ipecac! In the cat's milk!' Ruddock's face contorted with scorn. 'No, that's not the sort of thing you'd tell a woman, is it? You're damned right you wouldn't!'

'Now look here. I did not doctor any milk, I did not put down a saucer for your cat. There was no saucer in here when I left on Saturday morning — the cleaners will tell you that. I like your cat, all cats.'

It chose that moment to rush out and bite at his ankles.

'Go away!'

'Kick him if you dare!' Ruddock shouted.

'I'm not going to kick him! Oh dear, he's drawn blood.' Matthew lifted his trouser leg. A bubble of viscous red was bursting through the fine mesh of his sock.

'He knows. Dumb animals know their enemies.'

'Listen. I am not his enemy. I don't know who did this, but *I* did not. You must see that I am not a person given to what you call horsing around. Honestly, Doug, do you really think I am?

'Well ...' There was a long pause. Then, with surprising acquiescence, 'If you say so. All right, boy. Who did do it, do you think? I suppose it was that skunk Tiepolo.'

'He is certainly a likelier suspect than I am,' Matthew said rather crossly. 'And as he has been here longer, I dare say he would know where to obtain ipecacuanha. It is not a common remedy to have around the house.'

'No, I suppose you're right there. Well — sorry.'

'Not at all.'

'I wasn't blaming you about poor Emily. Old Parke did say something about was I trying to make a somewhat unusual case which might "gravely distress some people", but I guess he'd just been snooping around my office. He does sometimes, you know, when we've all gone home. He's got a passkey.'

Matthew felt, through his instant profound relief, unease at the thought of Dr. Parke finding out his own idleness.

'I told him he was on the wrong track,' Ruddock said, with a pale, ferocious grin. 'By the time the book comes out I'll be a hell of a long way from here, you can be sure.'

He made a sudden dive to the floor, hauled the cat out, sat it up on his knees facing Matthew, and put its front paws together in an attitude of prayer.

'Pussy says he's sorry,' Ruddock said sickeningly, 'he says he made a great mistake. Pussy says please forgive him.'

Matthew smiled sicklily in return.

'Well, *forgive* him!' yelled Ruddock, a backwash of rage overcoming him, 'forgive him, what the hell's stopping you? Say "That's O.K., Pussy, not to worry".'

'Quite O.K., Pussy,' Matthew said meekly.

' "Not to worry." '

'Not to worry.'

Ruddock rose, the cat pressed to his cheek, ginger-roseate hairs fanning out all over his nose. He departed with dignity and complacence.

Well, Matthew thought, in any case he can no longer be a serious candidate. (He was ashamed of the thought, though.)

During the three desperate days separating him from Thursday, he dined at fraternity houses hoping, though he would not admit this hope to the conscious level of thought, to curry favour with potential executioners. He sat before mock-baronial fireplaces, drinking the young men's whiskey, and accepting their eager homage: they sat or stood around him, firing innocent questions, and at dinner instructed him in their peculiar usages while the singing went on. It was their custom to tap with ring-finger on the table, both as an accompaniment to college songs, and as applause. He was not so unsophisticated as to assume that they would admire him once the party had broken up, though he hoped he might induce in them a certain kindliness when his ordeal came: but he did have the comforting feeling that, just at this moment, they gave him their admiration. He knew perfectly well that in American eyes he was something of a 'stage Englishman' — a type they despised and were a little charmed by. He knew they liked the clarity of his diction, while grinning inwardly at some aspects of his pronunciation. But in fact he liked them; he liked the young because, by reason of his good physique, his unlined face, his genuine enjoyment of their company, he did not feel sundered from them. Whether they felt sundered from him was, of course, another matter. He recognised the gulf, artificially induced by all means of public relations, which had grown up between his age-group and their own: and it saddened him to think that though he had had precious little in common (at the same age as theirs) with his father, he would never have regarded him as belonging to an entirely different species.

As he left Wednesday's fraternity house they pressed round him, promising him heartfelt support on the morrow.

For some reason, this broke the carefully-cultivated surface of his calm.

'If you bastards laugh so that I *know* it,' cried Matthew, who had perhaps drunk too much, 'I think I shall go off my bloody head!'

Whatever success he might have on the following evening, he was a great success then.

He woke on Thursday with a belt of nausea, perhaps four inches wide, and colour-banded from sulphur to apple-green, lying beneath his heart. He could not bring himself to go to the Boosie House for breakfast. Lying face down beneath the sheets, he tried to shut the horror out. Every morning, of every day that week, he had tried to compose his lecture-notes. All he had on paper was as follows:

'(1) Merlin b. 1919, Sydney, Australia, (m. Cosmo Hines.)
(2) 1941, poems (*Meanjin*, N.S.W.), *Times Lit. Supp.*
(3) 1955, *Joyful Matrix*, produced Group 22 Theatre, London.'

Something else must have happened to Dorothy between her birth and the year 1955, but apart from her constant breeding (she had seven sons) he could not imagine what. He had inserted slips of paper into the slim volumes of her verse — nine slips. He did not think he could bring himself to read a single line.

He talked to himself seriously.

'You live in an age, Matthew, when the preoccupation of Man (though perhaps it has become exaggerated) is not to be blown up. (This itself is meiosis: to be blown up is not the dread — that sounds brisk, immediate. The real dread is not to be expounded without an extreme of human indecency.) To imagine that an absurdly trivial academic failure on your own part would cause the slightest sensation *sub specie aeternitatis* is obviously absurd. Therefore, though it may be painful to yourself (since you must lack objectivity in this matter), a howling frost, even a howling riot of derision, will not matter in the slightest. If you keep your mind firmly on those things of supreme human importance, you will pass through your ordeal of tonight with a flick of the fingers, a toss of the head, and a tilly-vally, whatever that may mean.'

None of which comforted him.

He rose at eleven and sought oblivion in his bath, but no oblivion was there. He could eat no lunch — he did not try. All through the afternoon, he tried to implement his notes, to rehearse the reading from *Joyful Matrix*. It was no use. At one appalling moment, even the concept of Dorothy's name disintegrated. MERLIN. Meulen. Merlun. Myrlin. Myrlun. WƎЯ⅃IN. He was caught in the horror of the totally meaningless.

At six o'clock he forced himself to swallow some bread and cheese, to drink some milk. He dared not risk hard liquor, lest it should slow up such enfeebled reactions as he had. Head throbbing, mouth dried with smoke, he tried once more to complete a set of notes adequate enough to carry him through.

It was a symptom of his extreme terror that he, who loved light, had turned on nothing brighter than his reading lamp which, in the gloom of his house, was necessary at even eleven o'clock in the morning. He had forgotten about light. He was still struggling with notes and horror at seven-fifteen when the bell rang, the door opened, and following a rush upon the stairs Edith appeared to him, wild-eyed, like a ghost conceived by Fuseli, her pipe sticking up from her mouth as Excalibur from the lake.

'Oh, it's you,' said Matthew, too sunk in misery even to be surprised.

'I've come back!'

'Oh. Good.'

'Matt, I could not bear it. I knew I was ratting. I have an obligation to Cobb, and I'm going to honour it. Romeo or no Romeo, and damn Hefflinger, I'm back . . . Matt, what *is* the matter with you? Did you hear what I said? Matt, has anyone died?'

Though Edith was not specially feminine in some ways, she had a motherly heart. The moment she turned up the lights, she had perceived that Matthew was in trouble. 'Matt, come on: out with it!'

Somehow, he managed to tell her.

She despised him, of course; he knew that. The fear which had rotted his week, the fear which he had taken upon himself rather than submit to blackmail, would to her have been no fear at all. Nevertheless, she said:

'Do you absolutely swear it's as bad as that?'

'Worse,' said Matthew. 'Inconceivably worse.'

She contemplated him. Then she took up the pitiful page of notes, riffled through Dorothy's works. 'I see. Well, my lad, you have laryngitis. I shall explain that.'

'Laryngitis? Do you mean I can get out of the lecture?'

'You can, yes. But you must show willing. You must come with me, and speak in a faint, hoarse voice. Do have some guts, man! At least you can do that.'

'And there won't be a lecture?'

'Certainly there will be. I shall give it.'

'But, Edith dear, you know nothing of Dorothy's work——'

Her lips set grimly. 'No. But I know Dorothy.'

'Has she done anything to you?'

'Yes.'

'Reflected upon your work?'

'Certainly not. She is bone-ignorant.'

'What, then?'

'Miss Merlin,' said Edith, more tightly still, 'saw fit to criticise my way of dressing at a party in Oxford two years ago. I wasn't present, but these things get around. And in case you are worried about your professional reputation, or about myself as your surrogate, get it into your silken head that I am capable of lecturing on anything, if need be, from Beowulf to cybernetics. I shall not talk sense, of course. But I shall sound as if I do. There, now!'

She pounced upon him and gave him a hug. 'Your breath smells of hay and lilac, Matt. That means you haven't had a drink. Fortify yourself immediately, remember your larynx and we shall be off.'

He padded downhill at her side through the deep snow, hardly able, even now, to believe in his good fortune. 'You're sure——?'

'Perfectly sure. I have her horrible books to go on.'

Lights were blazing out from the Pump Room; there was a roar and sizzle of animation. The place was crowded, Faculty in the front seats, serious young men in the back ones, jocund young men on the piano and the window-sills. Dr. Parke, seated just below the lectern, sprang to his feet.

'Ah, my dear Matthew! A full house as they say. And Dr. Corall — can it be Dr. Corall? I was informed——'

'I've changed my mind, Dr. Parke. And poor Matthew here cannot speak to you, as he is pretty well stricken dumb with acute laryngitis. I am going to give the lecture from his notes. Don't bother to introduce me — I'll introduce myself and let Matt out at the same time.'

When she made her public explanation, a *frisson* of disappointment ran through the room like a cold wind through wheat.

'Yes, I'm sorry, too,' she said implacably, her stony blue eyes upturned to the window-sills, 'and so is Mr. Pryar — Matthew, please demonstrate your incapacity.'

Blushing like a rose, he got up and made a few croaking noises. The applause was tumultuous.

'So you see,' said Edith decisively. Her gaze fastened upon a figure in the second row. 'One moment, please, Dr. Hefflinger——'

He rose and bowed, his face smooth with delight. 'Delighted to welcome our colleague again——No, there is no need for fear.'

'Dead sure?'

'Dead sure.'

Edith waited for the murmurs caused by this curious exchange to die down.

Then she said, 'I think Mr. Pryar is in a draught. If someone who has not laryngitis — at the end of the third row — would exchange seats with him——'

Somebody did. There was silence.

Edith took off her green tam-o'-shanter and placed it over the lectern lamp. She propped Dorothy's works on the reading stand. She had forgotten to bring Matthew's notes, but did not seem put out.

She looked about the hall, shrewdly, slowly, intimately, as if preparing to make some statement later, in a witness-box, about everyone present. Matthew, adoring her technique, hugged his knees.

'Dr. Parke. Mr.——Ah yes, I knew I was right! I think I see the President lurking just inside the door. How very flattering. Mr. President, Dr. Parke. Ladies and gentlemen ——

'The works of Dorothy Merlin may be little known in this country.

143

Whether this is a reasonable state of affairs or whether it is not, is outside my jurisdiction. I propose to read some of her poems to you, and leave it to you to make your decision. You are, after all, as you so constantly — and so rightly — remind the world, a free country.'

Storms of applause here: the audience was getting over its earlier disappointment, and was hoping for good things.

'First of all,' said Edith, 'a personal note.' Here, to Matthew's stupefaction, she rattled off a list of the outstanding dates and events in Dorothy's life, ending with a roll-call, delivered at the speed of a Gilbert and Sullivan patter song, of Dorothy's sons, with their quaint Victorian names: Albert, Augustus, William, Frederick, Wilfred, Percival, James.

'Motherhood,' said Edith, 'is Miss Merlin's thing.'

A ripple of amusement.

'I should say, the thing of Mrs. Hines: that is why her poetry deals almost wholly with this aspect of the human condition.'

More laughter.

'Don't!' cried Edith, in a field-marshal voice Mrs. Merle would have envied. 'If it were not for motherhood, not a man jack of you would be here tonight. Nor should I. Nor, of course, would Miss Merlin.' She stood for a second with hand on her breast, like a knight keeping vigil over a tomb. Then she began again, *piano*. 'Let us, however, approach a lighter aspect of an almost abnormally serious poet. We come to love people through their surface frivolities, but it is not by these that we deeply understand.' Her voice grew strong again.

'Come. Let us love Miss Merlin. Here is perhaps the most engaging of her, let us say, *déshabillé* series, called *Light Thoughts*. (I need not labour the reference to Young.)'

Dr. Parke nodded deeply at this point.

Edith put on her glasses, which she did not need in the least, and pitched her tone high.

> ' "Don't bother — Mother,
> Or lather — Father——" '

At this point there was a moan of pleasure.

' "If you'd rather," '

Edith continued severely, her gaze raking the room,

' "I'll give you a plum." '

It is to Matthew's credit that he felt a pang of shame, of disloyalty. His ribs ached with their content of laughter withheld: but it is possible to be sick with mirth and thoroughly ashamed of oneself at the same time, and he was both.

The rest of the lecture proceeded in comparative silence, since Edith could quell a mob when she chose; and indeed, to bring it to an end in relative calm, she deliberately chose to bore them with a dry, uninflected reading of nearly the whole of *Joyful Matrix*. The ovation she got at the end was due partly to relief, and partly to the grateful memory of what they had received from her at the beginning. She left the hall in stately fashion, holding a muffled Matthew fast to her side, and permitting no one to talk with him.

'He must not tire his throat,' she insisted, 'or he will be dumb for a good fortnight, and when Mr. Pryar is dumb, then I am bored.'

She saw him back home. On the doorstep, under the fancy lamp, he kissed her for all the world to see.

'Edith, darling, you are the most.'

'Be quiet, or they'll find you out. And your slang is antiquated. What I did was not entirely for you. It was all for the benefit of Dorothy Merlin. You may tell her that I did her justice: it will take her a long time to catch up with the truth. I only hope they took a tape-recording.'

'Darling Edith, they did.'

23. 'Can't I See his Dead Eye Glow?'

It occurred to Matthew that Dorothy had better be mollified. Next day he sent her the following cablegram:

'PREVENTED LAST MOMENT ACUTE LARYNGITIS LECTURING YOUR WORK BUT EDITH CORALL COMMA IMAGINE THAT COMMA SUBSTITUTED SUCCES FOU LOVE.'

It was, he felt later, lucky he had done so, for one of the secretaries brought a further letter from her in his mail.

It was brief.

'If I do not hear from you soon *I shall fly over whatever the cost*, and there is a sort of revolting TV dinner in the tourist class. You must understand that I simply will *not* tolerate this silence any more. I am relieved that your part in the Sabine affair was misinterpreted, but if you had been doing your book on me you wouldn't have been walking in any woods, which just goes to show. Please report progress by cable. My patience is exhausted.'

This time, too, she failed to send her love. Well, she would have something, to satisfy her for the time being, or so he hoped.

He decided quite suddenly, without the slightest premeditation, that he would not write that book at all. How he was to get out of it was by no means clear: but it was simply not going to be done. The decision gave him a feeling of intense liberation. He walked about his room, feeling free as a boy at the end of term.

How should he celebrate? For celebrate he must.

It seemed to him that the pathetic fallacy was by no means so fallacious as people thought, for at that very moment the sun came out, and the trees cast across the snow shadows of the strongest, most euphoric blue. A small bird, bright as the drop of blood drawn from Matthew's ankle by the cat, dropped from a twig, descended in a diamond shower, and poked for worms. A boy kissed a girl in full public view: where he had found her, God alone knew, but it was a beautiful sight, promising a new spring and a new, perhaps more prepossessing, generation.

He telephoned to Anderson and ordered the car. His garage bills were enormous, but he was past caring. He would lunch today in Hamelin, at an Italian restaurant he had noticed on his way from the airport. He was tired of the Pickwick place at Piltdown.

Down the hills rode Matthew, humming to himself: this time, the song about *Trinki, trinki, trinki, tra.* Had he realised this he would have been horrified, as he thought it a detestable song: but he did not.

The restaurant smelt encouraging, and did not disappoint his expectations. All over the United States are these curious pockets of good food, though one comes upon them only by chance. The average Italian restaurant tries to live up to its name by dousing everything in tomato catsup: this one was different. Matthew settled down to golden *gnocchi alla Romano*, beautified with nothing but Parmesan cheese: to *pollo alla Bolognese*, chicken-breasts fried with ham and cheese, and sprinkled with (he could scarcely believe his eyes) white truffles smelling as strongly as chloroform and tasting like nothing else on this earth. The proprietor was not a Cypriot, a Greek or a Puerto Rican: he was a real Italian, old, bright-eyed, filled with the proper greed of the decent *maître d'hôtel* at the sight of every dish he waved towards the customer. With this superlative meal, Matthew drank half a bottle of that Orvieto which has a curiously medicinal taste and is engaging nevertheless, if only he could have with him some agreeable companion — here he thought for one flashing second of Mrs. Merle — he would have been supremely happy. As he ordered his coffee, he knew the beginnings of that beautiful digestive process which is like a lubrication, by the lightest, most refined of oils, of the whole internal system.

It was just then that he caught sight of Wohlgemutt, lunching alone, at the next table.

'I wondered when you were going to surface,' said his neighbour — perhaps disagreeably, perhaps not.

'I say, Dr. Wohlgemutt, what a really splendid place this is! I can't get over it.'

'Anyone could have told you.'

'But alas, nobody did.'

'So you see, damning everything out of hand is all very well if you don't know the score.'

'Or if no one tells you the score,' Matthew said mildly. He was too contented to be drawn.

Wohlgemutt was making his way through some pleasant-looking pudding, half-fruit, half-pastry. He was an untidy eater, letting a scurf from every mouthful decorate his lower lip, until it occurred to him to suck it in.

'Didn't get anywhere with your meeting,' he said.

'Oh, I don't know.'

'Well, did you?'

Matthew did not answer.

'I know this place. I know Parke. You condemned Parke.'

'Oh, but I didn't——'

'By implication. Have you the faintest idea of the life that old boy leads?'

Wohlgemutt was now spoiling Matthew's lunch.

'No,' Matthew said crossly.

'You must have seen that Bea is off her head.'

'I do not agree that she is off her head.'

'She tripped him once at Convocation.'

'I beg your pardon?'

Wohlgemutt's voice took on a quality which, in another man, might have been described as tremulous.

'Walking in procession, that poor old man, quietly, in his Harvard gown: and just as he was passing her pew she stuck her foot out and down he went, smack on his face. Don't you suppose,' he said with sudden fury, 'that anyone laughed! You could have heard a pin drop. And there she was, dead pan, pretending she hadn't done a thing.'

'I refuse to believe,' Matthew said, 'that she did such a thing on purpose.'

'No?' This was a sneer, drawing out the O into a kind of umlaut. 'Do you usually stick your feet out, when you're in pews?'

'I expect it was crowded.'

'You do? I tell you it wasn't. Well, that's the sort of man dear old Dom is. Not a word of complaint. Not a word of reproach. And that's the man you're trying to unseat.'

'I assure you, I am not——'

'You may have heard that Cobb sometimes appoints people from outside.'

Matthew said, as lightly as he could, that he had no idea of Cobb's procedures.

'But not from so far outside,' said Wohlgemutt. He looked with regret at his empty plate, his ferocity for the moment dampened by this emotion.

Matthew did not say — 'So far outside as what?' — which must have been expected of him. He sipped his coffee in silence.

Silence was maintained between them for some time. Then, stealing a glance sidelong, he was alarmed to see fire in Wohlgemutt's dead eye.

He thought to himself,

'Bright as 'twere a Barbary corsair's,
   That is, if he'd let it show.'

But Wohlgemutt was letting it show.

'You haven't a chance, Pryar,' he said. 'You can take that from me.'

'Do believe me, I haven't the least idea what you're talking about.'

'Must be pretty dumb, then.'

'Conceivably.'

The fire died. Wohlgemutt said slowly, 'That's the trouble with you people. A man like old Parke, maybe he isn't as efficient as he might be, not by modern standards. So you write him off, totally. In all ways. He's no good. That is, you wouldn't give him credit for a thing, not in his public life or his private.'

'I can't see what his private life has to do with it — admitting, as perhaps we may for the sake of argument, that he is in fact inefficient.'

'No.' The mathematician was drawing figures with a matchstick in a mess of breadcrumbs. 'You people never do. But a man's personal and private life are so much tied up together that no judgment can be any good unless it takes both into account. If you don't know that Hitler was fond of kids, then you don't entirely know Hitler.'

Matthew, a liberal in the 'thirties, protested, 'That makes Hitler better?'

'Who said so? I didn't. I only said, it makes him different. You slam a politician, you make out he's the devil, with horns and hoofs. But his wife loves him, and so did all his mistresses. So you're not slamming the *whole* man, see?'

Matthew dimly perceived that this attitude seemed to stem from an inner saintliness which he could not associate with Wohlgemutt at all.

'So you slam old Parke because he isn't always on the ball. But you don't think of his life with Bea, or the fact he had to keep his old mother and three useless sisters for years, or that he's had two coronaries already——'

'Look here, Dr. Wohlgemutt, you simply can't expect me to know all this!'

'Well, then, you ought to find out. Check, please.'

The mathematician collected his bill. Stolid as a rhinoceros heaving itself up from sleep, he pushed the table back.

'Can I give you a lift?' Matthew asked grudgingly.

'No, thanks. Motor-scooter.'

Through the steamy glass, Matthew saw him mount and ride off in a rude burst of noise, as if a giant had blown through blubbered lips. He ordered more coffee. He was upset, even in his deepest being. There are few things more disturbing than to find, in somebody we detest, a moral quality which seems to us demonstrably superior to anything we ourselves possess. It augurs not merely an unfairness on the part of creation, but a lack of artistic judgment. We should be horrified to find, lurking behind one of Veronese's golden balustrades, a clown by Rouault, or an angel by Fra Angelico, no matter how gloriously painted either was in its own fashion. It would be both a moral and an aesthetic jar for us. We demand that people should be true to the pictures we have of them, no matter how repulsive those pictures may be: we prefer the true portrait (as we have conceived it), in all its homogeneity, to one with a detail added which refuses to fit in. Sainthood is acceptable only in saints.

So, certainly, it was for Matthew, who was feeling sore and ashamed. He could not think of dear old Dr. Parke without wincing. Was this the man he had been so eager to dethrone? (It was for the moment immaterial that Dr. Parke had dethroned himself.) A blur of father-figures arose in Matthew's mind, all with soft, kind, hairy, silly faces. He regretted his protest-meeting and its revolutionary implications.

A mad wife. A dragging family. Two heart attacks. Tripped up in Convocation.

Oh dear, thought Matthew, how could I have done it?

He was so upset that his digestive processes, so smooth, so enjoyable up to now, were sharply arrested. His beautiful luncheon lay like a stone in his intestines. He even wondered whether it would not be better for him to be sick and get the whole thing over.

He climbed into the car and allowed Anderson to drive him home. He did not speak a word on the way.

24. Matthew is Compassionate

Nothing of any interest happened for ten days or so. In the meantime the snow hardened, the ice sealed the boughs, the ponds hardly squeaked under the weight of skaters. Matthew turned the heating in his house up to 80° and found an extra blanket in the linen-closet. He spent Thanksgiving with Mrs. Nash, and swam in her indoor pool, against a backdrop, not of snowflakes, but of icy blue sky. Some part of his unconscious mind was alert all the time for the appearance of Mrs. Merle: and it was disappointed. He ate his pumpkin pie and was aware, despite the surrounding comfort, of being more than a little bored. Though it could not be said that he returned to Cobb with relief, at least it was without the usual repugnance.

Could he conceivably be getting fond of the place?

Somehow his house seemed welcoming; even the ghost of the former owner had a degree of domestic appeal. The three rooms (out of twelve) which were familiar to him, had a strange air of home: and an air of home was something Matthew, even in London, was hardly used to. He dined that night in a fraternity house, where the young men sang songs, and afterwards sat around his inadequate knees. Humbly, he felt he was giving them little in exchange for their hospitality. He knew he was not particularly clever — he had never thought so: at Eton, they had never thought so, either, ('A slow boy,' his tutor had said of him.) But if the boys believed he was clever, surely that was enough? He entertained them with witticisms which, even in his own ears, rang sadly of Wodehouse. And they laughed. Like drains. Perhaps it was not so surprising, since Wodehouse had made more than one generation laugh at the pureness of his fantasy, the fantasy of a world that never was, but had nearly been.

He found, on the table inside the door, a note from Dr. Parke, asking him to dinner on the following evening.

'Mrs. Parke will not be with us, I am sorry to say, as she has to attend a meeting, so we shall be "stag", as I think one might put it.'

Matthew wondered who the hell was going to cook the meal.

As he plodded through the dark, fumbled through ghostly lanes high-stacked with winter, to Parke's house, he reflected that there were two Matthews whereas there should be one only. The first Matthew was fluid and decent in speech, his mind attuned to that gentleness which should make gentlemen. The second was given to thoughts of a crude and violent nature, such as — 'Who the hell is going to cook the meal?'

Matthew believed in the importance of the whole man. Indeed, before he came to Cobb, he had credited himself with being one. Now, he was becoming fractionated.

Fumbling through the muffled orchard trees, minuetting in search of a pathway, steadying his gaze on a pink-glowing lantern which must surely be the one upon the Parkes' porch, he said aloud to himself —

'Let us say that it would be fascinating to know who was going to prepare our dinner.'

A hearty voice rang out through the dark, that peculiarly hearty voice with a streak of strain in it which belongs only to very small men.

'Why, Matthew, have you brought a guest? Splendid! You are both welcome.'

'The spotty, pomegranate light of a torch danced at his feet, guiding him on.

'This way! This way! Be careful of the ditch. "Welcome, Gentlemen both", as Queen Elizabeth the First was said to have observed to the eighteen tailors.'

'There's no one with me,' Matthew said, finding himself, with startling suddenness, on the porch steps.

'But I distinctly heard you talking to a friend! And about your dinner!'

'I don't think I was,' Matthew said obstinately. 'At least, not about dinner. I may have been talking to myself, though.'

'Now, now, now! That's a bad habit for a young man. When you get to my age, all is forgiven you. But you — you must watch your step!'

He caught Matthew neatly as the latter stumbled into his arms. 'Dear, dear! I'm afraid we are iced up.'

The house was cosy as ever, logs glowing and crumbling in the hearth, some streaked still with the autumn's verdigris.

'My dear boy, I appreciate your making this journey on such a night, I do sincerely. Let me take your coat.'

They sat down before the fire. From within came a soft and rather alarming smell of some food Matthew was certain not to like.

'And is your throat better now?'

'Thank you, sir.'

'You want to watch throats. I always watch mine. A young man like you——'

'It is tremendously nice of you to call me a young man. I am, however, fifty-one.'

'Then don't tell another soul! No one would guess.' Dr. Parke clapped his little hands together. 'Do we want to give away all our trade secrets? A little sherry, that won't hurt you.'

Conversation was desultory, ranging from the dormitory extensions to Edith's splendid lecture. 'You bring us a breath from another world, Matt, perhaps an older world, but one with lessons for us yet.' Dr. Parke looked at his watch. 'Ten after seven precisely. I must remember what Mrs. Parke told me. "At ten after seven precisely, take the casserole from the oven, and don't forget the pot-holder or you will burn your poor hands." So I shan't forget the pot-holder, Matthew, and we shall both regale ourselves sound in wind and limb.'

The casserole contained some whitish meat in a whitish sauce. Matthew had once been repelled (at Eton, of all places) by a dish of tripe. This meat resembled tripe. He tried to eat it, but was taken by a terrible anorexia: his throat refused to move. He fell into a stream of inconsequent chit-chat, to cover the feet that he was hiding what he could of his dinner under a blanket of lettuce. This chit-chat would have deceived anyone in London: it merely bewildered Dr. Parke.

'You don't like the casserole? Oh dear! I wonder if we have anything else in the house. Eggs? Cheese? I think there was some corned beef left over from last night.'

'I'm terribly sorry,' Matthew said in despair, 'I didn't want to be a bore by telling you: but I had the most frightful attack of indigestion after lunch today——'

'Where did you lunch? At the Boosie House? What did you eat? This must be looked into!'

Dr. Parke was suddenly huge and Rhadamanthine.

'No, no, I didn't eat there,' Matthew lied, hoping the lie would not be nailed. 'I ate at home. I think one of the tins had been opened too long.'

Parke relaxed. 'Well, then, that's a relief! Because, you know, if I thought anything were below optimum condition — optimum condition, my dear Matthew — at the Boosie——'

Matthew renewed his assurances.

He ate some pie and some cheese. The two men returned to the fire for coffee, after Dr. Parke, looking upset and by no means unsuspicious, had returned casserole and dirtied plates to the kitchen.

Any man who has lived in the great world as long as Matthew can sense trouble coming a mile off. There need be no palpable indication of its approach: it is a miasma on the air, rather beautiful in its own way, of a colour between thunder-blue and the bluer ranges of violet. It has a musical component also, the colour wrapped about the unheard melody, which is sweeter, and more distressing, than heard ones. Matthew stiffened and waited, while Dr. Parke, simulating that extreme physical relaxation which is another augury of trouble on the way, cleared his throat.

'Matthew, I want to solicit your help.'

'Of course, sir.'

'It did come to my ears, I will not say through which source, that our good friend Doug Ruddock was taking, let us say, a somewhat disturbing line, in his book on Emily Dickinson.'

'Sir, I really wouldn't know.'

Dr. Parke looked piteous, and Matthew's heart was touched. He remembered the sadness of the old man's life (he, too, was coming to think of him as old), the putative dottiness of his wife, the parasitical family, the coronaries.

'You see, Matt, because of the named fellowship, she occupies a very special place in the corporate life of Cobb. If our Emily Dickinson Fellow were to produce some work which showed her in some — ah — painful light, it would cause much grief here in our little Grove of Academe.'

'Of course. But I'm quite sure——' Matthew was going to wipe out his own treason whatever the cost.

'I suspect that you would like a little Scotch,' Dr. Parke said, perking up to get it. 'It is, after all, a chilly night. "In the bleak midwinter——" ' It was one of his favourite quotations. 'Ah! but it is not midwinter yet. Yes, we have the hard months before us. Would you, in fact, like a little Scotch?'

Matthew accepted, and was poured a drink which was very little indeed.

'Now I shall have a Coke, as the youngsters do. Habit-forming, I know: but surely a small vice?'

Dr. Parke poked the logs and the sparks flew upwards, jolting into Matthew's mind an unlooked-for memory of the Quatorze Juillet at Antibes. He could smell the scent of sea and French cigarettes, the acrid scent of the powder. He had been there with Betty Hedingham, old darling that she was, at a party given by Elsa Maxwell. He smelt the great waft of Patou's *Joy* arising from Betty's cleavage. A little piece of yellowed, saturated cotton wool stuck up from one side of her brassière.

'Not a very dreadful vice,' he said.

'I dare not indulge too much, you know.'

'I'm sorry, sir.'

'Let us count our blessings, though. And, my dear boy, I have many.' He was obviously counting them, for his face was irradiated.

Not for long, however. 'Now, Matthew. I think it was you who suggested to my wife that Dr. Ruddock's thesis was likely to be of an unusual nature.'

'Look, I only meant that he was an unusual *person*. How could he produce anything that wasn't unusual?'

'And Mrs. Parke, who is quick off the mark——'

Matthew thought for a wild moment that this would do as an opening couplet for one of Dorothy's *Light Thoughts*.

'— suggested several things to you.'

'Sir, I wasn't listening. I don't mean that out of disrespect to your wife, who is always quite fascinating, but I was feeling most frightfully cold.'

'She said she fancied it was in your mind that Dr. Ruddock was making the specific suggestion——'

'It was not in my mind.'

'— that the most austere, the most shy, the most ladylike (if I may use the word in its true sense, lady — *hlaefdige* — the breadmaker for her lord and his household) of our American poets was something less than abstemious.' Dr. Parke flushed up with restrained, but profound indignation. His voice trembled.

'It is really too bad, too bad!'

'Mrs. Parke must have made the suggestion. I didn't.'

'She said you did not deny it.'

'I was perishing with cold. When I am cold, it often makes me deaf. It is a very curious fact. It puzzles my doctor, I assure you.'

'You are friendly with Dr. Ruddock.'

'Certainly.'

'So I am sure you must know the lines on which he is working.'

Matthew steadily denied this. He could feel the sheet of shame falling from his shoulders, see the slow reversal of his shield back into its normal position, feel the grip of spurs once more on his heels. He was saving his soul, Matthew was, and his honour also.

Dr. Parke leaned over to pat his knee. 'Good! Good man! I should think the less of you if you weren't loyal to your friend. But I must tell you, between ourselves, of course, that among the people being considered for my office, when I retire (which, as you know, will be soon), Doug Ruddock has high priority. Any thought that he might bring scandal upon Cobb would, of course, automatically debar him. No — don't say anything yet!'

Matthew did not intend to, for his mind was in turmoil.

'I should not say this to you if you were not, though in the most welcome sense, a stranger. No despised *forestiero*, though, my dear Matt, far, far from it! Trusted *because* you are able to take an objective view; a trusted arbitrator. I beg you to think carefully.'

'I don't know anything about Doug's work. I said nothing about drink. It is all an absurd mistake.'

'Ah.' Dr. Parke stared into the crumbling logs, now peeling back from the heart of the fire like petals from some wild orange rose. 'You think so?'

Matthew took the final plunge. 'I am sure.'

With that he felt houselled and annealed, ready to retire at cockcrow, not to hell, but to a reception committee of joyful saints, among whom he would now stand, as pure as they.

'I have a little idea which perhaps has not occurred to you. I may say that it is most unlikely to have crossed your mind. — A little freshening in that inhospitable-looking glass?'

'Thank you, sir.'

'Should our dear Doug Ruddock — I only say *should* — appear to be not quite so strong a candidate as some of us actually thought, we might have to look elsewhere. There is another candidate, I may tell you, but, alas, he is not so popular as he might be with some of our Trustees. No, it might be necessary to find quite a new contender.'

'Yes?'

Somebody came in through the screen door, through the inner door, dropped rubbers with a plop.

'There is nothing in our constitution to say that the head of the centre must be an American citizen. No, nothing. I have wondered more than once myself whether some friendly detached influence from another land might not——'

'He is thinking truly of you, Mr. Pryar,' said Beata, beaming down upon him with her terrible big smile, and pumping his hand.

Matthew sweated all over. He could hardly believe his luck. 'Me?'

'Of course he thinks of you — do you not, Dom? There is no need to go round a mulberry at all. He thinks of you. I think of you.'

'Oh, but I couldn't——'

'I was wondering if you would let your candidature go forward. It would be a blessing to Mrs. Parke and myself, and I am sure I may say to the President also, to have you with us often, often, practically one among us——'

'Positively one among us,' cried Beata. 'There is no need to juggle with your words, Dom.'

She looked on Matthew with such favour that he quailed. He was rather a modest man in sexual matters: many women had taken a fancy to him, yet he was astonished every time it happened. There was no doubt that Beata had done so.

'Of course,' said Dr. Parke, 'your candidature would depend entirely upon whether Dr. Ruddock seemed unlikely to be in the — ah — running. Entirely.'

'How a man such a beast could be,' boomed Beata, with such explosive force that Matthew jumped, 'to put pitch on the reputation of a poor dead woman! So she reeled, did she, she lurched? She was a nayword in Amherst, but the conspiracy of silence truly protected her? So she was raised from the sidewalk, carried home to her bed raving and shouting? That is it, so? Oh, for shame, for shame!'

Matthew got up. Temptation had come upon him once again with such force that he knew he must leave the house or yield to it.

'There isn't a word of truth in it,' he said, the effort almost choking him.

'Of course there is no word of truth!' Beata shouted. '*That* is the shame of it!'

'I meant, that Doug is after any such thing. Not that I know anything about it. It is all an invention. Forgive me, I must go. It has been quite splendid, and you left us such a delectable dinner, Mrs. Parke, but I have to be at my desk early in the morning. I am at a tricky stage in my own work.'

He was halfway across the room when someone else came in, with the same plop of rubbers.

This time it was the President, entering with his usual hunted look, slightly twitching his head as if he had a dried pea between his collar and his neck.

'An unexpected pleasure, Dr. Pickersgill,' Matthew said, relieved. His mind was not functioning very well.

'We see each other all too seldom,' said the President gloomily, 'all, all too seldom. I am so pressed.'

'But I'm afraid I was just leaving. As I was telling the Parkes——'

'No, no, don't go. Have another drink,' said the doctor.

'I won't, thank you so much.'

'Of course you cannot take your departure,' said Beata. 'You are not a foolish man. Your deep instinct must have told you that it is you our President has come to see. For he knows all, all!'

Pickersgill sighed, lowering himself in a chair as if expecting it to collapse softly beneath him. 'I fancy Dom was sounding you out. This sad business of Doug Ruddock.'

'Please listen, sir.' Matthew had decided to stand his ground. Indeed, with Beata between himself and the door, he could do nothing else. 'This is all moonshine, I am quite convinced. As I have told the Parkes, I know nothing, absolutely nothing about Dr. Ruddock's work. It is simply not my business.'

He began to suspect that Dr. Parke knew about it, though. He had remembered that pass-key.

'It is all very tentative,' said the President. 'But if a certain 'concatenation of circumstances arose, I hope you would let your name be presented.'

'And I!' cried Beata. 'Even though Mr. Pryar, as I am told, does not find life here entirely to his liking. He is accustomed to serving-men,' she added scornfully, though her gaze was still ardent, 'he is used to his breakfast in his bed.'

Matthew blushed, and wished he were not.

'Mind you,' said the President, 'your chance of election would be slim. I can't answer for the Trustees. I, however——'

'Ah, Matt!' Beata exclaimed, with acceptant familiarity, 'he would be on your side! He would be your sincere prop and stay!'

'Unless——' the President began.

'Oh, unless you have still your fancy for the rude man.'

'Ruddock?'

'The other.'

Tiepolo, Matthew thought, and wondered why he had never considered this dark horse. Here was a new problem to be faced.

'I don't know that I have any fancy,' the President mused. 'My mind is open.'

'Well?' Beata demanded.

'I beg your pardon?' said Matthew.

'My wife means,' said Dr. Parke, 'will you let your name go forward?'

'That is truly what I mean.'

'Well——'

'I think you will do it,' she said strenuously, 'for Dom and for me.'

What there was about her delivery of the line which made Matthew certain that Wohlgemutt, however correct he might be in other respects, was wrong about Beata's mental instability, he never found out: but he was suddenly convinced. She might be awful, but she was not off her head.

He decided that enough had been done for honour's sake.

'If you really think I'm remotely worthy, or remotely adequate — that is, that I should be adequate, given the chance——'

'I think you are sincerely adequate,' said Beata, on a bass note which tolled like a bell, and, like a bell, sent its echoes rubbing round the walls of the ensuing silence like a cat rubbing itself around a piece of furniture.

'But this drink business, President, is all nonsense.'

'We must hope so,' said Dr. Parke. The President gave his sad, sunken nod.

Matthew was allowed to go. At the door, Dr. Parke said to him,

'I hope you will not reconsider this, my dear Matt, if I may now call you so.' (He had forgotten that this was what he had called Matthew for some time past.) 'I am, I fear, getting old. Yes, and somewhat feeble, though I would not confess it to the world at large. I am a *tired* man, my dear Matt. Oh, by the way, I must beg you not to *count* on my vote — for I have one, on an equality with our good Trustees. Not to *count* on it.'

But Matthew was quite sure he could. Dear old man, poor dear old Dr. Dominick Maudlin Parke! He hardly remembered the long walk home, so elated was he. He skimmed the snow as if on skis, miraculously getting no whit of it into his rubbers. The sky had cleared, the stars were out. They sang to him in their ancient fashion, whirring round in a blissful choreography.

'Turn again, Pryar,
Director of the Centre for Visiting Fellows,
Turn again, Pryar,
O, Power in Hamelin!'

25. A Change of Heart

There was no question about it: Matthew was getting fond of Cobb. A hitherto unfamiliar tree became a landmark of his day, one that he tapped with his knuckles as he passed it on his way from breakfast to the Centre. The Boosie House, beautiful even to disenchanted eyes, became an aesthetic delight, in its poised whiteness; even his dark house was no longer a place to connect, necessarily, with a detested wife.

The art building, neo-Colonial, seemed to him an exquisite example of what a sensitive architect could do when he tried; and the senior dormitories gave him pure pleasure when, as he walked past them at sunset, their lavish windows were filled with gold, rose, apple green and cobalt blue. He liked the soaring slopes, thickly wooded, that tumbled down from Pilt-down to Hamelin, the frozen ponds, with a breath of jade on them by day and a sheet of silver by night. He loved all his new friends and — ah! — he loved America.

It is only fair to say that he had by now solved his eating problems, and had induced Anderson's sister to look in and make his bed every morning, in addition to her two-hourly commitment per week.

He would like a stake in this place. Moreover, he was going to have one. With any luck. His future stretched before him, clear and brilliant as the resident snows.

Mrs. Merle wrote him a nice letter in her huge, dashing hand (he counted nine words to a sizeable page) asking him to spend Christmas at her house. She was staying longer than she thought with her sister, as the skiing was excellent that year, but on the morning of December 24th she would be driving back, and would pick him up on the way.

Matthew looked forward to the stately process of the year (he had been meaning to return to England in January, but this might not be necessary if things went his way), the melting of the ice, the late, brief spring, the return of the lilacs, the sweaty, dazzling summer. He loved heat. Whoever would be out for the count during the torrid months, he would not. He was a happy man.

When Doug Ruddock came in with new discoveries, he was able to listen without the slightest touch of shame.

> ' "What Inn is this
> Where for the night
> Peculiar travellers come?"

'She was a damned peculiar traveller, Matt, you bet she was. Furthermore, I bet the whole neighbourhood knew it. It was a conspiracy of silence. Or listen to this:

> "Bring me the sunset in a cup,
> Reckon the morning's flagons up
> And say how many Dew——"

"Dew" my foot. Pulling wool over our eyes, that's what she was doing,' he added, with a note of admiring affection. 'Just think of her, remorsefully reckoning up all those flagons, promising herself she'd lay off next day——It makes me almost weep.'

As for Edith, she had made a superb return to her Cambridge form. She rode her bicycle with such gusto that students fled from her path, she was seen smoking a cigar in the Boosie House, she had been heard to call a distinguished mediaevalist 'cully'. Miss Groby was getting on with her work, and could now make her way along the corridor without clutching at the walls. Chuck seemed as bad-tempered as ever, but he was probably past praying for.

Matthew only realised the profound nature of the change which had set into his own being when, one night in a fraternity house, hearing the young men singing after dinner —

'Give a smile and a sob
For dear old Cobb
As we start along the Road of Life,'

he felt the dangerous waters prickling behind his eyelids. Dear old Cobb! Well, yes, indeed. Or rather, say: Yes — possibly.

The only outstanding matter that worried him was the affair of Ruddock's cat. Chuck had denied it: nevertheless, he and Doug were not speaking. This made a blot on an otherwise enchanting panorama.

'But. Doug, you cannot be sure.'

'I am willing to believe that *you* didn't do it, Matt.'

'Thank you.'

'So who is there left? Groby? Wohlgemutt? Edith? Can you see any of them poisoning a cat?'

'My dear fellow, there was no intention of poisoning. The idea, as I see it, was simply to incapacitate the poor creature. Incidentally, why have you never given him a name?'

'Cats are all called Kitty.'

'Surely he deserves better.'

Doug said shyly, 'When we're by ourselves I sometimes call him *La Fille Aux Yeux d'Or*.'

'He isn't a *fille*.'

'Well, he's neutered.'

'Nevertheless.'

'Or sometimes "My Snowy-Breasted Pearl".'

'Those are descriptions, not names,' Matthew said, pleased to have diverted his friend from wrath. 'I should call him Hugo.'

'Why?'

'I don't know. Hugo von Hoffmanstall seems a good name for a cat. A friend of mine calls hers Pushkin — that's probably the best of all. But only black cats are called Proust.'

'I will call him Ginger,' Doug said. 'That's a good name.'

'I think it's fine.'

'Do you really?'

'An inspiration,' said Matthew. 'No, no — I mean it. Something simple. One wouldn't want to make a fool of the poor fellow.'

Halcyon days at Hamelin: days with half a grain of benzedrine to every mouthful of fresh, exhilarating air, and through them all a thread of that mysterious promise which keeps Englishmen from the gas-oven, and Americans from carbon dioxide in the garage.

Halcyon days, however, have the knack of coming to a dramatic close. Darkness does not fall slowly, mercifully: it comes at one stride. It came with a letter from Dorothy.

'My friend George Peters will be passing through Hamelin in a week's time. He will call on you. Please have tapes of the Corall lecture ready for him, as I wish to hear them.

'And don't say there aren't any tapes when you know there are. If the tapes are college property, then please have a transscript made. Also, please let George have carbons of your book on me, so far as it goes, which I hope is quite a long way by now. After all, you haven't got anything else to do.

'PS. Duncan has taken up with Betty Hedingham, if you ever heard anything so *disgusting*, she must be fifty-five if she's a day.

'All send love.

'PS. Again. Believe it or not, there is an interminable article on *Daniel Skipton and His Times in Encounter*, which doesn't mention me. If I am not of his "times", who is?'

Matthew's normally sweet mouth hardened, and the mothy twitch of lip which to his friends had always indicated amusement, now indicated something quite different. Dorothy had at last mistaken her man. He had a future now: and in that future she was to have no part. He determined to let her have her damned tape, but not a transcript. He would not spare her an inflection of Edith's wiry voice. He would get the tape copied.

He put the matter in Miss Ehrlinger's hands, and within twenty-four hours she put Edith's lecture into his.

At the beginning of the next week, George Peters arrived. Matthew had expected him to be one of Dorothy's bravos, those young men she never had the slightest difficulty in recruiting, though she rarely held them for more than six months. Peters proved to be an agreeable surprise, when he looked timidly in on his way to a conference of educationists being held at Dartmouth. He was a small man with a wry, gentle face and a permanent tic. He presented Dorothy's compliments. 'Our common friend,' he pedantically called her, and Matthew felt rather snobbishly that no term could be more appropriate.

'I have had the tape copied for her,' Matthew said smoothly. 'I do hope she will be pleased.'

Peters thanked him warmly.

'How is she? And how is Cosmo?'

'Oh — Cosmo's better now. He had bronchitis. Dorothy is — er — Dorothy. She's — er — she's a stimulating person, isn't she?'

'Tremendously,' said Matthew, gleefully perceiving what was to come.

'She does make an impact.'

'I know nobody who makes a greater one.'

'The first time I met her, I was quite overwhelmed.'

'She does that to people, yes.'

'You know,' said Peters, 'it sounds idiotic to say it, but sometimes she quite scares me. Of course, that must seem absurd to you. You're old friends.'

His eyes were flickering in response to the flicker in Matthew's.

'I used to be intimidated,' Matthew said, choosing the word carefully. 'Not now, I think.'

'I suppose one could say she was almost intimidating.'

'One could say quite a lot of things.'

'I admire her, of course. But she does tend — do forgive me, saying it about a great friend of yours — to be a little overbearing. Now would you call that fair? Or not?'

'Oh, quite fair,' said Matthew. 'In fact——'

'In fact——'

They had both spoken at once.

Matthew grinned. 'You may get your blow in first.'

'Dear God,' said Peters, 'what a woman!'

'An appalling woman.'

'You think so, too?'

'Certainly. How did you get caught up?'

'Simply when I was in Cosmo's shop, buying some books. She came in and he introduced us. She — she — well, just sucked me in. And later, when she knew I was going to the U.S., she ordered me to intrude myself on you.'

'I am so pleased you intruded. But in fact you don't. Let's go and have some dinner. Have you got a car?'

'Oh, I mustn't impose myself further——'

'I beg you to,' said Matthew, 'and we will have a perfectly magnificent evening being rather less than gentlemen about Dorothy.'

They had a most enjoyable time and parted refreshed.

'I say, Pryar, is she going to be *pleased* with that tape?'

'How very perceptive you are. You might try to be present when she plays it. And drop me a line to let me know how the whole thing went.'

Matthew felt that the halcyon bird had flown back again, fanning the stars about with its wings of silver and indigo. Another of his troubles was over: he would never need to set eyes on Dorothy again. Of course he had an obligation to Cobb, to do a book of some kind: but he did not think they would mind very much if it wasn't about Dorothy. He wondered whether they would settle for a witty and not too voluminous study of Ronald Firbank. In his mind's eye he saw the work completed: about sixty pages of it printed on blue paper, with gilt edges, bound in watered silk, violet, with a powdering of tiny gold birettas.

Or perhaps another idea would occur to him. There was no need to make a decision now.

26. 'Had Tiberius been a Cat'

Next day Dr. Parke called at the Centre, and invited the Fellows to lunch with some of the Faculty. 'At the Boosie House, of course,' he said, 'in the Pump Room at twelve o'clock. I believe, my dear Matt —' he smiled teasingly — 'that there was some talk about pre-emptions. Well, now the Pump Room is going to be pre-empted for *you!*'

'So kind,' Matthew murmured, 'so kind.'

After the Doctor had taken his leave, Matthew went downstairs to the gloomy general lounge, for he had heard voices.

They were all there except Miss Groby.

'Has he got a nerve!' Chuck was shouting. 'After all these months he asks us to lunch at last. And where? In that god-awful place.'

'Don't look a gift horse in the mouth,' said Edith, 'even if it has got lavender teeth. After all I've heard about American dentistry——'

'I can't say I've noticed,' Wohlgemutt returned softly. 'I think he's rather a fine-looking old man.'

'He is not an old man,' said Matthew. 'He is about five years older than I am. But I appreciate that he has had a dreadfully hard life.'

For some reason Wohlgemutt blushed.

'I agree with Dr. Corall,' said Hefflinger, 'a gift horse always a pleasant animal is. — Excuse me, is always a pleasant animal.'

Doug Ruddock, the cat slung over his shoulder like a tippet, observed that the very fact that they all found it necessary to foregather to discuss an invitation was a curious comment on Cobb's hospitality.

Chuck moved up behind him and gave the cat's tail a tiny pinch. It snarled at him, orange eyes lambent with fury, but did not budge.

'I shouldn't do that,' Matthew murmured, 'they do so hate it.'

'Oh do they?' Chuck sneered, while Ruddock said, 'Just what did he do?'

'Matt's seeing things. By the by, Matt, isn't it time you gave another lecture?'

'No dice,' Matthew answered. He was learning a little of the language.

Chuck grinned.

'But what's all this about Dr. Parke's hard life?' Edith enquired. 'It's the first I've heard of it.'

'Well,' said Matthew uncomfortably, 'Dr. Wohlgemutt — Herman, here, if I may call him so — says his life with his wife isn't easy. And he has to maintain all his sisters. And he's had two coronaries.'

Ruddock jumped. 'What crap! He's never been sick in his life. I ought to know. He's my wife's first cousin.'

Matthew saw in a flash why Doug had been so strong a candidate. 'Her first cousin?'

'Yes. And he gets along fine with Beata, and he hasn't got any sisters.' He swung round upon Wohlgemutt. 'Just what is all this about?'

'Well, I heard it from somebody. I could have been wrong.'

'I'll say you're wrong. What's the big idea?'

'I think Herman was trying to alter my attitude to dear old Dr. Parke,' Matthew said gently, 'that's all. I think he objected to my — our — somewhat abortive revolt. You will remember that Herman was not really of our mind.'

'If you want to know, I thought it was pretty lousy, trying to make the old man's life miserable!'

'I was not trying to make his life miserable. I was merely suggesting that Cobb should have an inn.'

'And what could more pleasant be than an agreeable meeting place?' said Hefflinger.

'And what if he didn't want any goddamned inn?'

Wohlgemutt was shaking with rage. He glared at Matthew, all

the time automatically picking invisible bits of fluff from his smart suit.

'Well, others might have wanted it. Oh, and Herman——'

'Don't call me Herman.'

'So sorry. I was only trying to be friendly. Dr. Wohlgemutt, you simply *can't* have been wrong about Mrs. Parke tripping the old boy up in Convocation.'

'What?' Chuck yelled.

Matthew described the scene, with certain touches of fancy which made him proud. He was not, as a rule, a malicious man. But the rule was not operating on this occasion.

'By God,' Chuck said to Wohlgemutt, 'I have to hand it to you. I never thought you had any imagination. But, boy, you're the most!'

Edith gave a cackle of such high, uncontrollable laughter that she startled Ruddock's cat. Unfairly, it lashed out with a claw at Chuck's face, drawing a pinstripe of blood. He turned round with a roar and smacked at it. The cat avoided the smack, leaped from Ruddock's shoulder and went dashing around the room, growling in so terrible a fashion that they all backed away.

'My God, he'd kill you if he could,' said Edith, 'just look at him!'

Ruddock, white-faced, swung at Chuck with open hand, and caught him just over the scratch.

'You two-bit bastard!' Chuck staggered back, looking like a demon.

Ruddock stood motionless, his hand incarnadined with Chuck's blood. 'You tried to poison my cat! And you tried to put the blame on to Pryar!'

'I did not try to poison your damned animal!'

The cat, though it had not been hurt, was growling more horribly than ever, dashing at all available ankles in an unprejudiced fashion. Edith had calmly cocked her legs up on the table. 'Boys, boys,' she said, 'just stop this, if you please. In half an hour's time we shall all be fellow-guests at a delightful luncheon.'

'I'll knock your head off!' Chuck shouted at Ruddock.

'Go ahead and try it, you dirty poisoner! You damned Borgia!'

'Well,' Matthew said, hoping to mollify them both,' it wasn't actually poison.'

'It was ipecac,' said Wohlgemutt stonily. 'I put a drop in its damned milk. It was in and out of my office the whole goddamned time, so I thought I'd discourage it.'

'Ts, ts, ts,' said Hefflinger, 'he is only a poor animal to whom we should be kind.'

'You did! You!' Ruddock's face was the colour and texture of pale grey blotting-paper.

'I put milk down in my room and doctored it. There was no need for that animal to drink it, was there? He had only to keep out of my way. Do you know he piddled on my papers?'

'In that case,' said Matthew, 'if what you say is true, how did that saucer get into my room?'

They all stared at each other. Ruddock managed to catch the cat and hug it, in all its terrible wrath, to his chest.

'Oh dear, I am so very, very sorry!'

They all turned round. Miss Groby had come tottering silently into the room. 'Oh, I did not know, you must believe me that I did not know!'

'Why do they say "as good as a play"?' Edith enquired. 'I have never seen a play half as good. Just compare this with *Rosmersholm*!'

'What is it?' Matthew asked Miss Groby. 'Do tell us. I'm sure you didn't mean to do any harm.'

'Well, you were all out but Dr. Ruddock, and he was in the room with the door closed, and I looked into Dr. Wohlgemutt's room when I was passing, and there was the milk, and I am afraid I was terribly muddled, but I thought, knowing he hated pussies, that it must have been put there by mistake — perhaps one of the cleaners: and then I thought, Mr. Pryar is so kind, it must have been his thought, so I just took up the saucer and popped it into his office——Oh dear!' she burst into tears. 'I was so muddled. I am not nearly so muddled nowadays, but I was then.'

Edith jumped down from the table. 'Maud, do stop crying! Nobody's blaming you. Look, they're all smiling!' (Though only

Chuck and Matthew were, and Chuck's smile was filled with disagreeable exultation.) 'They're smiling brilliantly. They love you, Maud, we all do.'

'Of course we do,' said Matthew with warmth. 'Don't we, Doug?' He put some force into this.

'OK, OK.'

'And *no* harm was done, none at all.'

The cat escaped again and flew at Wohlgemutt. His choice of a foe was purely arbitrary: yet it seemed to Matthew a just one.

Wohlgemutt aimed a kick at it. Ruddock rushed at him, and was dragged back by Edith, who, though small, had muscles of steel.

'Gentlemen! Scholars all! What an unbecoming scene!'

Wohlgemutt turned smartly and went out. They heard him stamping up the stairs.

'You hit me,' Chuck said to Ruddock, softly. 'And I never did a damned thing to you.'

'You would have, though, if you'd had a chance!'

'Doug, I'm not going to forget this.'

'We are all going to forget it, cullies,' said Edith, 'because we have just twenty minutes to wash our hands and go bounding merrily off to the fiesta.'

The clock in the tower struck the quarter.

She looked at her watch. 'In fact, we have fifteen minutes. Come on, now, and no nonsense.'

Hypnotised by her forceful calm, they followed her from the room.

Halfway up the stairs she stopped and, leaning on the banisters, fell into a *fou rire*. 'Tripped him in Convocation! Oh Lord, tripped him in Convocation! That enormous womanly foot! Oh do stop me, somebody! It never happened, did it? But it should have. Oh yes, by the nine gods of Lars Porsena, it should have.'

27. Ruddock is Ruined

They sat about a big round table in the Pump Room, looking as though butter would not melt in their collective mouths. At the head of the table — despite its roundness, it had a head — sat Dr. Parke, in his element as host. With the six Visiting Fellows, interleaving them, as it were, sat five members of the Faculty, carefully selected so that each Fellow should have a chance to talk with an expert in his own field. In honourable positions to Dr. Parke's right and left sat the women: Edith Corall and Maud Groby.

Matthew realised that he must have seen the Faculty members before: yet they appeared to him as total strangers. They might have been gathered together, selected by a dip in the bran-tub, from all parts of the United States. He thought he recognised the Head of the English Department who sat at his right hand, but the thought was flimsy.

The sun poured through the windows, pointing out the elegancies of the beautiful room, the icing-sugar moulding on the ceiling and over the chimney-piece, the lofty proportions of the windows. It also seemed to point out that the food was even more deplorable than usual, since choice had been denied. They began with cottage cheese salad, continued with hot roast beef sandwiches, sodden and tepid, and ended with a slice of pumpkin pie.

'Punkin pie!' Dr. Parke exclaimed, 'that is what we call it! Not pumpkin — p-u-n-k-i-n. How I remember my boyhood, playing around the yard, and my mother calling to me — "Hurry, hurry, Dominick, it's punkin pie today!" '

Matthew gagged, and was ashamed of himself. He drank a whole glass of water. A student thoughtfully renewed his coffee.

The Visiting Fellows, though shaken by the morning's scene, were behaving well: that is, unsensationally. Conversation was dull and courteous.

'If only Dorothy Merlin could go into paperback,' said the Professor of English, 'it would help. The boys will buy anything. But as it is, you have a hard row to hoe. Yes, a hard row.'

At one point during the pie, Dr. Hefflinger rose, blushing, excused himself, and made for the cloakroom. When he returned, he had no handkerchief in his breast-pocket. Matthew guessed that he had had a spider in it (probably Susie) and had now shut her, handkerchief and all, into his briefcase. When Hefflinger returned, he was looking more at ease.

Miss Groby, though tipsy (she had stoked up before the meal), was talking earnestly to her neighbour about the original hagiography of the Tornovo Empire. Edith was on the livelier subject of the Albigenses. Hefflinger was claiming preferential treatment for all *araneae*. Wohlgemutt was buttering Dr. Parke. Only Chuck was silent and surly.

Dr. Parke was obviously enjoying himself. His face, like a small, crumpled rose, shone with pleasure, his blue eyes twinkled. 'How very pleasant it is to see you all here! How very, very pleasant! I am sure this is a day that will go down in the by no means undistinguished annals of Cobb.'

Matthew could not imagine why it should.

'And here am I among the ladies! I have the privilege of absorbing the attention of the only two ladies present — charming ladies both! I must say it hardly seems fair. I really think I must implore you all to breathe no word of it to my wife!'

This raised a titter.

'She would be jealous, I am sure. And Mrs. Parke is a very formidable woman, I must tell you, despite her mild exterior.'

This was meant to provoke laughter, but in fact provoked only puzzlement.

'Yes, yes, her mild exterior. So we must keep mum, eh? — Even though I see that one of our waiters is the new editor of the college paper.'

The boy coloured and wagged his head.

'And as we are a free country, how can we presume to censor what he chooses to write about this very happy occasion? For I am sure you are all as happy as I am!'

'I think we have reason to be,' said Chuck suddenly. 'I mean, from what I hear we're all pretty advanced in our work. I ought to be through with my book in ten days — I may say I've already sold the serial rights to the *Saturday Evening Post*. For ten thousand bucks.'

This was greeted with truly vivacious applause, since the scholar admires worldly success as much as the next man.

'But let that go.' Chuck tried to look modest, in spite of the aura of blue smoke which seemed to be blooming on the surface of his swart, satanic face. 'Others are as far advanced, I believe. Miss Groby——'

'Oh, I am making great progress now!' she said earnestly. 'I feel I have really settled down. And I have made so many good friends.'

She meant Mrs. Briggs, Mrs. Merle and their glittering circle, but the company took this to themselves, and murmured with gratification.

'Our entrancing Edith——' Chuck continued.

'So-so. I'm plodding along.'

'And Matt has almost completed the first draft of his thesis, I believe, so that we can anticipate the day when the whole United States knows about Dorothy Merlin——'

'I am slightly more behind than you think,' Matthew said stonily. He was not going to be a hypocrite.

'Doc Hefflinger,' Chuck continued, 'tells me everything is going swell for him.'

'Ja, ja,' Hefflinger put in eagerly. 'I think I have some nice new suggestions to make, some quite startling! I am learning so much about the digestive tract of the *araneae*, you would not conceive! There is something so strange about the chitinous lining of the foregut——Though I must not be proud, no, I must not. I have, by the way, found out, as a by-product, we might call it, the amazing capacity of affection between the *Avicularidii* and the human master.

Oh yes. The cat is a pet, eh?' He seemed to have forgotten the morning's tension. 'So shall little fluffy one be. Soon, I hope, he will be in high demand at the petshop!'

'And,' said Chuck remorselessly, 'last but not least, there is Doug Ruddock.'

'Ah! I hope that our old friend and colleague is going to surprise us all.'

'Look,' said Doug, 'I'm only at the preliminary stages.'

'The hell with that! Anyone who works the way you do must be pretty far ahead. I tell you, Dr. Parke, Doug's the envy of us all.'

Matthew, who had become strangely fond of Ruddock, was alarmed. He tried to head off Tiepolo. 'Oh rather, certainly he is. I sit in my room all day wishing I were like him. Dorothy Merlin is very difficult to handle, you know: it's all so simple on the surface——'

'Not to me it isn't,' said the Professor of English.

'— but so infinitely subtle. And her verse-forms are so odd: when you're up against pure originality it does tend to throw you——'

'Originality,' said Chuck loudly. 'That's what Doug's got, haven't you, Doug?'

'Now look, I——'

'After all, we think we've got most of the stuff about Emily Dickinson. But Doug here is prepared to throw a monkey-wrench.'

Matthew realised that whether or not Dr. Parke was given to prying into the offices of the Visiting Fellows, Tiepolo certainly must be.

'A monkey-wrench?' Dr. Parke said blandly, but his eyes lost a shade of colour, and the muscles around his mouth tightened somewhat.

'Emily was a queer fish, wasn't she, Doug?'

'This is my damned subject, not yours!' Ruddock cried, losing control far too soon and wrecking his hopes of escape.

'Doug thinks Emily was a wino.'

'*Not* a vino! I never said any such thing.'

'Well, it could be rum. I think Doug has some ideas on that subject.'

The table was still.

'My dear boy,' Dr. Parke said at last, in a tone mild as the patter of raindrops on mashed-up leaves, 'you are taking us for a ride. Yes, I am quite sure of that.'

'What right does he have to talk about my work?' said Ruddock, who seemed near to tears. 'Can't a man be private in this dump?'

The last word was fatal; he would never have used it but for his distress.

'Dump?'

'This place.'

'Of course you have a right to privacy.'

'Well, then——?' Ruddock, desperate and inflamed, swung round on Chuck.

'Oh, come off it, Doug, you told me all about it yourself, and you didn't say there was any secret about it.'

'I never told you any such goddamned thing!'

'My dear Doug,' said Dr. Parke, still with his soft patter, though his eyes were colder than rain, 'are you really trying to prove what Dr. Tiepolo suggests?'

There was a silence so tense that thoughts inscribed themselves upon it, standing out as clear as the writing on the wall.

Ruddock burst out, 'It's all there! Only a moron could miss it!'

Tears stood in his eyes, a big one apiece, each standing up straight and silvery as a thermometer in a glass of alcohol.

'Well,' said Dr. Parke. 'Let us change the subject. There may be some mistake, indeed we must hope there is, besides it is not fair to Dr. Ruddock to make this into a public discussion.'

He brushed the whole thing aside, as a judge does when he learns the verdict, has pronounced sentence, and has no further thought but to get back to his wife and his dinner.

'Let us speak of something else.' He stood up, rosily smiling. 'Ladies and gentlemen, I have, alas, some troublesome news for you. No! Don't be alarmed. Not bad news. Just troublesome. From tomorrow, for five days, the Boosie House will be closed for meals of any kind.'

'My God, and I've only got a bicycle!' The first reaction was Edith's.

'We have to repair the heating-system, so I am afraid there will be sad disorganisation. Still, I know you are all able — more than able! — to fend for yourselves. The young men can eat in their own dormitories and fraternity houses, so there will be no trouble there. Our Visiting Fellows will, I am sure, stock up their larders, and be as co-operative as we have always found them.'

'Won't make any difference to us,' said Wohlgemutt, with a sickening smile. 'Don't you worry, sir.'

'I shall drink,' Miss Groby said in a hurried, distraught whisper. 'I know I shall. I shall drink.'

Ruddock said nothing. He was still sunk in despair. He looked at no one, not even at Tiepolo.

Dr. Parke glanced at his watch with the feverish anxiety of the White Rabbit. 'Dear, dear, this won't do! I have a class at two. Well, I must thank you all for making this such a very pleasant occasion!'

They straggled out into the sunshine. Ruddock went off in one direction, Tiepolo in another. The remaining Fellows stood in the snow, eyeing one another silently.

'Means no breakfast,' said Hefflinger, who, like Matthew, could not cook.

'I shall drink, I know it,' said Miss Groby.

'Now look here,' said Edith, 'this is not to be endured. Matt, you must call another meeting. Tonight. And Parke has got to come, if we have to drag him there. I'll get after him now and catch him before his horrible class begins. Can you have us at eight o'clock, Matt? I'd offer my own room, but it's so poky. Herr Wohlgemutt' (this was nasty), 'I hardly imagine we can count on your support.'

He walked away.

'Dr. Hefflinger, if you would be so good as to contact Ruddock and Tiepolo, though I imagine that neither will be at the top of his form——'

'It was not kind, Dr. Corall. No; it was not kind. I think Dr. Tiepolo should not have done what he did so unfortunately do.'

'Chuck is a skunk,' said Edith decisively. 'Well, "each to your offices" — no, I don't mean your rooms, I mean each of you get out on the job. Have you enough liquor, Matt?'

'I think so, yes.'

'We'll all chip in with the cost.'

Matthew refused to hear of this.

'Bless you. Eight sharp, then.' Edith set off at a run to find her bicycle.

As he welcomed them that night, as he might have welcomed guests on Betty Hedingham's behalf, in her huge hideous hall where Matisses wrangled with suits of armour, Matthew had a perfectly explicable sense of *déjà vu*. The only unfamiliar figure in the gathering was Dr. Dominick Maudlin Parke, who could not have seemed more co-operative. Wohlgemutt, naturally, was not present and they were not talking to Chuck if they could help it. Ruddock had brought his cat, which was for the moment quiescent.

Dr. Parke accepted a tiny Scotch, indicating the size he desired by putting his two little fingers together.

'Now, I am not going to talk to you, you are all going to talk to *me*. You know me well enough, I am sure, to be convinced that if there is any way in which I can help you, I will!'

'We are going to have a pretty rough time during the next few days,' said Edith. (Matthew had cunningly appointed her spokesman, since he himself did not wish to be in Dr. Parke's black books.) 'Three of us, Mr. Pryar, Dr. Hefflinger and myself, cannot cook.'

'And I do not care to!' Miss Groby intervened with unlooked-for spirit, tossing her untidy head, forcing her all-too-mobile lips into a straight line, two inches in length.

'Come,' said Dr. Parke, 'there are splendid places round about. Pete's Diner, for instance, in Hamelin, provides a true English breakfast, lavish and delectable.'

'Mr. Pryar,' said Edith, 'does not drive. Nor does Miss Groby. Nor myself.'

'Ah! But I have thought of that. Now, at six-thirty each morning, a bus stops at the Boosie House, and continues on to Hamelin. So we have a storm in a breakfast-cup —' he chuckled, 'now haven't we?'

'I shall not catch any bus at six-thirty. Nor will Miss Groby. And I shall be astonished if Mr. Pryar does.'

'Well, no,' said Matthew meekly, 'I am always dead asleep at that time.'

'In that case, perhaps Dr. Tiepolo might be persuaded to take you all in a little later.'

'Listen,' said Chuck, 'that's crazy. I don't get up before seven-thirty, and by the time I've collected this bunch and got them all into Hamelin, it'll be getting on nine. What time do we all get back? Say half an hour for breakfast — back at ten if we're lucky. And I'm usually at my desk an hour before that. No go.'

Dr. Parke smiled ruefully. 'Ah dear, what a collection of lie-abeds! Mrs. Parke is working in the garden by six. That is, in the autumn and spring.'

'This is the bleak midwinter,' said Edith remorselessly. 'Snow on snow.'

'I could perhaps make do with orange-juice and crackers.' Hefflinger was wavering.

'I could not.' Edith was stony. 'Breakfast is the basis of my day, and I cannot face my Cathars without it.'

Dr. Parke sat down. 'Well, now! I said, *you* must talk to *me*. What have you to suggest?'

'Perhaps one or more of our great buddies on the Faculty could take us in for breakfast,' said Chuck, leering.

'And that,' Edith said firmly, 'is a splendid scheme. I don't always see eye to eye with Chuck, but this——'

'None of them lives very near,' Dr. Parke protested, 'except the President and myself. How would you get to their homes?'

Chuck reeled off a list of Faculty members who did, in fact, live on the campus. Dr. Parke found a convincing damper in each case. Also, he pointed out, nearly all these people were at their desks by half-past seven.

'I do not see,' said Hefflinger, with his gay, worried air, 'why they must so early start. They do no more work than I do, and I myself find the hour of ten quite civilised.'

'When in Rome——' Dr. Parke began.

'My dear doctor, I'm afraid you have forgotten, just for the moment, that I too am an American citizen!'

'So you are, so you are! Dr. Hefflinger, I apologise. But Miss Groby, Dr. Corall, Mr. Pryar, I fear they are accustomed to the morning hours of the British Civil Service.'

'Which is the best Civil Service in the world,' said Edith. 'It tolerates a cup of revoltingly weak tea only twice a day, works like mad, and takes time off to write poetry.'

'You mustn't suppose I was criticising——'

'Just for the record,' said Edith.

Silence fell.

'Dear, dear,' said Dr. Parke, 'I am afraid I haven't been able to help you much! — No, nothing more, thank you, Matt. Still, I am sure you will all cope manfully with a situation which affects not only ourselves but the entire student body——'

'Why should it affect them?'

'Any disorganisation upsets the boys. No, you will all be magnificent, and before you know where you are, it will all be over, and you will be back in the dear old Boosie.'

'Matthew,' said Edith, 'now that we have expressed our open revolt, I feel a Pushkin speech is called for from you.'

'Well, frankly, there doesn't seem anything much to say.' Certainly, he did not propose to say it. He had learned by chance that afternoon that a Trustees' meeting had been arranged for Saturday.

'Then I will take my leave.' Dr. Parke rose and shook hands all round. 'Goodnight, Pussycat, too,' he said, bending to stroke Ruddock's animal, which had been wandering miserably about the room sniffing in corners. 'Oh — one thing more. *In camera.* I may count on no word leaking outside this room?'

Matthew felt a twinge of excitement. Could this be about his candidature?

'Go ahead,' said Ruddock, speaking for the first time.

Dr. Parke drew himself up, and a shade of quite unwonted majesty fell across his face. 'You are all scholars, therefore all one of another. Because you are privileged by virtue of your high intelligence, you are also subject to certain obligations.'

They were all puzzled.

'As Director of the Centre, I can't pass certain things over, much as I would like to — ah, much as I would like to!'

'Oh, my God!' Chuck muttered.

'What did you say? I didn't hear you.'

'It's getting late.'

'Dr. Tiepolo, it was to you I wished particularly to speak.'

'What have I done?'

'I tell myself,' said Dr. Parke, 'that your references at lunch to the nature of Dr. Ruddock's work were — ah — well-intentioned. You wanted, perhaps, to praise the enterprise of a colleague, not considering how little to the taste of some of us his enterprise may be.'

'That bastard——' Ruddock broke out.

'You call me a bastard and I'll kick your teeth in!'

'Gentlemen, gentlemen!' cried Dr. Parke. 'This isn't becoming, not at all. If you will listen to me——'

They were quiet, eyeing him in puzzlement and rage.

'You must have realised, Carlo, for so I may call you even at this difficult moment, that you did Dr. Ruddock a certain amount of *damage*. I am only too glad to have been warned, Doug, of what you had in mind — but perhaps not in such a manner.' Parke really looked like an old man now. He was flushed: the colour stood up in peaks, like raspberry ice, on his crinkled cheeks.

'I cannot exculpate Dr. Ruddock——'

'But I'm right!' Doug shouted, 'I'm right! Do you mean, you'd suppress the truth? What sort of a place is this?'

'— however, I must say to Carlo, gravely, and in front of you all, that he should not have revealed the nature of a colleague's work in such a fashion. No, indeed not. We must — ah — "love one another or die".'

'In that case,' Edith muttered to Matthew, 'they'd better alert the funeral parlours. There's a windfall coming.'

'Damn it,' said Chuck, 'if you think I'm going to stand here and be lectured like a kid in second grade because I tried to give Doug a boost——'

Dr. Parke raised his hand episcopally. 'I have nothing more to say. Goodnight to you all.' He moved statelily towards the door, Matthew thankfully following.

At that moment Chuck grabbed up the cat and whizzed it across the floor like a cannonball. It skidded like lightning between Matthew's legs, nearly throwing him.

It did throw Dr. Parke.

He went down the entire flight, rolling over and over, to lie still and silent at the bottom.

Matthew tore down, the others after him. He was terrified. He bent over the doctor, who, to his stupefaction, opened his eyes and gave him a look of unutterable reproach. He spoke no words: but the words unspoken were as clear to read as the top line of an oculist's testing chart. They were:

Et tu, Brute!

28. Pushed

Dr. Parke was not, of course, hurt: such men are indestructible. First he sat up cautiously, flexing each limb: then, assisted by Edith and Hefflinger, unsteadily arose. He refused to let Matthew touch him.

He said loudly, '*I was pushed.*'

'Oh, you weren't,' Edith cried, 'it was the cat!'

'I beg your pardon. I know when I am pushed.'

Matthew, who had seen nothing at all, was utterly bewildered.

'The cat took a run——' said Miss Groby. She looked bitterly at Tiepolo. She would not give him away, none of them would: but she was trembling with contempt.

'Let us say no more about it.'

'Are you sure you're all right?' Matthew asked him. 'I say, do sit down for a bit. It must have been a shock.'

'Yes, Mr. Pryar. It was a very great shock. Physically (thank you, I need no assistance), I seem to be unharmed. A few minor bruises, perhaps. Otherwise, I — I will not say what I think.'

'Look here, sir, I swear nobody pushed you.'

'Then I am in honour bound to accept your word, Mr. Pryar, am I not?' A terrible reproach lay in his eyes.

'For God's sake, you can't think that any of us——'

'I should much prefer to say no more about it. Now, if you will forgive me, I should like to go home. No; nobody is to go with me. If you please. I must insist.'

He fended off all their attempts to help him. They watched him as he stepped gingerly out onto the swept path, went tottering along into the moonlit road. He paused for a second. Then he walked away, fairly briskly.

Edith turned round and smacked Chuck's face.

'You just try again!' he snarled at her.

'I don't wish to. Once is enough.'

'What have I done, for Chrissake?'

'You threw the cat at him.'

'I did not! I only tried to pick it up and it got away from me.'

'You *howling* liar!'

'Get this,' said Chuck, 'you may be a lady, but if you say that again, I'll put you over my knee and spank your fanny.'

'Oh, please!' Miss Groby moaned.

'Alas,' said Dr. Hefflinger, 'the poor old gentleman believes he was pushed by our friend Matthew here. No, one cannot doubt it.'

'If I thought you were fooling with my cat again——' Doug began.

'I can't help the antics of your damned cat!' Chuck replied to Ruddock, while still glaring at Edith.

'He cannot,' said Matthew helplessly, 'he cannot have thought I pushed him.'

Where there can be no proof, however strong suspicion may be, people are inclined to create a *tabula rasa* in their minds. Before they parted, they all more or less agreed that Dr. Parke had been the victim of mischance, and that he could not conceivably go on believing in Matthew's guilt. It was just not on. Even Edith was persuaded to disbelieve the evidence of her eyes, though she would not express regret for her action in striking Chuck.

'You can take it in payment for your dirty trick at lunch.'

'If a lady socks me,' he said, with an air of gallant conceit, 'I say to myself she can't be one hundred per cent indifferent. I didn't know you loved me, Edie.'

Matthew had to hold her back.

After that, there seemed nothing more to say. They took leave of one another, quietly, sadly. They were all worried and confused.

When they had gone, Matthew thought he had better enquire about Dr. Parke, so he made a long trudge between the drifts to his house. Beata opened the door.

'Yes, yes, it is no thanks to you that he is alive!'

'Is he all right?'

'No thanks to you if he is!'

'I say, do let me have a word with him.'

'He is not fit for words. He does not want to see you.'

'But has he broken anything?'

'His heart, perhaps,' said Beata dramatically, and having a sense of style, shut the door in Matthew's face.

29. A Man of Bad Character

It would not have happened if Matthew had not, at nine o'clock at night, been seized with a splendid idea for a book he might write: and, excited by drink and semi-starvation, had decided that he must at all costs go back to the Centre to fetch a work of reference which was stuffed away in the bottom drawer of his desk.

Although the Centre would be locked up, he had been told that his office key was also a pass-key to the back door. He walked briskly across the campus through the freezing night, went round the back of the building and tried the lock. The key would not turn. Swearing to himself, he wondered where he had slipped up. 'The back door,' Pat Ehrlinger had said: positively: he could remember the sound of her voice. Then could there be another back door? There was. In a fuddled way he recalled it. It led into a small lobby which, in its turn, led into the general lounge. It was a narrow door, tucked away beneath a sloping roof from which hung a sparkling prettiness of icicles. Matthew tried the key, and this time it worked. He stepped into pitch darkness, but below the inner door, which was a mere slit in a thin partition, there was a strip of light, and clearly through that door came voices. Parke's voice. Tom's. Walters'. Two voices he did not know.

There can be no question that Matthew, had his metabolism been undisturbed by privations, would have retreated at once; there had been three cardinal sins in the eyes of his family, lying, eavesdropping and being rude to the servants. The first sin he had, of course, learned to commit fairly frequently in a white and modest fashion — a man must grow up. But he had not yet committed the other two. He paused, not with the intention of listening, but to try to work out how he might get to his room without passing through the lounge at all. He had a frustrated vision of the book he now so ardently wished for, a decadent historical novel of the early thirties called *The Damask and the Blood*. Never in his life had he wanted to read anything so much. Was there really no other way of entering the Centre? Of course there wasn't. But by the time he had worked that out, his attention had been captured by the tenor of the conversation within.

For it was, in fact, a Trustees' meeting. He had forgotten all about it, despite the fact that he had seen Tom Helliwell driving along the main road only that morning.

'. . . so we come to the most important item on the agenda,' said Dr. Parke. 'The choice of my successor.'

A murmur of regret that the choice should be necessary.

Matthew stood still, hardly daring to breathe.

'Well, it seems we've got three candidates,' said one of the alien voices which was a very loud one, 'I vote we take them one by one.'

Tom's fresh, youthful voice: 'I suppose the hottest is Ruddock.'

'Despite all things' — Dr. Parke sounded more than grieved, 'he would still be mine. Yet——'

Another new voice said sharply, 'Disgraceful. If anyone had told me Doug was that irresponsible——'

'Could be he's on to something,' said Tom, but without much conviction. 'So far as the job goes, he's an able fellow and they all seem to like him.'

Loud-voice said, 'We don't want to be here all night. I say no.'

Nothing from J. L. Walters.

'This is not easy for me,' said Dr. Parke. 'As you know, Doug and I have been friendly for years; indeed, as Beata's cousin — not that I would let that make a difference. Nepotism, no. It would lay us too open to criticism. But I am afraid his very curious theories — and in such poor taste — put him out of court. Oh dear, I never thought I would have to vote against Doug. But I do.'

'I do,' said Tom, 'but not so much because I have anything against him. I just happen to prefer Pryar.'

Matthew jumped. He had, up to this moment, been on the point of retreat, but the sound of his own name was sufficient to pin his feet to the floor. He hardly heard the inner voice that kept saying to him, in schoolmistressy tones, 'This is disgraceful, Matthew. You should be ashamed of yourself. Go away at *once*.'

'J.L.?' Parke enquired. 'You know how we value your opinion.'

'Then I say, Nope. Not Ruddock.'

Loud voice and sharp said together, 'No.'

'Which brings us to Pryar, then, as the name has been mentioned.' There was something very strange in his voice. Had his voice been a cat, the animal would have arched its back.

'Well, from all I've heard,' said sharp-voice, 'we might do worse. He seems popular. And if we have an Englishman, the losers may not feel so badly about it.'

'I think they'd feel worse,' said loud-voice, 'I vote against. This is America.'

'It's not unheard of for Englishmen to get boss jobs,' said Tom. 'Why, at the Ford Foundation——'

'We're not the Ford Foundation,' said loud-voice, 'this is a sort of family concern. A real Cobb concern, not a national one.'

'Well, I vote for Pryar,' Tom went on. 'He's a good man, efficient, gets on with people — I think he'd be accepted. Also,' he added thoughtfully, 'the boys like him.'

'Yes,' said J. L. Walters, 'because of that sex business with the girl.'

'But that was his bad luck——'

'So he says. So they all say. I have my own suspicions.'

Matthew had a vision of his own foot, swollen to colossal size, smudging J. L. Walters right into the carpet.

'Besides,' said J.L., 'there's something else about him. He's a tight-wad. I can't bear a man who's a tight-wad.'

'You say, a tight-wad?' Dr. Parke enquired. He did sound surprised at this.

'Money-grubbing.'

Matthew groaned internally at the thought of the five dollars he had, in his pettishness, snatched back.

'If a man's a tight-wad,' said J.L., 'then I don't trust him. Give him charge of the Centre, and he won't so much as get a broken window repaired if he can help it. Money-grubbing. Tight-wad. Don't talk to me about Pryar.'

'Well, look here,' said Tom, 'we've got two for, two against. I guess Dom gets the casting vote. What do you say, Dom?'

There was a long pause. Matthew had stopped breathing.

When the doctor spoke, his voice was silvery, high and sad. 'I have never disliked saying anything so much in my life. For I was fond of Pryar — yes, I admit it. And Mrs. Parke was wholly on his side. Oh, she could say nothing too good for him! But . . . *he is a man of bad character.*'

This produced an excited babble.

Matthew had to restrain himself from bursting into the room with a great cry — 'I'm not! I'm not!'

'Bad character, Dom?' Helliwell sounded bewildered. 'What on earth do you mean?'

'I am not at liberty to say. Indeed, I could not speak of a certain incident, the truth of which, alas — or perhaps I'm glad it is so, — can't be proved. But I have reason to believe that Pryar has a certain impulsiveness which might be most dangerous, which already (alas) has endangered a life.'

'Dom, you can't leave it like that! Matt endanger life? I've known him for years.'

'I wouldn't put anything past that fellow,' said J.L. 'When a man is a tight-wad, he can do anything. I'm never wrong. The first time I set eyes on Pryar, I knew. And I never make mistakes.'

'You must *go*,' said the schoolmistress voice to Matthew, 'you make me ashamed. You are disgusting. I have never been so filled with disgust. You must go.'

'The Centre,' said Dr. Parke, on a peculiar reedy note, 'is my life. I will not say it comes before my wife and children. Yet perhaps I could not love them so much if I did not in a sense love Cobb and the Centre more, to paraphrase the poem. I have a responsibility to them both. And I cannot, even though I have nothing but a grave suspicion to go on, vote for *a man of bad character.*'

191

'Well, then,' said loud-voice, 'that's Helliwell and me for, you three against. That disposes of Pryar.'

'Certainly it does,' said J.L., 'and I may say that if you had elected him I would have resigned.'

There was a dense silence, filled no doubt by that mingling of relief and horror which follows escape from disaster.

'Poor old Matt, though,' said Tom, rather bravely, 'I'm sorry. And Dom, you'll have to tell me all about it sometime, because I've got to clear the man. Damn it, he's a friend of mine.'

'That I know,' said Dr. Parke, 'and these things are all the sadder when they affect a friend. Well, Ruddock and Pryar are out. That brings us to our final candidate who will be, on the face of things, who must be, our choice.'

'GET OUT, YOU SNEAK!' shouted the inner school-mistress, with such force that Matthew stumbled backward, gripped the door-handle and found himself in the street.

Not since childhood had he been so near to tears. Misunderstood, his reputation under a cloud, he stared up at the grinning moon, waiting for the waters of his eyes to subside. He had lost the game, lost it hopelessly, and all because a silly old man had fallen downstairs.

'Oddly enough, he could bear the failure of his candidature rather better than the thought of Parke's hostility. Silly old man he might be, but he was fundamentally a good one: he meant well: he was not without the milk of human kindness, though rather poor at getting it distributed. He was the kind of man whose respect people could not help seeking, even though they might regard him as something of a fraud. Anyway, nobody likes to lie under suspicion of attempted homicide — Matthew checked himself: there was no point in exaggerating. Even the old boy couldn't believe that.

He amended it: nobody likes to lie under suspicion of attempting to cause bodily harm.

He prayed that Tom would indeed save him. But how was he to raise the matter with Tom, when he could not admit to overhearing the meeting of Trustees?

He began to walk, slowly, heavily, not noticing where he went:

and since he did, in the classic manner of the distraught, walk in circles, he found himself in the road, at the front of the Centre, precisely at the moment when two things happened simultaneously.

At the top of the steps the door opened, flooding the snow with amber, as if it were the stage of a theatre, and voices burst out in friendly chorus.

Anderson's cab skidded up to the kerb, and out of it stepped a small, dark, fuzzy-haired, furious woman, wearing a brutal shade of orange.

'So there you are!'

'Why, my dear Dorothy,' said Matthew.

30. Big Scene

It was so plainly a confrontation of a dramatic order that the men on the steps, by common consent, stood still at Matthew's back, like a Greek chorus holding its tongue while the protagonist prepared to chew the rag for twenty-five minutes.

With the passing of the immediate shock, Matthew felt adrenalin pumping into his system. He forgot his failure, his disgrace. All he knew was that before him stood Dorothy Merlin, hideous in gumboots and glaring like a fiend.

When she spoke again her voice was penetrating as a train whistle cutting the green cheese of the night.

'Don't you dare to call me your dear Dorothy!'

'But it's splendid to see you. Why shouldn't it be? What can you be doing here? Oh, by the way, Peters has your tape.'

'*I* have that beastly tape!'

'Oh, but that's not possible.'

'Yes, it is! I got a chance to come to this filthy cold country, and I just caught George in New York, before he could sneak off by plane.'

Matthew asked her why Peters should sneak. 'He seemed to me a frightfully open sort of fellow.'

'Because he *knew*! Because you told him! I expect you two played the ghastly thing together, and jeered your guts out! Oh, it's a fair cow!' Dorothy, in moments of high tension, recalled the Antipodes.

'Now, Dotty,' Matthew said, 'hadn't you better dismiss Mr. Anderson, or are you going on somewhere else for the night?'

'Do you think I'd stay in this howling desert? I've booked a room in some ghastly place called Piltdown, and the least you can do is to pay for it. Oh, you cad! You lousy, deceitful cad and snob! When I think of all I've done for you——'

Dorothy might have been a harridan of the eighteenth century, so fluent was her abuse and so formal her gestures: a bit player in *The Beggar's Opera*, that was Dorothy. She stormed away at him in a manner Matthew felt to be magnificent, since he had for some time felt free of her influence. He was even proud of her. When she paused for a second to take breath, he announced her to the group at his back.

'This is Miss Dorothy Merlin, our tremendously distinguished poet. Dorothy, permit me to present——'

'Where's that book? How much have you done? I don't believe you've written a single word of it!'

'Why, Dotty——'

'Why do you say you have when you know you haven't? Why do you pose as being a gentleman when you're a moral guttersnipe? Why do you make me travel thousands of miles on a disgusting dinner in a plastic tray, and drive through the night over ghastly roads——'

'So many questions, Dotty,' Matthew protested. 'I do think you ought to put them one at a time.'

'I feel sick to my stomach, I feel sick in my *womb*!' Matthew turned his head aside. He did not care for Dorothy's imagery at any time, but he disliked her maternal line inordinately. He was a prudish man.

'And you let that Cambridge show-off make a fool of me, here in this very place——'

'Well, not exactly here. Over in the Pump Room.'

Dorothy appeared to swell. Anderson, leaning out of the window of the cab, absorbed in the proceedings, guffawed. She advanced steadily over the sidewalk, sinking up to her ankles with each step, thus giving the welcome impression that the ground was actually swallowing her up. But Matthew backed a little.

'Matthew! Do you, or do you not, mean to write a book?'

'Why yes, of course.'

'About me?'

'Oh, that. Well, no.'

'Did I hear you say no?'

The Greek chorus was losing its impassivity; Dr. Parke was making shocked noises. Tom was sniggering. Matthew was somehow aware that another figure had come out from the Centre to join them.

'I did say no; yes, Dorothy.' He paused, then added joyfully,' I am going to write a study of the life and work of Daniel Skipton!'

He had heard of people giving screams of rage, but had never known anyone actually do so. The noise Dorothy made was between a screech and a gasp, a rising whine of breath blown out simultaneously through mouth and nose. It was rather a terrible sound, seeming to exclude the possibility of further speech. He looked with distaste at her bulging eyes; in the golden light, he fancied he could see her uvula.

'Good as a movie,' said Anderson. 'Go to it, lady, don't mind me.'

Nobody budged. It looked as though it might all go on for ever.

Then Matthew found Dr. Parke at his side, little, erect, stately, all prepared to smooth things over.

'Miss Merlin? It is, I am sure, a privilege to meet you. We have naturally heard so much about you from our good colleague——'

She switched her terrible attention to him.

'Let me get this straight. Are you the head of this Centre, or whatever you call it?'

'No,' said an unexpected voice, harsh, flat and penetrating, 'I am.'

Matthew swung round to see, descending the steps like a Caesar among the legionaries, Herman Wohlgemutt.

31. Confiteor

'Elected this very night,' said Dr. Parke with desperate jollity. He was afraid of Dorothy because he thought she was mad. 'A great night. We are very proud. May I present to you Mr. Helliwell, Mr. Walters, Mr. Egan, Mr. Van Eyck?'

She took not the slightest notice of him, but addressed herself to Wohlgemutt.

'If you're the Head, or whatever you're called——'

'I am the Director of the Centre for Visiting Fellows.'

'Then you ought to know what's going on under your nose. You pay Mr. Pryar here good money for working on *me*. Is that right?'

'Mr. Pryar's subject is his own choice,' Dr. Parke said, looking shocked but a little less scared, since Wohlgemutt stood between him and Dorothy.

'But that's what you *understood*!' she cried. 'If you imagine I'd have let him come here otherwise——'

Could her megalomania really have reached to such a pitch, Matthew pondered?

'Lady,' said Anderson, 'I might tell you it's started to freeze again, and if I've got to get up those darned hills I'd rather do it right now.'

'You'll wait till I'm ready!' She turned on him in an orange rush.

In reply, he let the clutch out and trundled the car a few yards along the kerb.

'Don't you dare!' Attempting to run after him, she slipped, righted herself, was stuck fast in the snow.

'I really would say "please" if I were you,' Matthew said, enunciating his words beautifully.

Anderson, no sadist, did not wait for this to be enforced. He reversed and trundled back. 'Come on, Miss Mervyn, step on it.'

Matthew assisted her out of the drift, from which she emerged with a sucking noise. His arms ached. 'Honestly, Dotty, I do think you'd better.'

'My name is *Merlin*, Mr. Anderson!'

'It would look just about the same on a tombstone, if we get into any trouble tonight.' Anderson revved the engine encouragingly.

She was frantic, not wishing to go, not quite daring to stay. Anderson sounded the horn at her.

'Mr. Whatever-your-name-is,' she hurled at Wohlgemutt, 'Mr. Pryar is taking money under false pretences! I hate to say it, yet say it I must. He is here to work on my poetry. I am a poet of distinction in my own country. I claim — yes, I claim, consideration in yours! *Hommages littéraires!*'

He looked at her stonily. Matthew wondered, in a detached sort of way, whose side he was on.

But he was never to know. 'C'm *awn!*' said Anderson, reaching suddenly for Dorothy's arm and hauling her to the car, so that she came flying, all legs and wings. 'Now get in, will ya?'

She was still shouting as he slammed the door and drove off with her.

'I guess that poor lady's a case for the head shrinkers,' said the man with the loud voice, who turned out to be Mr. Van Eyck.

'Oh, not really,' said Matthew with a stir of queasy loyalty, 'she can be quite nice when she likes. But she does get excited. I assure you, she is precisely the same in London.'

'A very distressing incident,' Dr. Parke said, 'and perhaps better forgotten. Well, gentlemen——' He hesitated.

'Do accept my congratulations,' said Matthew to Wohlgemutt, who nodded irritably.

Everyone began to shake hands with everyone else.

Matthew made a decision. 'Tom, come back with me and have a nightcap.'

'I'm supposed to be at the President's, we all are.'

'Please, Tom. Just ten minutes.'

'Well——'

'Please.'

The two middle-aged men who, because they were limber, small-buttocked, long-legged, looked like youths in the starlight, walked as quickly as they could across the campus, hugging themselves in an attempt to keep warm. The slight thaw of the afternoon had been succeeded by a cold that made them gasp, and poured like ice-water into their lungs when they did so. It was not unlike the sensation of drowning. A wind was blowing up from the ponds, where the bare trees strained and groaned.

Back in Matthew's house neither could speak for the moment. They blew out icy ectoplasm into the hot room, stamped their feet, tugged at their numbed fingers to restore the circulation.

'Bit better,' Tom said, after a while.

They went upstairs into the chaotic sitting-room: Anderson's sister had not turned up that day.

Now that his chance had come, Matthew found it hard to begin. He did not know which he disliked the most: feeling a knave or feeling a fool. He caught himself humming beneath his breath, *O that we two were Maying*. Well, he would rather have been maying or doing any other damned silly thing than what he must do now.

'Tom,' he said at last, 'I think I could confess to a murder without much difficulty.'

'You can't have done one, chum. Nobody's missing.'

'But this sticks in the throat, somewhat.'

Tom glanced covertly at the clock.

'I was there, at your meeting.'

'Oh, were you?' He was interested, if only mildly. 'Where?'

Matthew told him the circumstances. 'I should have got out. But old Parke started on about me, and I couldn't. I only went when I'd been disposed of. I didn't want to find out who had been chosen. Tom, I'd give anything if it weren't true.'

'Wohlgemutt? Don't blow it up. He's an oaf, but he'll be adequate. I'd far rather have had you or Ruddock, you must have heard me say so.'

'No, no: I mean, if I hadn't listened.'

'Oh, that! Apparently we were flanked by ears on both sides. We'd just got through when the new Director walked in, looking oh so surprised to find us there. Said he'd been working in his office. Of course, while you had your ear glued to one door, he had his glued to the other. We were a sort of aural sandwich,' Tom said gaily.

'Thank God!' Matthew felt the mantle of guilt slip from him, then realised that even if it had, it should have done no such thing. 'Two wrongs don't make a right, though.'

'I always think two wrongs are a little less chilling than one. I mean, they can get sort of friendly with each other and that makes for a warmer atmosphere. I expect you found the evening pretty exciting, even if you didn't enjoy it.'

'It's simply not a thing any decent man ought to have done, far less have enjoyed, which I did not——'

'Oh, for God's sake! If I'd been in your shoes I'd have listened like crazy. Though you didn't hear any good of yourself, I'm afraid. Why does old Parke think you're a man of bad character?'

Matthew drearily explained.

'Well,' said Tom, 'I think I can get that out of his head. I mean, it's a question of knowing a man. You and I — how many years is it?'

'On and off, a good many.'

'Well, *I* know you're not the type to shove a nice old guy down a flight of stairs. He doesn't, see?'

'In that case, I should have thought he was rather lacking in psychological insight,' said Matthew, with a touch of revivifying tartness.

'Of course he is. He's never had any at all. He once misheard something somebody said and came to the conclusion that Pickersgill was a sex-maniac'

'Does he still think so?'

'Oh no, no. He soon realised the improbability. Now I'll straighten things out for you — that's a promise. By the way, who did push him? That thug Tiepolo?'

'The cat. Propelled by Tiepolo, or so Edith says.'

' "*It was the cat*" ' Tom sang. ' "*It was the cat.*" Did you ever go for Gilbert and Sullivan? I did.' He paused. 'Look, if J.L. had been on your side, Parke could have broken his neck for all the effect it would have had. Your real mistake was to ask J.L. for that five bucks. It was crazy, man, crazy.'

'And the worst thing, Dorothy will be back here tomorrow. She's bound to be.'

There was such a distressful note in Matthew's voice that Tom sat down brotherly beside him and laid a hand on his shoulder.

'No, boy. She will not.'

'How can you tell?'

'I know the climate of these parts better than you do. Weren't we frozen up like brass monkeys when we got in?'

Matthew agreed.

'Tomorrow, my fine-feathered eavesdropper, the road between here and Piltdown is going to be impassable. Anderson knows that. He knew that if he hijacked her, as he did, he'd just about make it there and back before the siege set in. Put your mind at rest. Dorothy is going to be skyed in that godawful place for at least a week.'

'Tom,' Matthew said simply, 'you are the most splendid friend a man could conceivably have.'

'Sure. I do my best. But I must get going.'

'You won't make it. Not comfortably. Ring up and say you've ricked your ankle, and you're staying with me for the night. Isn't it *nicer* here?'

There was a long pause.

Then Tom said, 'Yes. It's far nicer.'

32. 'Good-Bye, Good-Bye, to Everything!'

Matthew was given to humming a great deal but he rarely sang: which was a pity, for he had a tuneful and pretty light baritone and that peculiarly young note in his voice common to Peter Pears, Fischer-Dieskau and Frank Sinatra.

On the morning of December 22nd, however, while he packed his cases for the holiday, he was singing away happily, at the top of his voice, singing Robert Louis Stevenson, so far as he knew, though he had to invent most of the words.

> 'Farewell, the farm, farewell, the spring,
> Goodbye, Goodbye to everything!'

The young men were pouring away to the four points of the compass, jalopies piled high with bags, books, sports equipment. Jane Merle was calling for Matthew at eleven o'clock. Dorothy was still stuck fast in Piltdown which, had she known it, had anyone warned her, was just about five miles too high up the mountains to be a reliable place if the winter were uncommonly severe. And this year it was.

Naturally, Matthew had disconnected the telephone.

> 'The sun was shining on the sea,
> Shining with all his might.'

Matthew had changed to Lewis Carroll, this time inventing the tune. For the sun was shining on the blue-scooped snows, the red birds dazzled like rambler roses as they garlanded the whiteness, picking and poking for seeds, and the bells were ringing. It was ten o'clock.

A brass band was coming down the road, a student band, by the sound of it.

He looked out, delighted by the splintering of sun on brass, and on blossomy faces. There was a small troupe following the band, a troupe with banners. Matthew, who had always been edgy about Christmas, began suddenly to know the emotions of the reformed Scrooge.

The noise was deafening. To his astonishment, band, banners, followers, lined up in the roadway — before his house.

There were three banners.

One was in Latin, but he had long forgotten his, and did not know what it meant.

'SOLVENTUR RISU TABULAE, TU MISSUS ABIBIS.'

The second read,

'MERRY XMAS, SANTAMATT!'

The third,

'UP WITH RAPE!'

For twenty minutes, while he smiled and waved, they played him all the traditional Cobb songs. He did not know when he had felt so happy or had loved the young more. He had, like most middle-aged men, been in the habit of ignoring the young pretty completely, suspecting that when they were not silly they were hostile, and that they were usually both. But the boys of Cobb made him feel fatherly: and their friendliness tinged his pleasure with that shade of regret which makes pleasure supreme. Oh, why had he not married? Why was not one of these glorious, lusty juvenals his own? Why had he deprived himself of the joys of fatherhood?

'You and Dorothy,' said the inner voice he so much resented, 'would have made a pretty pair.'

So he stopped thinking any such thoughts, and the band played on.

Edith came up the path, her ruddy face upturned, her blue eyes beaming. 'Come to wish you a Merry Christmas!' she yelled.

'Do come up.'

She came, and hugged him.

'Edith,' said Matthew, 'do you understand Latin?'

'Of course I do, you born fool. How else should I get my work done? Golly, what a send-off!'

'Well, what does that one mean?'

' "The tables of the law will fall to bits in a wave of laughter. You will leave the court without a stain on your character." '

'American boys,' said Matthew, meaning it, 'are unsurpassable, anywhere.' He waved wildly to his admirers, who by now were bringing the concert to an end. 'Good God, they even *know* things!'

Edith was more doubtful. 'At least they know where to look things up.'

'I say, had you the faintest idea Wohlgemutt was in the running?'

She looked astonished. 'Of course I had. Hadn't you? All that sucking-up. No one was allowed even to suggest that old Parke wasn't St. Francis of Assisi. Though you,' she added thoughtfully, 'according to our musical friends outside, know more about *poules*.'

The band was marching away. He gave them one last wave, they gave him one last cheer.

'A remark in such dreadfully bad taste, Edith dear.'

'No free soul worries about taste. Is it true that you've abandoned your Merliniana?'

'Quite true.'

'What are you going to work on, though? You'll have to do something.'

He told her.

'Well, if you must. It doesn't matter. No one here will know the difference. Oh, Matt, in the spring I really can go home! Just in time to catch the Backs at their best. And I shall see Milly——'

Milly was her friend. Her eyes filled.

Miss Groby joined them. 'To bring you Greetings, dear Mr. Pryar, from Grandfather Frost!' (He guessed that she was becoming increasingly Russianised.) 'And to thank you for all you have done — oh, how much it is! For I am spending Christmas with dear Mrs. Briggs, and Professor Zondenbok will be there.'

The next visitor was Dr. Hefflinger, merry as ever, bearing a little pierced box.

'Don't you dare!' Edith screamed.

'Now, my most esteemed, my most beloved Dr. Corall, this is like all good Christmas presents, it is not to be opened till Christmas morning. So there is no need for you so to unnerve yourself. Mr. Pryar, please to accept a very small, very loving companion, with the good wishes of your old fond colleague, Rudolf Hefflinger.'

'How big?' Matthew asked apprehensively.

'No more than just the joint of my little finger! But she will grow, never fear. No harm can she do, and she is fluffy one, also. And rare, ah, rare!'

'In that case, I do wonder you can spare her. Are you perfectly sure you can?'

'Her mamma she became *enceinte*; this little one, she is one of many.'

He went away, after a series of crushing handshakes.

'Matt,' said Edith, 'I implore you to put that in the wash-basin and turn the tap on.'

'I should not be so cruel to a dumb animal. Before I go, I am going to pop it into Wohlgemutt's mail-box.'

'You promise?'

'Cross my heart.'

Meanwhile he locked Hefflinger's gift in a drawer.

Edith, who was looking out of the window, called out, 'Here comes that swine Tiepolo!'

Matthew looked down. 'It's no go, Chuck. I don't want to see you.'

'Can't take a joke, huh?'

'Not your kind of joke.'

'That's a lot of crap! Come on, Matt, loosen up, it's Christmas.'

'I won't. I'll say good-bye from here.'

'I didn't mean to get him with the cat, honest, I didn't.'

For some reason not immediately plain to Edith and Maud Groby, Matthew now chose to become involved in conversation, his boyish voice pealing down the side of the house.

'Do forgive me, Chuck, but I'm by no means sure what you are talking about.'

'Of course you know! When old Parke went ass over teakettle down your stairs. He thought it was you.'

'I know he fell. But I do not yet quite know what the cat had to do with it. Perhaps you'll explain.'

'Well, Matt, I grabbed it — wanting to make friends with it, you know——'

'What a very curious time to choose!'

'— Anyway, I did. What's wrong with that? But then the animal started clawing as usual, and I just tossed it away, not hurting it, and whizz-bang, it went right between the old boy's legs!'

'You mean Dr. Parke's legs?'

'Of course I do,' Chuck replied, the picture of bewilderment, 'who else's legs should I mean?'

From behind him rose an old, mellow, strong voice, filled with horror.

'Matthew, what have I done? Matthew, I beg you to accept a thousand apologies!'

Chuck looked round, sidestepped, stood for a second in consternation, then bolted.

Dr. Parke came into the house, ran upstairs, wrung his hands and looked at Matthew imploringly.

'My dear, dear boy——'

'You are a silly little man ever to have believed such a bloody silly thing,' Edith said warmly. She was by now seized of the situation.

'Tom Helliwell was telling me only this morning that you could not have done it, Matthew,' said the doctor, who was near to tears, 'and of course I said I must accept his word, and I came here to tell you, since this is the season of goodwill to all men, that I proposed to forget the whole matter. Then this — this——'

'You must not believe,' said Matthew, hypocritically, 'that Dr. Tiepolo intended any personal harm to yourself.'

'No, I must not, I must not. It is a terrible lesson. I see one can believe nothing. I must hurry home and tell Beata, she will wish to see you, to apologise, and I know our President will. Beata will put on her coat and come running at once, if I know her. She will be distressed!'

'There is no need for Mrs. Parke to visit me,' said Matthew, 'as I shall undoubtedly see her after the holidays and we can sort the whole thing out then, or better still, forget it. Anyway, I'm expecting to be fetched any moment now, so if you'll forgive me——'

He got rid of them. Dr. Parke went first, looking hang-dog. But repentance won't get me my lost job, Matthew thought. He watched the doctor picking his way down the path and along the road, under trees frosted like maytime, even the smallest twig blossomed thick with snow. At the corner the old ulster flapped: and was gone.

'Give me a kiss, cully,' said Edith, 'you are vindicated.' She hugged him.

'I too,' said Miss Groby,' if I might dare, and if you wouldn't mind——'

Her little kiss on his cheek was as fresh, as timid, as sweet-smelling as a child's. Touched, he realised to his surprise that she must once have been quite pretty, in a Kate Greenaway fashion. Although she had withered in loneliness on her scholarly plinth, her youth had never gone from her. It was preserved, shrunken but still perceptible, under the glass bell of age. It would be easy, he thought, to pity her: yet he doubted whether she had ever pitied herself. If she had wanted love enough, she could have had it — verve and beauty are far less compelling than the sheer desire of flesh to be taken. She had not wanted men, but she had wanted her work. She had wanted success after her own fashion. She had been perfectly happy in her way, and it was pure sentimentality to wish that her way had been otherwise. You might as well give a man a space-suit when what he wants is Proust, in two volumes, boxed.

'A stirrup-cup,' Matthew suggested, feeling fanciful.

But neither woman would accept. Edith had to get to the library, Miss Groby had planned to begin keeping her New Year's Resolution a good ten days before she had to. 'Then it won't come as such a dreadful shock,' she said wistfully.

When they had gone, Matthew stole out to Wohlgemutt's house, which was a couple of blocks down, and deposited Hefflinger's present in the mail-box, as he had promised he would. He returned to find Ruddock on the step.

'Come in, my dear chap.'

'Well, only for a minute. There are just a couple of things I want to draw your attention to.'

'Emily?'

'I suppose she lost me the job,' Doug said, his face clouding. 'None of them has any idea of the morality of scholarship. Not one of them.'

'I do wish it had been you, Doug.'

'Oh well. Worse things happen at sea. I won't have an easy time with Wohlgemutt and Parke sniffing round everything I do and begging me not to publish. Me, I'm going to be your Duke of Wellington. "Publish and——" They'll damn me, all right. But I don't care. Matt!'

The frog face filled up with light, like a pond brimming with the early dawn.

'Just get a load of this:

"And so, I always bear the cup,
If, haply, mine may be the drop
Some pilgrim thirst to slake——"

No! Don't say anything yet. I want you to think it through. Take this one:

"I could not drink it, Sweet,
Till you had tasted first,
Though cooler than the water was
The thoughtfulness of Thirst!"

208

Well? What do you say to that?' He was rigid with excitement.

' "Thoughtfulness of Thirst," ' Matthew replied rather feebly, 'it's a splendid line, isn't it?'

'That's not the point, man! Don't you see, it gives me quite a new slant?'

Matthew, apologizing, said he could not see.

'Why, it's the classic alcoholic deception!'

'I beg your pardon?'

'The excuse had to be made. Otherwise she couldn't have lived with herself. *So she put on a show of social drinking.* "I could not drink it ... till *you* had tasted first." Obligation to keep it in the house — get that? And the one before — Emily bearing the cup just in case she ran across a thirsty pilgrim. Pathetic, isn't it? Of course, in it's way, not unsublime.'

'No, not unsublime at all.'

'I imagine that's what she told the grocer when she went stealing in at the back door in her little white dress.'

Matthew protested. Doug could not have known that she did any such thing.

'Oh be your age, man! They had to keep a supply of sherry — rum, sometimes, maybe, for callers. But it was never enough for Emily. So she had to get more. How would she get it? Openly? The family would soon catch on. They'd spot it on the bills. So she must have gone out herself, with her heart thumping, poor girl, and her mouth dry as a kiln, driven by need. "Let me not thirst with this Hock at my lip," she was praying: she was panting like some poor animal for "many a lay of the Dim Burgundy" to "chant for Cheer" .... It makes you weep to think of it, Matt! She *had* to confide in the grocer. She hadn't any choice. So what did she tell him? That she had to have extra liquor in, in case guests arrived or strangers were taken sick on the doorstep. Can't you see him,' Ruddock went on, with rising indignation, 'smiling behind his hand? Sneering? Because he saw through her. Oh yes, he saw through her. The bastard!'

At that moment a car hooted outside, hooted forcefully: three times, twice, three times again.

'After the holidays,' Matthew said feverishly. 'We'll go into it then, Doug, line by line, word by word.'

'So you think I've got something?'

'I'm sure you have.'

'You're not kidding——?'

Matthew flung open the window.

Her clear voice rose up to him, silvery as a bugle.

'Matt-Matt! I'm here!' She shouted to a cluster of tan and chocolate dogs who were occupying the back seat. 'All people be quiet, I can't hear myself talk! Matthew! It's time to go!'

33. Mrs. Merle Makes a Suggestion

She smiled at him restfully as he emerged with his bags. She wore Irish tweeds again, this time in a green both strong and soft: the hills of Connemara, the mountains of Mourne. Under a kind of green deerstalker, her hair whisked up in sparkling wings, silver-gilt, a girl's hair.

'Get in, get in, go on. The dogs always have the back. They can have the bags, too, we won't bother to open the trunk.'

Softly, speedily, the car sped away, Mrs. Merle's toe controlling it.

'We'll have to go slow,' she said, 'or pretty slow, till we get to Brattleboro.'

It was not slow by Matthew's standards.

Cobb receded into a petrified dream of delicate verticals. No doubt, far behind, out of Matthew's world, Beata was making her horrible white stews, the President sat in gloom, his gaze upon the frigid campus, the Visiting Fellows waited for transport to take them elsewhere. To Dorothy, Matthew gave no thought at all.

It was warm in the car, and Mrs. Merle's neat, sharp profile, the high, questioning curve of her cheek, were steady against a blue sky. Her nose was delicately beaked, a splendid little nose.

'Well, was it ghastly?' she said at last.

So he told her: the good and the bad. It took a long time. He omitted nothing, neither his personal problems nor the problem of Cobb as a whole.

'Do not expect me to receive Miss Merlin. I am dead sure I would not like her.'

'Oh, I shouldn't expect it,' Matthew said hastily and very sincerely.

He had never felt so much at home in his life. Owing to the excellent heater, he and Mrs. Merle were insulated from a sour and stubborn earth. Others might wish to fight hot wars, cold wars or, worse, tepid wars: it astonished him, feeling himself in a state both mescalined and mentally acute, that it had occurred to no one how appallingly dangerous a tepid war might become, once it got under way.

He had never talked so much in his life: or, to be precise, had never talked so freely. Mrs. Merle, no great talker herself, liberated him.

At Brattleboro, she drew up to a Howard Johnson's, which, in its orange and peacock whimsy, its impeccable deanliness, seemed to him suddenly like the ultimate desire-image of the whole of the human race. If the world did not blow up, it would with the centuries be covered all over with places such as these, planted in the deserts, the jungles, the swamps reclaimed: french fries for all, and a pretty wonderful thing too. Already all over America these pretty, Disneyesque buildings proliferated, offering nowhere a disappointment: for everything you were offered, any old place, would be precisely the same, not even a variation in the thickness of a hamburger.

'Coffee,' said Mrs. Merle, 'I think we could do with it. I have something up my sleeve for lunch.'

She had other things up her sleeve, for as she waved Matthew out of the car, clattering beauties tumbled to her wrists: emeralds and amethysts in gold, turquoises in silver.

Nothing is quite so intimate as a small table in a Howard Johnson's. Americans had perhaps ceased to notice it: Russians, when they got the equivalent, would discover it. Between Matthew's nose and Jane Merle's was no more than eighteen inches.

'Dorothy,' she said incisively, 'is not my kind of person. I am terribly uneducated, Matthew: therefore your Dorothy would terrify me.'

He did not believe that sixteen tribes of Kipling's Fuzzy-Wuzzies, cavorting in battle order, would cause her to miss a heart-beat.

'She can be an old sweetie,' he said with doubt in his voice, 'in so many ways.' But the phrase was her friend Duncan Moss's, not his own. He himself could find nothing to say for her.

'You haven't made them very clear.'

'Well, I suppose she's a poet.'

'And what,' said Mrs. Merle, unanswerably, 'makes poets better than us? A good poet might be a perfectly awful man. Odd as it may seem to you, I have never had a strong feeling for Lord Byron.'

'Nor have I.' How well they agreed!

'Most of my English relations have.'

'So much the worse,' said Matthew firmly.

'Oh, my dear! Indeed. *Much* the worse. I should never have invited him for a week-end. He would have shown off *all* the time, which I cannot bear.'

They drove on, down, ever down, the great slope of America. Hedges showered them with confetti, roads crackled under them.

'Did I tell you we were going to New York?' Mrs. Merle asked him suddenly.

'No, I don't think you did.'

'Not nice in the country, not just now. I thought my apartment would be far cosier. Anyway, all the servants are there. Do you object to New York?'

'Far from it!'

'So that couldn't be nicer,' said Mrs Merle, rounding a corner at such speed that a shower of diamonds flew and the earth turned.

She asked him even more about Cobb and himself: and though he believed he had exhausted both subjects earlier in the day, he found himself still full of information. A wonderful woman! With Jane Merle, time flew. That is, it flew if it could be said to exist. For Matthew, it couldn't.

She took him for lunch at a pleasant place not far from Amherst. In Massachusetts the snow was thinner, and the main roads were clear. The inn was not Pickwickian but Early American, and though a little cluttered with spinning-wheels and dark portraits of ladies and gentlemen with cake-like faces, had an agreeable air of belonging where it was. The food, surprisingly, was French.

Mrs. Merle took off her topcoat and slung it over a chair. When

Matthew asked if he might hang it up for her, she told him not to fuss. The dining-room was full; but after her arrival nobody else seemed likely to get much attention. Matthew sat happily within the golden pentagon of her fame, feeling as safe as houses. He realised that he was humming, though inaudibly, 'All is Safely Gathered in Ere the Winter Storms Begin.'

She frowned at the menu. 'Escargots! I think not. Too far from their native land. What's our main dish? We'd better base our choice on that. Matt? I suggest the *coq au vin*, they do it well.'

'It is particularly good today, Mrs. Merle,' the *maître d'hôtel* murmured, as if wanting to press its claims without a show of immodesty.

'In that case, we had better start with *petite marmite* and a little piece of fish. Matt?'

She swept on before he could agree or disagree.

'Right, then. And Jules: *plenty* of Parmesan. You know how I like my soup.'

'A cocktail, Madame?'

'Matt?'

'Well, if you are——'

'I'm not, no.'

'Then neither am I.'

'But we will have a bottle of Beaujolais. Have you any of the '47, Jules?'

He mumbled.

'Of course you have.' Her eyes shone like the Angel of the Annunciation's. 'You keep it for me, you know you do.'

Apparently he did.

'Not a stone's throw from here,' Mrs. Merle said, 'lived that darling Emily Dickinson. Oh, but I forgot. She's your Dr. Ruddock's sore point.'

'Not his sore point. Far from it. Dr. Parke's.'

' "Empress of Calvary",' she mused. 'I feel like that sometimes. Do I strike you in that light, Matt-Matt?'

'Certainly. The Empress part,' he replied tactfully.

'No, but suffering. You know, being too much on my own.'

He said he hardly knew her well enough to judge, but could not imagine she need be much on her own if she chose otherwise.

'Perhaps you can't. Well, well! "The bride without the sign." Me. Yes, I'm sure it was meant for me. Don't look embarrassed, Matt, just drink your nice soup-soup.'

They had a delicious meal, after which Matthew felt a little drowsy. Mrs. Merle was as brisk as ever.

They must be on their way, she said, or they would not make New York by dinner-time.

They made such good speed that the sun had only begun to set when they reached the Merritt parkway. Birds were speeding home across a sea-green sky to unlisted addresses, and the evening petrifaction was on the trees. Lamps shot up in the windows, patching the dusk. 'Tired?' asked Mrs. Merle.

'Not very. In fact, not a bit.' (Though he was.)

As they stopped to pay a toll-keeper, they heard a bird singing.

'Jane Blackbird!' cried Matthew, inspired, poetic.

'What?' she rasped at him, as she drove on.

'A Merle is a blackbird.'

'How nice. What's a merlin?'

'Another kind of bird, I think.'

'Or perhaps some repulsive form of fish. I hope so. I don't see why all your friends have to have much the same name. Do try to do something about it in future.'

He promised that he would.

'Do you think it would be a good idea for us to get married?'

He was so jolted by what he fancied he had heard (though he knew he couldn't have) that the breath slammed out of him.

'Poor boy is deaf-deaf.'

She had neither increased nor slackened speed. The car sped on through the darkening air.

'What?' said Matthew, sounding unmannerly for once.

'Naturally you couldn't ask me, that is, if you thought it was sensible, because I have so much money. Men find it an embarrassment.'

'Jane, you cannot honestly mean——'

'Say at once if you don't want to, of course. We're not in love with each other, and I'm older than you are, but I don't look it, and we do have fun. I think we might have marvellous fun — a much nicer time than most people do.'

Matthew, though he felt every cell in his brain and body had switched places, was not entirely devoid of spirit. 'I do think if we could just draw up somewhere for a moment——'

'Don't be silly, we're not allowed to, anyway not for another five miles. And we don't want to be sentimental at all, only happy. That is, if you are.'

'Jane, you know my position.'

'Perfectly, dear. You have been explaining it for over six and a quarter hours. Now do tell me what you really think. I've always wanted to marry an Englishman, and I'm very lonely. You have plenty of money of your own, so although I shall pay for most things, you will never seem disgusting. There won't be a lot when I die because it's pretty well all tied up in foundations, and anyway, I won't die for a very, very long time. Both my grandmothers lived well into their nineties, and so shall I. Well, what do you say? Will we get married?'

As the numbness of shock faded in Matthew, a new kind of numbness took its place: the numbness of sheer bliss. Of course he would marry her! He was unattached, so was she: they would poke and shovel pearls for ever out of the oyster of the world.

'I wouldn't, of course, make demands on you. Nor should I refuse them, if you felt that way. That kind of thing would simply have to be unimportant now, don't you agree?'

She did not stop at the next rest-area, but put her foot down and tore past it.

'Oh, certainly,' said Matthew, 'but it is not entirely inconceivable that sometimes I might.'

He saw the arc of a smile pressing up her firm, biscuity cheek.

'That's fine, then. In that case, when do you think it ought to be? I see no sense in waiting very long, do you? By the way, you realise you will only be my second husband? I don't go around marrying all the time like some of these women. And I had Calvin for thirty-five years.'

While he was struggling for words in which to accept her proposal, he realised that he had unwittingly done so already. He was not, however, altogether cowardly. He said, 'I should very much like to marry you, Jane, and it is tremendously nice of you to think of it.'

'Good. So that's settled.'

At once she began to put her mind to practical things, ordering their future life together as if planning a military campaign. She had everything worked out. She had never, of course, for one second feared a refusal.

Ahead of them, a great blur of pale lights, flottant, sprawling as the Milky Way, announced New York.

'Of course you won't go back to Cobb.'

'Jane dear, I have to! I haven't earned my keep. And I have commitments.'

'Nonsense. I'll explain to them. Also, I'll give them another donation. To build an inn with. If they say no, they will get no nice money and no nice Matthew. So won't that be wonderful for everybody?'

Putting out her small wiry hand, she patted his knee.

'All settled. That's what I like. That is always how things should be.'

34. Night-Piece: New York

Matthew was in the national press again.

Almost immediately after Christmas, when the social wires began to hum all round the world, he had resolutely moved out of Mrs. Merle's apartment into the Plaza.

'I know it's only a wretched cot,' she said of her twelve-room apartment on Park Avenue, 'but there's masses of space for you. I do wish you wouldn't be so middle-class!'

Though he flinched at this, feeling its innate unfairness, he would not budge. And perhaps she admired him for it.

Of course, the move made him more vulnerable. Mrs. Merle's telephone number was so closely guarded a secret that he had found himself relatively safe from the world's press. At the Plaza it was different. Newspaper-men waylaid him at every turn and the telephone rang incessantly. After two of the less respectable papers had referred to him as 'British Cinderella Man', Dorothy called him up. She was still snow-sieged at Piltdown, and furious.

'How could you do it?' she stormed. 'Oh, you *ponce*!'

'Come, come, Dorothy. That's positively discourteous.'

'No one will ever want to speak to you again.'

'I think you may be surprised how many will.'

'You are — you are——'

'What am I this time? Don't be so angry, it's terribly bad for you and will only upset your work.'

'How dare you even mention my work? You — you Anti-Hero!'

Matthew laughed joyfully. He simply could not help it.

'Don't you dare to laugh! Oh, don't you *dare*!'

'But, Dorothy, you did ask for it.'

He hung up: then requested the hotel exchange to take no further calls from New Hampshire that day. He would have refused calls from all quarters, but for the irresistible excitement of seeing who it could possibly be this time. Also, the caller might be Jane Merle, by whom he was now entirely ravished.

He was waiting one evening a week later for her to fetch him (they were to dine in her apartment) when the bellhop brought up the usual quota of cablegrams. Among them was one from Dorothy, despatched from Idlewild. At last she had thawed out, and was blessedly on her way back to Europe.

'SO SORRY SO SILLY REALISE NOW HAD CHILL HIGH TEMPERATURE ANYONE MIGHT BE FORGIVEN LOVING CONGRATULATIONS YOU MUST BOTH DINE WITH US WHEN IN LONDON REGARDS YOUR JANE LOVE DOROTHY.'

Good God, Matthew said to himself, 'Regards your Jane!' He tore up the wire and threw it into the wastepaper basket.

He stood above New York as it bloomed in harlequin colours out of the sunset into the night. He was as yet unable to realise the whole of his happiness, the fabulous character of his future. There was a tiny crack in the sill, just where his hand lay, and the only touch of icy air in the room just spiked his forefinger. For a moment he was struck with sadness and something like shame, knowing there was a world elsewhere and that it was the real one. With any luck he might never know reality again (if he had ever known it), need never raise his own mild eyes to eyes like stone. And of course never write a single line, about Dorothy, Daniel Skipton, or anybody else. But would he feel at ease with himself, be able to live with himself, consoled by the knowledge that the real world, however tragic, could not be made more so by the fact that just one minnow had slipped through the net?

Well, yes. Being Matthew, he would.

Unlit windows were filled now with the last rays of the falling sun, and above the single great united palace of the city the sky was green, not so much with the hue of apples but with the taste of them. A precipice below, the traffic lights flashed and changed, first scarlet, then jade, switching back and forth the whole mood of the evening. The beetling cars showered their bright arrows over the streets, making a mysterious Agincourt. In a garden enclosed, fourteen stories below, lamplight shone on the few remaining snail-tracks of snow.

Yet he saw none of it. In his mind's eye was something quite different. He saw Cobb in the imperial splendours of autumn, the young men streaming from their classes to the Boosie House, which was slender and white as peeled willow against violet creeper and vine. He saw the INN rising, first the scaffolding, then the neo-Georgian brick. Miraculously, rough earth became a garden, the bare planks of the door were suffused with paint, curtains fluttered waterlights against the sashes. The door opened and his friends began to gather, Edith, Maud, Doug, Hefflinger, even Chuck Tiepolo — no, not Wohlgemutt: he would by now be remote and beastly, set apart from them by office and by conceit. But the others would go into the ripeness of the inn, as into the Mermaid Tavern, they would lounge on foam-rubber, they would be happy. Maud would drink like a fish, but a joyful, uninhibited one.

Dear Cobb! O my America, my old-found land, America regained!

He had felt no lump in his throat when he left Eton. Eton had never made itself into a happiness-symbol, a green sprig of innocence.

Cobb, however, had.

Matthew swallowed.

'Penny for them,' said Jane, very English, coming into the room light-balanced in Balenciaga. 'What are you thinking about?'

He could not control a flash of feeling that a penny was a pretty slender offer, all things considered.

But he said, 'About my youth.'

THE END

Lightning Source UK Ltd.
Milton Keynes UK
UKOW04f0327071015

260012UK00001B/42/P

9 781447 215547